C000078396

Indomitable

by M.F. Frosolono

ISBN 978-1-63393-989-9

Published by

210 60th Street
Virginia Beach, VA 23451
800–435–4811
www.koehlerbooks.com

INDOMITABLE

A NOVEL

M.F. FROSOLONO

VIRGINIA BEACH
CAPE CHARLES

In honor and memory of my beloved and indomitable
Andrea Cheek Frosolono

CHAPTER 1

On Sunday morning, an angry and sobbing Theodora Nelson called her mother, Dr. Pamela Kendal, who was nearing the end of her shift in the emergency room at Grady Memorial Hospital in Atlanta.

"Teddy, is something wrong?" Pam asked.

"A lot. Thompson tried to rape me this morning. I fought, but he was too strong for me."

"What?"

"Mom, I said Thompson attempted to rape me, right here in my bedroom."

Pamela forced her medical persona to override her maternal instincts.

"Are you bleeding anywhere? Did he hit you?"

"I'm not bleeding. He slapped my face a couple of time as I was fighting him."

"Did he penetrate you?"

"No, although cum—I mean semen—was all over my crotch."

"You're saying he ejaculated before penetrating you?"

"Yes. Some of his semen may have gotten into my vagina."

"Teddy, listen carefully to me. Do not shower or bathe. Don't try to clean the semen off you."

"I feel gross and sticky."

"I know. Did you by any chance scratch him?"

"I marked his face with my fingernails before he pinned my hands to the bed."

"Don't wash your hands. I want to get his skin residue from under your fingernails."

"Mom, you sound like someone from *CSI*."

"Where is Thompson now?"

"I think he was getting ready to try to rape me again when Giovanni pounded on my door yelling that Frank Gordon wanted to see Thompson immediately."

"Thank God."

"Mom, one more thing."

"What?"

"Thompson told me he would kill you if I told you what he had done to me and would do in the future."

"The hell he will," Pam huffed. "I'll be there ASAP."

Pam rushed to get a rape kit and a high dose of levonorgestrel, commonly referred to as Plan B, from cabinets in the ER.

On her way home, Pam marveled at Teddy's fighting spirit, which until now had mostly been unleashed on the tennis and basketball courts.

She certainly is her father's daughter, Pam thought.

***

Pam examined her daughter, collecting her skin and semen samples, and then let Teddy shower.

"Get dressed, Teddy. Pack a small bag with enough clothes and cosmetics for a few days. Also, you'll probably want your laptop. I'll do the same. We can buy anything we need that we don't bring with us."

"What are we going to do? I don't want Thompson to get anywhere near me unless I have a gun so I can shoot the SOB."

"I may deprive you of that outcome by shooting him myself," Pam said.

"Where are we going?"

"Durham, North Carolina. I have friends from my time at Duke. They can take us in for a while until we figure out what we can do about Thompson."

"Can't we go to the police here in Atlanta?"

"Frank Gordon probably has someone in the police department on his payroll."

Once the mother and daughter were in Pam's BMW and driving toward I-85 North, Pam asked, "Did Thompson say anything that would explain why he tried to rape you?"

"Thompson said he had seen me masturbating many times and knew I wanted, and needed, a real man to satisfy me. He said I would enjoy it much more than masturbating."

"He said he saw you? Where? How?"

"Yes. He must have hidden a camera in my bedroom."

CHAPTER 2

Jason Andrews Jr. walked through the exit doors at the Delta terminal in the Atlanta Hartsfield-Jackson airport late Sunday morning. His erect posture and lean frame reflected his twenty years of military service, first as a graduate of the US Naval Academy and then as a jet fighter pilot. His lithe economy of movement derived from many years of martial arts training.

A new, red Ford F-150 truck with *Andrews Poultry Industries* emblazoned on the front doors abruptly stopped in front of Jason at the curb. Jason saluted the driver, tossed his carry-on bag into the bed of the truck, and climbed into the cab.

The driver, Martin Andrews, was about twenty-five pounds heavier and three-inches taller than Jason. Martin looked as if he could easily resume his former career as a professional football player, his arms and chest still thick.

"So, bro, you managed to sell the Ruskies our dark meat?" the driver said as he steered into the thick airport traffic.

"I did, Martin, all we can produce."

"Like I been telling you for years, dark meat is the sweetest."

"Even so, I like a tender piece of white meat." Jason smiled.

"You brokered a good price?"

"Miz Lizbeth will be happy to hear the details. It's the new global economy."

"How about London?" Martin asked.

"What do you mean?"

"You know exactly what I mean. Will the Lady Burgess be joining you in holy matrimony?"

"No."

Martin drove the truck onto I-85 North. He checked to ensure his way was unobstructed and pushed the speed to eighty miles per hour, moving easily with the traffic through midtown Atlanta.

"What happened? Did your studliness fail to close the deal?"

"Seems that way. Philippa has decided to marry Sir Percival Talbot."

"Sir Percival! Surely not a descendent from King Arthur's Round Table?"

"They're friends from childhood. Both sets of parents want Philippa and Percival to marry, to unite the family fortunes, and to provide for continuation of the bloodlines."

"Did you have sex with Philippa before this decision?"

"I did."

"Then, afterwards, she informed you that a great time in bed didn't trump family status?"

"She offered to be available whenever I could come to the UK."

"What did you say?"

"Thank you and hell no."

"Good for you, though Miz Lizbeth will be powerfully disappointed you won't produce children for a while."

"You're taking care of that. How's Shanna?" Jason asked.

"About to pop."

"There you go. Miz Lizbeth will have a grandson."

"Not the same as you fathering a child."

"How so?" Jason asked.

"I'm the African-American member of this family. Miz Lizbeth will highly appreciate a grandchild from your white loins. You need to do your duty."

The two men rode in comfortable silence for almost an hour while listening to WABE, the Atlanta NPR station. "Dang," Martin said, watching the outside mirror on the driver's side of the truck. "Look at this BMW."

A white sedan passed their truck as if it were standing still. Martin caught a glimpse of a young girl in the passenger seat who mouthed "Help" as the BMW flew by. An older woman drove the sedan, both hands on the steering wheel with eyes locked on the road ahead.

"Looks like damsels in distress." Martin pushed the accelerator.

Seconds later, a black Suburban with dark-tinted windows passed the truck, presumably in pursuit of the BMW.

"Punch it," Jason said.

"We'll see how fast our new truck goes." The F-150 jetted to 120 miles per hour as it crossed over the Alexander County line.

"Time for my Glock," Jason said, removing his holstered .40 caliber Model 22 pistol.

"Glove compartment," Martin ordered, keeping his eyes fixed on the road.

Jason reached in. "Is this a gun or cannon?" he jested.

"Yes, it's my Dirty Harry," Martin said, referring to the .44 magnum Smith & Wesson Model 29 revolver that Clint Eastwood made famous in his Dirty Harry movies. "You know perfectly well I won't go to Hotlanta without adequate protection."

"Or anywhere else except church, and I'm not entirely sure about that."

When questioned why they carried concealed weapons permits and were typically armed, Jason and Martin would routinely invoke their Second Amendment rights. This truthful response hid the primary reason the two brothers carried arms.

A long-standing personal and business competition with the Whitfield clan, another prominent family in Alexander County, Georgia, had resulted in the death of the brothers' father, and serious permanent injury to Jason's mother.

Martin spotted the BMW, which had been forced off the interstate highway and into the embankment on the right side of the secondary road leading to Mercerville, the Alexander County seat. Steam erupted from the hood. Two burly men, one of whom carried a tire iron, left the Suburban and approached the BMW. The man with the tire iron pummeled the passenger's side rear window, shattering the glass.

Martin skidded the F-150 to a stop in between the BMW and the Suburban. Jason and Martin quickly exited the F-150, pistols in their right hands behind their backs.

"What's happening, fellas?" Jason asked the two men, who halted their assault upon the BMW.

"None of your business," one of the assailants snarled.

"We're making it our business," Martin said, his voice ice cold.

"Get away from the BMW," Jason ordered.

"You've got me confused with someone," the first man said.

"With who?" Martin asked.

"Someone who pays any attention whatsoever to you."

Martin's pistol boomed, and its .44-caliber slug passed between the two men, who had reached inside their sports jackets.

"See, here's the situation," Jason said, his Glock sighted and steady on the first man. "If you two idiots think you can get to whatever you have inside your jackets before my brother and I put bullets between your eyes, go right ahead." The men hesitated. "Pull those weapons out slowly with your thumbs and forefingers. Toss the weapons on the ground or you're dead," Jason said.

The men complied. "Do the same thing with the pistols in your ankle holsters," Jason said. The men again grudgingly followed Jason's orders.

"Martin and I can shoot the two of you before you even think about charging us." The two men moved away from the BMW. "Martin, I've got them in my sights. Why don't you get the two ladies out of the car?"

Martin went to the driver's side of the BMW and saw the deflated air bags. He motioned to the attractive woman behind the wheel to open the door. Obviously shaken, she struggled out of the car.

She held Martin's arm and he felt her tremble. "Stand behind my brother." Martin went to the passenger door, signaling the teenaged girl to get out of the car. The tall and pretty young girl resembled her mother. "Missy, please walk with me to stand with your mother. Ladies, whatever happens, keep my brother and me between you and these two men."

"They aren't men . . . they're assholes," the girl spat. She glared at Martin as though she recognized him.

"Ladies, why are these two assholes chasing you?" Martin asked.

"They're trying to take us back to my perverted stepfather, the sexual deviant," the girl said.

"Teddy, shut your face," one of the men barked. "This affair stays within the family."

"Well, you for damn sure aren't part of my family, and we're not in your crime family," the girl said.

"Teddy," the man shouted, "shut up!"

Teddy let loose with a torrent of profanity. When she paused to take in a deep breath, her mother said, "Language, Theodora, language."

Jason spoke to the woman, who had regained her composure. "Ma'am, I'm Jason Andrews and this fierce-looking gentleman with me is my brother, Martin Andrews."

"I'm Dr. Pamela Kendal. Thank you for your bravery in rescuing us."

Jason nodded. "Dr. Kendal, your daughter tells the truth?"

"She doesn't exaggerate. My husband, Theodora's stepfather, sexually assaulted her earlier today. We're trying to get away from him."

"Pam, shut your mouth or you'll be really sorry. Our orders are to bring Teddy back to Mr. Kendal, with or without you."

The more vocal assailant glared at Martin and Jason. "Teddy comes home with us. For all we care, Pam, you can stay here with these two turkeys."

Jason looked quickly at Martin. "Brother, are we missing something here?"

"No, we aren't confused. These wannabe tough guys don't understand the tactical situation."

"Screw you," the man responded.

"Dr. Kendal, do you know these men?" Jason asked.

"The one in front of your brother is Giovanni, and the one in front of you is Alberto."

"Do they have last names?"

Teddy laughed. "Asshole One and Asshole Two."

"Theodora, act like a lady!" the mother demanded.

"I think we need to enlighten Giovanni the loudmouth and Alberto about current reality," Martin said.

"What do you have in mind?" Jason asked.

"A marksmanship contest."

"Between you and me?"

"Well, we won't give these two idiots their guns," Martin said. He paused as if thinking. "On the other hand, if we have a shootout in which we definitely will prevail, be no loose ends to clean up."

"Except a lot of unnecessary paperwork," Jason said.

"Do it! Kill them both!" Teddy encouraged.

"Please define the terms of this shooting contest. I can beat you at whatever you have in mind," Jason said.

"Highly unlikely. Here's the deal. I bet I can shoot off the hanging down part of Giovanni's ear before you can do the same to Alberto."

"Which ear?"

"The one on my right, Giovanni's left ear."

Jason nodded. "And I shoot the same ear on Alberto?"

"You gotta shoot only the earlobe, or you lose."

"You're on," Jason grinned.

"You and your nigger brother don't know who you're dealing with," Giovanni said.

"Well, Giovanni, you best be real still or this nigger's most excellent aim might be off," Martin said. His pistol roared, and Giovanni stumbled backwards when the slug passed within a half-inch of his ear.

"What the hell?" Giovanni bellowed.

"You missed, brother. Alberto, it's my turn, and I won't miss." Jason took careful aim.

"Wait a minute, bro. Look at the front of Giovanni's pants." A dark wet stain had appeared on the man's trousers. "I think I hit him after all. I bet he's also crapped his britches."

"Doesn't matter. I win if I shoot off Alberto's earlobe," Jason said.

"Jason—" Teddy began.

"Theodora, he's Mr. Jason. You haven't been given permission to call these two men by their first names. They're adults; you're still a teenager," Pamela chastised.

"Misssterr Jason, please let me have your gun and I'll shoot off Alberto's ear, unless I miss and put a hole in his head," Teddy said.

"Missy, I gotta admit you got spirit. You should understand, though, my brother's a military man and always tries to be proper with his terminology," Martin said.

"What do you mean, Misssterr Martin?"

"The proper terminology for what he has in his right hand is weapon, firearm, sidearm, or pistol—not gun."

"Whatever. Mr. Jason, I would greatly appreciate your letting me take a shot at Alberto's earlobe."

"Have you had any firearm training?" Jason asked Teddy.

"My perverted, sexual deviant of a stepfather taught me to shoot."

"With a pistol?"

"A Sig Sauer P328."

"A nice pistol for a young lady," Martin said.

"Even so, better if I shoot Alberto's earlobe," Jason said.

"If I miss, you can have the second shot and still win the bet," Teddy said.

"If you manage to hit only Alberto's earlobe, my brother will never let me hear the end of this matter."

Martin snorted. "You're right about that. I'll spread the word that you let a young lady perform your manly duties." He shook his head. "No, missy, better to let my brother have his turn at winning this bet."

A siren whooped, announcing the arrival of an Alexander County sheriff's patrol car.

CHAPTER 3

The stocky officer, whose uniform appeared to be about to rip apart around his neck, approached. "Good to see you, A-Team."

"Hey, Deputy Dog. Glad you're here," Martin replied.

The officer kept his hand on the pistol holstered at his waist.

"Let me introduce myself to those of you who don't know me. I am Captain Covington of the Alexander County Sheriff's Department. Jason and Martin, what's going down?"

"These two guys, Giovanni and Alberto, ran Dr. Kendal and her daughter, Theodora, off the road. Jason and I got here before Giovanni and Alberto could break into Dr. Kendal's car. We were holding them until you arrived," Martin said.

"We made a citizen's arrest," Jason added.

"Is that right, Dr. Kendal?" the captain asked.

The mother waved Teddy to silence. "Captain, Jason and Martin rescued us. My husband sent these two after us when he discovered we had left him."

"My mom means my sexual pervert of a stepfather," Teddy interrupted.

"Is what your daughter said correct?" the captain asked.

"I have incontrovertible proof of the molestation," Pam affirmed.

Giovanni tried to regain control of the situation. "I'm telling you for the last time, Pam and Teddy, shut your mouths. Teddy goes back to Atlanta with Alberto and me."

"Is that right?" the captain asked.

"You have no idea who you're dealing with. Teddy goes with us. Try to stop us and you'll be sorry," Alberto said.

The captain's expandable defensive baton whipped through the air, striking Alberto's left shoulder. He fell to his knees, screaming in agony. The captain backhanded the baton across Alberto's back, driving the man to the ground, and to silence.

The tip of the captain's baton twitched in front of Giovanni's face. "We don't talk to law enforcement personnel or women in such a disrespectful manner in Alexander County."

Alberto, on the ground, reached for his pistol. The baton whipped through the air to strike his hand, eliciting another scream.

"Dispatch, send a couple of cars and four deputies to the Mercerville exit off of northbound I-85," the captain said into his hand radio. "I have two malefactors and a vehicle for transport to the county jail."

A Georgia State Patrol car pulled up to the group. The trooper left his car and approached Captain Covington. "Bruce, looks like you have the situation in control. Have you called for backup, or do you want me to help?"

"Thanks for the offer, Charlie. My deputies should be here any minute. I hear their sirens."

The state trooper introduced himself to the mother and daughter. "Trooper Charles Lane of the Georgia State Patrol, ladies. Sorry to meet you under these circumstances. You're in good hands with Captain Covington, and with Jason and Martin." He grinned. "Are Jason and Martin playing heroes again?"

"That they are, thank goodness," Pam said.

"They're good people, well-known in this county, with

excellent reputations," Trooper Lane said before turning to the captain. "Bruce, we received several calls about a kidnapping taking place on I-85. Are these two men you have in custody the perpetrators?"

"I made the calls on my cell phone," Teddy said.

"The calls brought me here. The A-Team prevented me from being the hero," Captain Covington said.

"What charges do you plan to bring against . . ." Trooper Lane started.

"Giovanni and Alberto. We haven't had time to discover their last names," Jason interjected.

Captain Covington bestowed a mirthless smile on Giovanni and Alberto.

"If the two ladies and the A-Team are willing to testify, I believe we can bring charges of attempted kidnapping, attempted vehicular homicide, resisting arrest, and attempted assault of a peace officer against the men without any question. We probably can add a charge of abetting the sexual assault of a minor. I'll have a meeting with the county DA tomorrow."

Giovanni glowered and shook his head. "Mr. Kendal will have us out of your Podunk jail as soon as we call him."

"Is Giovanni talking about your husband?" Jason asked Pam. "Is he a lawyer?"

"My husband's a criminal defense attorney in Atlanta."

"The pervert has only one client—Frank Gordon," Teddy said.

"You could be dealing with a tough situation, Bruce," Trooper Lane said.

"You know this Frank Gordon and Lawyer Kendal?" Captain Covington asked.

"They're familiar to law enforcement in Atlanta."

Two Alexander County patrol cars arrived. Four deputies waited for orders.

"Ladies, gentlemen, I'll take my leave. Bruce, I'm going to the truck stop for a break. Care to join me there?" Trooper Lane asked.

"I'll be there directly." Captain Covington turned to the four deputies. "Handcuff these criminals, pick up their weapons, get their cell phones, and take the men to the jail. One of you drive the Suburban. I'll be at the jail after I have coffee with Trooper Lane. We'll book these malefactors when I get to the jail. Don't let them have access to a phone."

"Pam, we'll be back to get Teddy," Giovanni said with malevolence.

"You won't get out of our jail until Monday afternoon at the earliest, even if Judge Watkins agrees to give you bond," Captain Covington said. He spoke to Martin and Jason. "I suspect the good judge abides in his cabin on the lake. If the fish are biting and he's laid in a good supply of Black Jack, he may not be back until mid-week."

Captain Covington returned his gaze to Giovanni and Alberto. "As for you two, our jailhouse phone is out of order and you can't have your cell phones. You'll have to enjoy our county's hospitality for an indeterminate time." He ordered the deputies, "Take 'em away. No need to be particularly gentle."

The deputies shoved Giovanni and Alberto into the back seats of separate cruisers.

"Dr. Kendal, we can't leave you stranded on the side of the road with no place to stay. What can we do to help you and your daughter?" Captain Covington asked.

CHAPTER 4

"Is there a nearby BMW dealer where we can send our car to be repaired?" Pam asked.

"About forty-five-minutes away in Anderson, South Carolina," Captain Covington answered.

"Ma'am, we have an excellent mechanic here in Vickery. He's what we call a 'car shark,'" Martin said

"Rufus repairs anything with wheels and a motor. I'll have him pick up your Beemer and take it to his shop," Captain Covington said.

"I don't want the car damaged further," Pam said.

"You can trust Rufus," Jason said.

"All right. Teddy and I need a ride to a local motel," Pam said.

Martin motioned Captain Covington to be silent and turned to Jason. "Here's your opportunity to redeem yourself with Miz Lizbeth."

Jason took the hint. "Dr. Kendal, we'd be honored to have you and your daughter stay with us at the Big House for as long as necessary or for as long as you like."

"Dr. Kendal, the Andrews family will see to your wellbeing. You shouldn't stay in a motel unprotected," Captain Covington said.

"What's the Big House, a prison?" Teddy asked.

"Everyone around here calls the Andrews home the Big House because of its size," Captain Covington said.

"Dr. Kendal, Theodora. We'll put you in one of the wings to the house," Jason said. "You'll have as much privacy as you wish, although we'd like for you to share meals with us."

"Let's do it, Mom. We've been rescued with a promise of safety," Teddy urged.

"Thank you, Jason and Martin. We'd rather stay with you and your family instead of being alone in a motel."

"Good decision. I'll call Rufus and wait here until he comes for your car," Captain Covington said.

Martin moved near the captain and spoke in a low voice. "No reason for Rufus to hurry with the repairs. You feel me?"

"I do."

"We have a plan. Dr. Kendal, if you'll give me your keys, we'll get your luggage transferred to our truck and be on our way," Jason said.

"Please be sure to get my black bag and the blue cooler," Pam replied.

"And my laptop," Teddy added.

***

"Wow!" Teddy exclaimed when Martin drove the F-150 into the circular driveway at the front of the Andrews residence. "A big house for sure."

"No place like home," Jason said.

A tall, stately man came out the front door of the house and walked to the truck. He inclined his head to Jason in the passenger's seat before walking to the driver's side to open the rear door of the truck and help the doctor out.

"Welcome, Dr. Kendal. We received Jason's call that you and your daughter were coming. I'm Jackson Williams. We're happy to have the two of you with us."

Jason opened the rear door behind him, and Teddy left the truck. Jason escorted the two women to the front steps while Martin and Jackson retrieved the luggage. A woman pushed through the screened front door with her wheelchair. "Ladies, I'm Elizabeth Andrews. I hope my two sons have treated you respectfully."

"Mr. Jason and Mr. Martin are our heroes," Teddy said.

"They do have their moments."

Mrs. Andrews motioned the group to come onto the wide porch. Jackson stood by the luggage and looked inquiringly at her. "Please put the bags in the north wing, Jackson." She looked at Jason. "I'm assuming these two ladies will be with us for a while?"

"For as long as they want to stay. Dr. Kendal and her daughter, Theodora, will be under our protection," Jason said.

"Dr. Kendal, Theodora, we're pleased to have you with us as guests. Do you want to sleep in the same room, or do you prefer separate bedrooms? We can accommodate either in the north wing," Mrs. Andrews said.

"Together tonight, probably separate bedrooms afterwards, please," Teddy said.

"Can you put the contents of the blue cooler in a refrigerator?" Pam asked.

"Make it so, Jackson," Mrs. Andrews said in an accidental imitation of Captain Jean-Luc Picard on the television series *Star Trek: The Next Generation.*

"I will." Jackson moved the luggage and cooler inside the front door.

"Dr. Kendal and Theodora, perhaps at cocktail hour you can tell us about your adventures with my sons. I suspect you might first wish to rest and clean up. I understand you've had a hard day," Mrs. Andrews said.

A tall, beautiful woman with milk chocolate–colored skin came through the front door. The last stages of pregnancy did not detract from her regal bearing. She kissed Martin on his check. "Welcome home, husband."

Teddy's eyes widened. "You're Shanna Graves, and Mr. Martin was a player and coach with the Los Angeles Chargers. That's why he looks familiar to me!"

"Well, child, you've tagged us," Shanna said.

"Mom, Shanna's a supermodel. Everyone's been wondering why she dropped out of sight."

"How do you know about this lady and Mr. Martin?" Pam asked.

"I read *Entertainment Today* and *People* magazines."

"I'm here in the wilds of northeast Georgia in order to avoid publicity over this birth," Shanna said. "I'd like to have the boy-child in a quiet and peaceful place whenever he finally decides to make his belated appearance,"

"When's your due date?" Pam asked.

"Two weeks ago."

"Your first birth?"

"Yes. I saw Jackson taking your luggage and a small black bag to the north wing. Are you a physician?"

"I am. I work, or at least I worked until today, in the ER at Grady—Grady Memorial Hospital—in Atlanta."

"Enough chit-chat for now. Our guests must rest." Mrs. Andrews smiled at Teddy. "Theodora—"

"Teddy, please, ma'am," the girl said.

"Teddy, I know how you young people like to keep in touch on social media; even so, please don't let anyone know that Shanna stays with us. We can't allow the paparazzi or even legitimate reporters access to the property."

"Theodora, you understand the importance of Mrs. Andrews's instruction?" Pam asked.

"I do."

"Mrs. Andrews, as I'm sure your sons will inform you, Teddy

and I have no wish to alert anyone to our presence here. Thank you for your hospitality," Pam said.

"Let's not be formal. Most everyone calls me Miz Lizbeth."

"Thank you, Miz Lizbeth. Please call me Pam or Pamela."

"I'd like to keep up with what's happening back in the world, although I definitely won't tell anyone we're here, Miz Lizbeth. Do you have Internet access at the Big House?" Teddy asked.

"We do. You'll see Andrews Poultry Industries when you turn on your laptop. LizJasMarJackson is the access code."

Jackson came back to the porch. "If our guests are ready, I'll take them to their rooms."

"By all means. Pam, Teddy, cocktails will be available in about an hour. Someone will knock on your door," Miz Lizbeth said.

Teddy brightened. "Adult libations?"

"I imagine Miz Lizbeth will have soft drinks for you," Pam said.

"We'll offer Miss Theodora a variety of non-alcoholic choices," Jackson said. He escorted Pam and Teddy to the north wing.

"Jason and Martin, unless you two are exhausted from your heroic deeds, I'd appreciate your telling Shanna, Jackson, and me the backstory," Miz Lizbeth said.

"A pre-happy hour drink of Jameson's would help," Jason said.

Martin shook his head. "I'll have a real man's drink, Wild Turkey."

Miz Lizbeth motioned to Jason. "Wheel me into the den. I'll need a martini while we assess the implications of what you two have done. In addition, Jason, I want a summary of the deal you closed in Moscow with the 'Evil Empire.'"

"In view of my precarious condition," Shanna laughed, "ice water for me."

CHAPTER 5

Miz Lizbeth greeted Pam and Teddy when they came into to the den an hour later.

"I hope you've had a good rest, ladies. Please sit with us. Jackson will prepare whatever libation you wish."

"A single-malt Scotch on ice for me," Teddy said.

Pam shook her head and looked to Jackson. "Don't waste a single malt on her, Mr. Jackson. Please give her something like Dewar's diluted with a lot of water and ice."

"Mom!" Teddy protested.

"Dr. Kendal, what may I fix for you?" Jackson asked

"A dry martini, please, if you have the ingredients."

"Gin or vodka?"

"Gin, with only a few drops of vermouth."

"I have Noilly Pratt extra dry vermouth and Beefeater's gin. Up or on ice, ma'am?"

Pam sank into an easy chair next to Jason. "Up and very cold."

Miz Lizbeth held up her own martini glass for Jackson to refill. "Teddy, please sit beside me." Teddy sat in a large overstuffed chair next to Miz Lizbeth's wheelchair.

"Let's review the bidding from this afternoon. Pam and Teddy, from what I've been told, my sons prevented two hoodlums from abducting you, from taking you back to Atlanta," Miz Lizbeth said.

Pam sighed. "They primarily wanted Teddy."

"Giovanni and Alberto had orders to return me to my perverted stepfather," Teddy said.

"The two men work for Frank Gordon, my second husband's primary, maybe his only, client," Pam added.

"He's a mobster in Atlanta, probably mafioso," Teddy said.

"Pam, I take it that Teddy is your daughter from a previous marriage?"

"That's right. Her father, Theodore Nelson, was killed in action, but we don't know where. He was a captain in the Army; he led a Special Forces team."

"You subsequently remarried?" Miz Lizbeth asked.

"I did, to L. Thompson Kendal, a lawyer. Teddy's last name is Nelson."

"Despite Thompson's objections, I presume?" Miz Lizbeth asked. "You've been happy in this marriage?"

Pam took a deep breath. "Problems surfaced in recent years."

"Martin, Jackson," Miz Lizbeth said, "perhaps you'd best check on the fence lines and assess the progress with our dinner while we ladies talk. Jason can stay with us."

When the men left, Teddy stomped her foot. "Miz Lizbeth, it is what it is. I don't mind telling all of you what happened."

"You have the floor, Teddy, to whatever extent you wish to share," Miz Lizbeth said.

"Thompson tried to rape me this morning. He said he would kill Mom if I protested or told her what had happened."

"How old are you?" Miz Lizbeth asked.

"Almost sixteen. I have no doubt Thompson would have had Mom killed if he knew I revealed what he had done, and what he intended to do again." Teddy took a deep breath. "Thompson said he had been watching me masturbate, and knew I needed a real man to have sex with."

"Have your mother killed?" Miz Lizbeth shook her head. "His own wife."

"He probably doesn't have the balls to do it himself," Teddy said. "He'd have contracted with Giovanni and Alberto to kill her."

"You left today?" Miz Lizbeth asked Pam.

"When Teddy called me to report what had happened to her, I took a rape kit and a dose of levonorgestrel—Plan B—home with me," Pam said. "I called Grady Hospital, and told them I needed a leave of absence for personal reasons."

"Plan B?" Miz Lizbeth asked.

"It's a very high dose of the active ingredient in many birth-control pills. Plan B can be used to prevent pregnancies under circumstances of rape, like with Teddy, and other instances of unprotected sexual intercourse. I for damn sure don't want Teddy to become pregnant."

"Me neither," Teddy said.

"I performed an examination on Teddy and collected samples for the rape kit," Pam said.

"It's in the blue cooler?"

"Yes. I hope to have the rape kit analyzed to provide evidence against Thompson."

"We can help with having the rape kit processed by law enforcement," Jason offered.

"Captain Covington?" Teddy asked.

"He'll send the rape kit to the appropriate lab," Jason said. "Your husband may raise an objection to the findings based on the chain of evidence."

"I used my cell phone to record the examination Mom did on me and how she put the rape kit in the blue cooler," Teddy said.

"Where is your cell phone, Teddy?" Jason asked.

Teddy retrieved the iPhone from her jeans pocket. "While we were resting, I copied the video from my iPhone to my laptop."

"I suggest some more duplication of the video," Jason said, "in case something were to happen to your laptop. I'll give you my email address after dinner and you can send the video to me."

"What did you do next, Pam?" Miz Lizbeth asked.

"Teddy and I headed north, until Giovanni and Alberto ran us off the road."

"Where were you going?"

"To Durham. I went to medical school at Duke and still have friends there. I thought they might give us shelter until we figured out our next move."

"Pam, Teddy. You may stay with us for as long as you want. I concur with what Jason declared earlier: You are under our protection," Miz Lizbeth said.

"Thank you, Miz Lizbeth. Nevertheless, you need to know that my husband associates with some dangerous men, like Giovanni and Alberto."

Teddy laughed. "They didn't look too dangerous this afternoon when Mr. Jason, Mr. Martin and Captain Covington dealt with them."

"Frank Gordon has many more men at his disposal," Pam said.

"Did you know about your husband's association with this Frank Gordon before you married Thompson?" Miz Lizbeth asked Pam.

"Thompson told me he was a criminal defense attorney. As time went on, I learned that Frank Gordon was his only client, and I heard news about Gordon being a mob boss. Thompson kept Frank and several of his associates, including Giovanni and Alberto, out of jail. Thompson's a great lawyer, and he's well-paid."

"This association didn't concern you?"

"Thompson explained that all persons, even reputed mobsters, were entitled to adequate legal representation. I accepted the concept by analogy to the fact that I treat all patients who come into the ER, regardless of their background and status."

"How did Giovanni and Alberto come into the picture with you, Teddy?" Jason asked.

"They often took me to school and brought me home when Mom was busy at the hospital. If I wanted to go to the mall, they would take me, stay with me."

"Were you able to see your friends without Giovanni and Alberto?"

"Those two guys were always in the background. Mostly, my friends came to our house."

"Teddy, you say Thompson saw you masturbating?" Jason asked.

"He must have put a camera in my bedroom," Teddy said.

"The camera was probably transmitting images somewhere where Thompson could view them privately," Jason said. "Do you have any idea where?"

"Probably in his study. He spends a lot of time there, ostensibly working," Pam said. "I'll bet he recorded her."

"Teddy, you are a brave and resourceful young lady who has been thrust into a terrible situation," Miz Lizbeth said. "I'm sure Pam will arrange for appropriate therapy for you . . . and for herself."

Teddy smiled weakly before her face darkened. "The best therapy would be for someone to shoot the bastard in his testicles."

"What kind of pistol would you use?" Jason joked.

"The Sig Sauer P328 that he taught me to shoot."

Jason grinned as Martin stepped back into the room. "Just like I said earlier, that's the perfect pistol for a young lady."

Miz Lizbeth spoke to her sons. "Enough already, you two."

Jason changed the subject. "Pam, you're right; he probably set up his equipment to record Teddy. Do you have any idea where he might be keeping the recordings?" Jason asked.

"In a safe in his study," Teddy said. "I went into his study one night to ask him something about the law for a homework assignment. He had his laptop open on his desk, and he quickly put the laptop in his safe and closed the door." Teddy shrugged. "That's all I have to say today, except . . . thanks, to all of you." She swept her hands across the room.

Jackson entered as if he had been summoned. "Need anything, Miz Lizbeth?"

"Jackson, unless Pam strenuously objects, please pour this brave young lady a generous portion of the twenty-five-year-old Glenmorangie single malt. She deserves it, as well as our respect and admiration."

"Mom?" Teddy asked.

"Of course. Don't expect to make a habit of it."

"You all look like you've been put through a wringer. Shall I refresh everyone's drinks?" Jackson asked.

"I think we deserve refills. And please tell the ladies in the kitchen we are ready for dinner."

After Jackson left, Miz Lizbeth resumed the conversation.

"Pamela, Theodora, this unfortunate business cannot be over until the legal system becomes involved or the situation is resolved through other means. I remind you about what I said earlier; the two of you are under our protection for as long as necessary." She held up a hand to forestall any comment. "I will not have this family's friends, new or old, endangered. Our family lawyer will be in her Vickery office tomorrow. We must confer with her."

"Thompson knows how to work the legal system," Pam said.

"We have our own fearless barracuda who has helped this family on many occasions. I have complete confidence in her," Miz Lizbeth said.

"Thank you," Pam said.

Jackson came back into the room. "Miz Lizbeth, time to eat."

"So it is. Please lead our guests into the dining room and get them seated. My sons and I will follow directly. Shanna will act as hostess until I get there."

When the room cleared Miz Lizbeth spoke to her sons. "We'll have a nice dinner and you two will be on your best behavior. After dinner, you must set up some security. Get Jackson to recommend a few of our most reliable men to take turns guarding the roads coming into the property. Make sure they have cell phones."

"You want them armed?" Jason asked.

"For damn sure. We face monsters. Our men should exercise restraint and call the Big House first when someone unknown comes onto the property. If fired upon, they should fire back." She propelled the wheelchair to face the hallway leading to the dining room. "One of you wheel me to the table. I'm starving."

CHAPTER 6

Vaguely aware that Teddy had left the bedroom an hour previously, Pam smelled the faint odors of breakfast on her way to the bathroom opening off the spacious bedroom. She splashed cold water on her face, and brushed her short, sculpted blond hair. Satisfied that she looked reasonably presentable without makeup, Pam dressed in fresh clothes and followed her nose to the kitchen.

"Good morning, Dr. Kendal," one of the two female cooks greeted Pam. "Breakfast will be ready for everyone in about half an hour."

"Thank you. I'd like some orange juice, if you have it, and some of that, please," Pam said, pointing to several pieces of bacon draining on paper towels.

"Of course." The cook gave Pam three pieces of bacon and a tall glass of orange juice with copious amounts of pulp. "Will this tide you over until breakfast?"

Pam crunched on a piece of the perfectly cooked bacon. "Wonderful." She downed the orange juice without pausing.

"Miz Lizbeth wants all of us to make sure you have what you need. May I get you something else, perhaps a cup of coffee?" the cook asked.

"Coffee would be outstanding. I hope you have lots more of this bacon."

"An abundance. Mr. Jason and Mr. Martin will be starved after their morning tennis match." The cook gave Pam a large cup of coffee. "Sugar or cream?"

"No way."

"The family, except for Mr. Jason and Mr. Martin, are on the side porch." The cook grinned. "Just follow your ears to the bloodletting."

"I don't know your name."

"Sally Williams," the cook replied. "The other lady with me is my sister-in-law, Ann Johnson Williams."

"Thank you, Sally and Ann," Pam said as she made her way out of the kitchen.

"Mom, you gotta see what's happening on the tennis court," Teddy said when Pam came to the porch. Jason and Martin were battling on the grass tennis court at the side of the house. Teddy held out her hand.

Pam gave Teddy one of the remaining pieces of bacon. "There's more in the kitchen."

"I'm not leaving the porch until Mr. Jason and Mr. Martin finish this match. They play like professionals," Teddy said.

"Who's winning, Teddy?"

"Jackson said they've been at it almost three hours. They each won a set and are even in the third. Neither ever concedes, according to Jackson."

"What's the scores in the sets?"

"They each went to tiebreakers, 7-6, 7-6. Now they're at three games each in the third set."

"Good morning, Pam," Miz Lizbeth interrupted. "I trust you and Teddy had a restful night."

"We did. And I'm looking forward to breakfast. We're enjoying watching your sons ravage each other on the tennis court."

"Yes, quite a sight. You'd think they were playing for the Wimbledon championship," Miz Lizabeth chuckled.

"Why is there no rim on the basketball backboard by the tennis court?" Pam asked.

"Jackson and I grew tired of having to restrain my two sons from attacking each other when they played one-on-one."

"They're fierce competitors, I take it?"

"As you can see on the court. The sibling contests pale in comparison to the two of them against non-family competitors."

"Mom and I saw a version of that competition when Mr. Jason and Mr. Martin rescued us," Teddy said.

Miz Lizbeth smiled. "Please enlighten me."

"They had a marksmanship contest using Giovanni and Alberto's ears as targets. Our two heroes said the two . . ." Teddy looked at her mother. ". . . criminals didn't understand the tactical situation."

"Were my two sons actually shooting at the two men?"

"Only at their earlobes. Mr. Martin missed his first shot at Giovanni. Captain Covington arrived before Mr. Jason could take his turn with Alberto."

Miz Lizbeth chuckled wryly. "Teddy, I can assure you that Martin missed on purpose. Both of my sons are remarkably good marksmen. What was the distance between my sons and the two criminals, as you called them?"

Teddy indicated the distance from where she was seated to the nearest end of the porch. "About that far."

"Martin probably wanted to frighten this Giovanni and get his full attention."

"Giovanni wet his pants."

"I wish I had been there," Miz Lizbeth said.

"Captain Covington called Martin and Jason the A-Team," Pam said.

"That's right, for the Andrews Team. Bruce, Jason, and Martin played football together in high school. The high school team won the state championship in their senior year. And then both sons were state champions or runner-ups in tennis each of their four years in high school."

"Who won more championships?" Teddy asked.

"They each won two championships and were runner-ups to each other twice."

"Did they play doubles together?" Teddy asked.

"They were the state champions four years running."

"Teddy won the all-Atlanta youth tennis championship for her age bracket earlier this summer," Pam said.

"Teddy, maybe you can play against my sons while you and your mother are here," Miz Lizbeth said.

"Miz Lizbeth, I'd very much like to play with them. They'd need to ease up a lot or I'd be blown off the court."

"They probably won't 'ease up' much on you. If you stick with them, you might well become as fierce on the tennis court as they are. Do you play tennis, Pam?"

"Mom would be an excellent player, if she had more time," Teddy said.

"Seems like mixed doubles are in order. That way my sons could be influenced toward more gentlemanly behavior on the court."

"What did your sons do after high school?" Pam asked. "From Teddy's comment last night, I understand Martin must have played professional football."

"Martin went to the University of Georgia where he played wide receiver on the football team, as he did in high school. He was an all-American in his junior and senior years. The Los Angeles Chargers drafted him, and he played ten years for them before joining their coaching staff."

"Yesterday, Mr. Martin said something about Mr. Jason being a military man," Teddy said.

"That's right. Jason went to the US Naval Academy after high school and then flew jet fighters for twenty years. He retired with the rank of commander."

"What type of fighter did he fly?"

"F-18 Super Hornets, he told me."

"The twin tail monsters?"

"Ask him to show you the pictures he keeps in his bedroom."

"Did he go to Top Gun school like in the Tom Cruise movie?"

"The Navy wanted Jason to be an instructor there when I summoned him and Martin to come home."

"You summoned them?" Pam asked.

"I did. I want to keep this place and all our business interests in the family."

"They came willingly?"

"They came and are thoroughly involved in the businesses."

"What about after Shanna has her baby? Will she stay here or go back to her modeling career?" Teddy asked.

"That matter remains under discussion. I think Shanna wants to live here and work selectively as a fashion model." Miz Lizbeth laughed. "Jackson and I raised two fine sons, so I guess we can see to the upbringing of a grandson when Shanna travels, if she returns to modeling."

"May I ask you something personal, Miz Lizbeth?" Teddy asked.

"You want to know about the parentage of my two sons?"

"Yes, ma'am, if you don't mind telling us."

"I'll give you the short version. Jason was a year old when we left him here with a babysitter while my husband, Jason Sr., and I went out to dinner with friends. On the way home, we were in an . . . an accident with a pickup truck. Jason Sr. was killed instantly, and I ended up in this wheelchair. While I recuperated in the hospital, Jackson brought another little boy for me to see. Turns out my husband, who was a force of nature, had fathered the child. The mother worked for us and died in childbirth while I was recovering in the hospital. Jackson wanted to know what should be done with the child, Martin. I told Jackson, Martin's uncle, to bring the baby to the Big House and oversee his care until I came home. Jackson was already caring for my son, Jason. When I recovered sufficiently, I formally adopted Martin."

"Weren't you angry about your husband's behavior?" Pam asked.

"Neither angry nor surprised, only disappointed."

"Astounding," Pam said.

"I wanted my husband's second son to be a full member of the Andrews family to honor Jason Sr.'s memory. Jason Jr. and Martin grew up in all respects as full brothers; can't you tell?" Miz Lizbeth grinned, looking to the tennis court. "What's the game score in this interminable match? I've lost count."

"Thirty to forty, in favor of Mr. Jason," Teddy replied.

"Jackson, please get ready," Miz Lizbeth said.

Jackson reached inside the door to the house and retrieved a Browning 16-gauge shotgun. "Say the word, Miz Lizbeth."

Martin served a viciously twisting ball that hit the tape on Jason's backhand side. Jason's attempted return drive went into the net. Miz Lizbeth asked, "This match is tied?"

"Yes, ma'am," Teddy said.

"Perfect. Jackson, now."

"If you say so, Miz Lizbeth." Jackson fired two shots in rapid succession into the air. Jason and Martin looked to the group on the porch. "Breakfast is ready, gentlemen, and our guests are powerfully hungry."

"We need to finish this set," Martin declared.

"You will cease and desist or the next time Jackson shoots, it will be at the ball," Miz Lizbeth shouted.

"That's not fair. I have Martin on the ropes," Jason said.

"I don't care; fair isn't my concern. The welfare of our guests takes precedence."

Jason and Martin looked at each other, shrugged, and left the court. "I figure Jason needs to regain some energy," Martin said.

"Enough is enough. Wash up and join us for breakfast," Miz Lizbeth commanded.

"Yes, ma'am," both brothers replied.

"Jackson, please wheel me into the dining room. We'll talk later about what we must do next."

CHAPTER 7

Miz Lizbeth spoke to the assembled group on the porch after breakfast. "Let's discuss our next moves. Jackson, you have reliable men stationed on the roads to our property?"

"Hidden on either side of the roads, front and back entrances, behind the gates."

"You issued firearms to them?"

"Shotguns only."

"Miz Lizbeth, aren't you overreacting to this situation?" Pam asked. "I doubt my husband can find this place."

"I prefer to be well-prepared," Miz Lizbeth insisted. "You and Teddy are under our protection. At the same time, we also must be on guard for the safety of my sons. I'm confident Giovanni and Alberto, or their boss, will seek revenge."

"Mom, Miz Lizbeth's right. Thompson will employ all his resources to find us, and he'll allow Giovanni and Alberto to try to kill Mr. Jason and Mr. Martin. That's the only way those two . . . guys can recoup their honor after what happened yesterday," Teddy said.

Jason and Martin both held up their hands. "You two have something to contribute?" Miz Lizbeth asked.

"In view of all that's happened and our developing relationship, Martin and I would be more comfortable if Teddy simply calls us Jason and Martin."

"Pam, do you have any objections?" Miz Lizbeth asked.

"No, not at all."

Miz Lizbeth smiled. "All right, Jason and Martin it is, Teddy, except when non-family members are present. And Pam and Teddy may call me Elizabeth. Agreed?"

"Yes, Miz Lizbeth," Teddy said.

"Thank you." Pam reached out to touch Miz Lizbeth on the shoulder.

Miz Lizbeth placed a hand over Pam's hand and squeezed tightly. "Now that we have the nomenclature settled, we'll get back to business. Jason, I want you to take Pam and Teddy to see our attorney after lunch. I've made the appointment. We need to ascertain our legal options." She turned to Martin. "For the present, I want you to stay with Shanna while helping Jackson with the security to this place."

Martin agreed.

"Pam, after you finish with Allison, Jason will take you and Teddy to Rufus's garage. He can give you an estimate of when your car might be repaired."

Miz Lizbeth noted Teddy's expression of concern.

"No matter when your car may be ready, I strongly urge you and Teddy to remain with us. You are now part of this family and I hope you will stay with us until we resolve this unfortunate matter." She looked quickly at Jason.

Pam began to cry, tears streaming down her cheeks. "Thank you," she said.

Jason knelt before Pam. "We'll take care of you and Teddy, no matter what."

Pam put both hands on Jason's shoulders. "You have no idea of what you may be getting into with Thompson and Frank Gordon."

Jason leaned forward to kiss Pam's forehead. "You've seen only a small fraction of what Martin and I can do to our enemies." He put his hands over Pam's, still on his shoulders. "Your husband, Alberto, Giovanni, and Frank Gordon have become this family's enemies." Jason stood up and pulled Pam to her feet and embraced her.

Racked with sobs, she put her arms around Jason to hold him tightly.

"Mom, we have knights-errant who will slay our dragons," Teddy said.

"The A-Team to the rescue," Martin said.

Pam tilted her head back to look directly into Jason's eyes. "A long time has passed since I had a champion."

"You have one from this time on," Jason said. He guided Pam back to her chair.

"We're all your champions, Pam and Teddy," Miz Lizbeth said. "No one is likely to try to harm us until Giovanni and Alberto are released from the county jail. Jason, do you have an idea when that unfortunate circumstance might take place?"

"Depends upon when the good Judge Watkins comes back to town, unless Mr. Kendal can find a sympathetic judge outside Alexander County."

"Judge Watkins is probably holed up in his lake cabin drinking and fishing, probably more of the former."

***

Jason drove his Honda Accord to the front of the Big House. Pam took a seat beside Jason; Teddy sat in the rear. "Jason, I thought you would have something sportier," Teddy said once they were underway.

"I do, a Porsche 918 Spider in the garage. I use this Accord as my go-to-town car."

"When may we take a spin in the Spider?" Teddy asked.

"Later," Jason said.

"Jason, please tell us about this Allison we're going to see," Pam said.

"Allison Jameson has been our family lawyer for many years. A few years ago, Allison moved her home and some of her legal practice to Athens. Her husband, Eric Jameson, a former minister at our church, was assigned to a much larger church in Athens. Allison kept her office in Vickery and comes here for two or three days a week, depending upon her local caseload."

"Why do you sometimes refer to your mom as Miz Lizbeth and other times you call her mother?" Teddy asked.

"I think Mother already told you that Martin is the son of my father and a lady who worked for us?"

"And we know Miz Lizbeth formally adopted him," Teddy said.

"That's right. Martin knew the whole story from an early age. When we were about six or seven, Martin started calling my mother Miz Lizbeth, like most people do. He, of course, never knew his father or mother. Most of the time when Martin's around, I call my mother Miz Lizbeth so he won't feel I'm trying to put him down."

"You were that perceptive when you were six or seven?" Pam asked.

"Martin and I are very close," Jason said.

"What's the relationship between Martin and Mr. Jackson?" Teddy asked.

"Uncle and nephew. For all practical purposes, Jackson functions as our father." Jason parked the Accord in front of Allison's office. "More of our family history will have to wait until later. Let's get started with Allison."

CHAPTER 8

Teddy and Pam entered the Big House, leaving Jason alone with his mother on the front porch. "Did you talk with Allison?" Jason asked.

Miz Lizbeth nodded. "Allison gave me a thumbnail summary with the understanding you'd provide more details."

"Allison advocates getting the legal system involved to bring Kendal to justice. Although the rape kit will help, without more corroborating evidence, we probably won't do more than embarrass the guy."

"Does Allison know Kendal?"

"Of him, not personally. Evidently, he's well known for the way he practices criminal law, ruthlessly and successfully."

"I'll bet Allison isn't afraid of him."

"She wants him punished for what he did to Teddy, and Allison would like to be involved in bringing him to justice."

"Did Allison mention the possibility of a civil suit, if we can't bring criminal charges against Kendal?"

"She did. We would face the same difficulties. We need corroboration, otherwise it may be Teddy's word against Kendal's."

"The videos, if they exist?"

"Open and shut case if we have them. Allison's smart, as you know. She bluntly asked Teddy and Pam if Kendal has any markings or abnormalities on his genitals that only they would know about."

"What did Pam and Teddy say?"

"Pam said no, but Teddy vowed Kendal would be lacking his penis—well, she actually said his cock—if she could get to him."

Miz Lizbeth clapped her hands. "A remarkable young lady."

"A true description."

"I hope Pam doesn't suffer too much emotionally over this affair. She must feel terribly inadequate as a parent," Miz Lizbeth said.

"Perhaps you could talk with Pam, help her to understand that what happened to Teddy was in no way Pam's fault."

"A better idea would be for you to talk with her."

"Me?" Jason asked.

"Yes, you."

"Mother, are you playing matchmaker?"

"Well, you haven't been all that successful with your own efforts."

"I will only say that I find Pam alluring, and I like Teddy."

"Alluring? An interesting choice of words."

"I chose the word carefully."

"While I would very much like to have Pam and Teddy in this family, you must do as you think best," Miz Lizbeth said.

"I think best would be for me to proceed slowly in working out a relationship with Pam."

"You're interested?"

"Yes, Mother, I'm interested."

"Is your interest more than saving a mother and her daughter from harm?"

"I've gone beyond that stage. I don't know how Pam feels."

"I'm reasonably confident Teddy would like the two of you together."

"How do you know?" Jason asked.

"I'm an astute observer of human interactions."

"I'll accept that statement. What does your astute observation say about how Pam views me?"

"Proceeding deliberately would definitely be appropriate. Let's move on," Miz Lizbeth said.

"Let's."

"Do you have any ideas about how we can get our hands on the videos and laptop Thompson Kendal presumably has secreted away?"

"I need to talk with Martin and Hack."

Teddy came to the porch and sat beside Miz Lizbeth. "Who's Hack?"

"He takes care of our computers here at the Big House and at the company," Miz Lizbeth replied.

"Hack heads our IT department," Jason said.

"With a name like Hack, he must be quite good at his job."

"Raymond 'Hack' Lawrence is the son of good friends to this family," Jason said. "When Hack was younger, he ran afoul of the law by utilizing his, shall we say, less than legal computer skills. Allison convinced the judge who heard the case against Hack not to send him to prison and that we would provide him with a legitimate job and ensure he ceased his unsavory activities."

"Has he?"

"With whatever time he has left over from his responsibilities to the Andrews family, he's become a day trader."

"Is he any good at day-trading? I've been tempted to try my hand," Teddy said.

"I think Hack may now be one of the wealthiest young men in Alexander County."

"Why do you want to talk with him?"

"He has certain skills."

Teddy smiled. "I'm going out on a limb here. Based upon what Counselor Allison told us this morning, you probably think this Hack person can help us get the videos out of Thompson's safe."

"Do you know what plausible deniability means?" Jason asked Teddy.

"I do."

"Then don't go any further with this conversation."

Pam came onto the porch and sat beside Jason.

"Teddy, can you drive?" Miz Lizbeth asked.

"I have my learner's permit."

"You won't need a permit or license on this property. Do you think you could drive one of our new trucks?"

"Like the one that brought Mom and me here?"

"That's right. My sons convinced me the business needs six of those monsters. I haven't had the time for a joyride. Would you drive me around this property, if Pam agrees?"

"Yes, ma'am. Just the two of us?"

"You might enjoy seeing the property, and I haven't been around the perimeter road in a couple of weeks."

Teddy looked perplexed. "The cabs are pretty high off the ground. How will you get into the front seat?"

"Jackson has built—rather, caused to be built—several different ramps that help me get in and out of vehicles. Someone will push me up to the cab in my wheelchair and I'll move into the passenger's seat with the help of my strong arms." She laughed. "Alternatively, my sons can lift me from the wheelchair into the cab."

"What will you and Teddy do if you have an emergency or need to leave the truck for some reason?" Pam asked.

"We won't be more than half an hour away from the Big House. In any event, Teddy and I both will have our devil's creations."

"Miz Lizbeth has only grudgingly accommodated to cell phones," Jason explained.

"I am reconciled to their utility in certain situations," Miz Lizbeth conceded.

"I assume the perimeter road will not be suitable for Teddy's tendency to drive fast?" Pam asked.

"We'll go at a sedate pace, I promise you."

"Then you two will have plenty of opportunity to talk."

"I'll make sure Teddy keeps her eyes on the road."

"Mother?" Teddy asked.

"Have fun," Pam answered.

Martin joined the group. "Teddy, come with me for a few minutes and I'll acclimate you to one of the trucks, make sure the driver's seat and rearview mirrors are placed correctly for you."

"You'll also show me how to start the beast?"

"And how to stop it. Once we get the fundamentals out of the way, I'll ride shotgun while you take a spin around the driveway."

"Let's do it."

***

Teddy sedately steered the F-150 out of sight from the Big House. "Miz Lizbeth, what do you want to talk about with me?"

"How do you know I want to talk with you rather than simply enjoying a ride around our property?"

"With all due respect, Miz Lizbeth, I'm confident something's on your mind that you want us to discuss."

"Am I so transparent?"

"I think you keep your cards close to your chest." Teddy resisted the urge to speed up. "I also know that you've taken the opportunity to bring my mom and Jason together."

"And if I have, would that disturb you?"

"I'm pleased, not at all disturbed. Mom needs a real man in her life, and I'd like a real father."

"Did you know your biological father?"

"No, ma'am. He was killed before I was born."

"Teddy, when we are alone, please call me Elizabeth, as we agreed, and dispense with the 'ma'am.' This occasion will be the last time we worry about nomenclature, at least for the time being."

"Yes . . . Elizabeth, for the time being."

"Back to business. I want an honest answer to my next question."

"You want to know if I really would kill Thompson, provided I have the opportunity."

"I do. How did you know that was my question?"

Teddy steered around what appeared to be a deep mud puddle. "We left that subject hanging the other night."

Miz Lizbeth sat back in her seat. "First of all, I think you would be entirely justified in killing him, but our legal system may not agree. Don't even contemplate such an eventuality."

"If you say so." Teddy continued her cautious drive around the perimeter road.

"Teddy, when you were with Allison, did you reveal in any fashion whatsoever that you would kill your stepfather given the opportunity?"

"I kept my mouth shut about that subject. I had plenty to say about the sexual abuse."

"You revealed everything except your intentions about Thompson?"

"I did."

"Hear me clearly, Theodora."

"I'm listening, Elizabeth."

"Your intentions—no matter how justifiable—about Thompson must never, ever be voiced again. Do you understand me?"

"I do, and I understand the reasons. Elizabeth, can you and your sons really protect Mom and me?"

"Beyond the shadow of a doubt. My family has always protected its own."

"Was Jason ever married?"

"Only to the Navy. He was involved for a number of years with a lady, an aristocrat he met in London. That relationship hasn't worked out, and I'm glad."

"Why?"

"Philippa lacks the robustness Jason needs. I saw that deficiency when Jason brought her to spend time with us."

"You think my mother has that robustness?"

"For damn sure once she recovers from the trauma of recent events. Go that way." Miz Lizbeth pointed.

"Elizabeth, I see four long and narrow structures ahead. Are they chicken houses?"

"We raise broilers without antibiotics in these four grow houses. We won't get too close."

"Without antibiotics? Are chickens usually raised with antibiotics?"

"Mostly. The antibiotics promote rapid growth despite their risk to society."

"Antibiotic resistance?"

"How did you know?"

"Mom rants and rails about her patients with MRSA." Teddy pronounced the abbreviation as "mersa."

"You mean, methicillin-resistant Staphylococcus aureus?"

"You're familiar with the problem?" Teddy asked.

"I am. The poultry industry isn't the sole cause of antibiotic resistance. The cattle industry also contributes, and physicians over-prescribe antibiotics."

"Mom thinks many physicians lack the good sense and willpower to resist prescribing antibiotics except when truly needed."

"Please stop here. We can't go any further without being decontaminated."

Teddy stopped the truck. "How large are those chicken houses?"

"We call them grow houses. They are five hundred feet long and fifty feet wide with fans and heaters to control the inside temperatures. Each house can accommodate up to twenty thousand broilers, which are raised for meat. We also have a number of hen houses elsewhere on the property."

"Hen houses?"

"For production of eggs. We supply broilers, hens, and feed to farmers who contract with us. Vickery Bank and Trust provides mortgages to poultry farmers to help them build grow houses on their properties."

"Andrews Poultry Industries manufactures the feed?"

"We're an integrated operation. Go to downtown Vickery on Wednesday afternoons and you'll smell the feed being prepared in our factory."

"Are the chickens raised in cages inside the houses?"

"They run free on the floors, which are covered with bedding material like wood chips, rice hulls, or peanut hulls. The houses are equipped with automatic watering systems we call nipple drinkers so that the bedding material doesn't get wet when the chickens drink. The chicken feed is also dispensed automatically."

"If the chickens run free, don't they mess up the bedding?" Teddy asked.

"We can't stop them from crapping."

"Have you ever had an infection in the antibiotic-free grow houses?"

"Never. We're very careful about decontamination. Anyone who enters the houses must wear a sterile gown over their clothes and wash their rubber boots in a decontamination bath."

"How do you get the mature chickens from the grow houses to a processing plant?" Teddy asked.

"Better that we show you one day rather than trying to describe the process. If you see what's done, you'll need a strong stomach," Miz Lizbeth said.

"I figure I can stomach whatever you do to put food on my plate."

"I'll ask Jason to take you with him the next time we harvest them."

"I'm game. If you don't think poultry farms are the only reason for antibiotic resistance, why do you raise chickens without antibiotics?"

"To prove we can do it, and also to provide chickens to customers who want meat raised without antibiotics," Miz Lizbeth said.

"You probably charge a premium for the chickens that come out of these."

"I see you have a good head for business."

"Thank you. I don't yet know what I want to do after high school and college."

"You don't need to decide for a few years. While you're here, you might like to learn more about our poultry industries and even the banking business."

"I would." Teddy stopped the truck again. "Elizabeth, if Mom and I stay here, I'll need to go to school in a couple of weeks in order to graduate on time."

Miz Lizbeth motioned for Teddy to drive on. "We'll enroll you in Alexander County High School. We'll get Allison to handle the residency details. Our high school graduates with good grades in advanced placement courses have no difficulty in gaining admission to many colleges."

"You think Mom and I will be here for a long time?"

"Teddy, I sincerely hope for that eventuality."

"I'm worried about what Thompson might do. He could have someone abduct me from a school bus or even from the school."

"He will not. You won't ride a school bus. You'll be transported to and from school with a family member or our employees. Our county schools don't allow anyone to enter without proper identification. I'll make sure the high school will permit only our family members and specified employees to drop you off and bring you home. And you will identify anyone who comes for you. Rest easy."

"I will, as much as I can."

"Take the next road to the right. It will bring us out to Sweet Gum Road," Miz Lizbeth directed.

"OK." Teddy looked both ways along the highway in preparation for leaving the Andrews property.

"Take a right, watch for traffic."

Teddy soon had the truck on Sweet Gum Road headed south toward Vickery. "What now?"

"Keep looking for traffic but floorboard it!"

"What?"

"Floorboard it, Teddy. I want to see how fast this monster will go."

Teddy pressed the accelerator and the truck lurched. "What if some type of law enforcement stops us?"

"I'll take care of it. You're in Alexander County."

When the truck reached eighty miles per hour, both Teddy and Miz Lizbeth's cell phones rang. Teddy slowed and extracted her phone from her jeans pocket. Miz Lizbeth answered first.

"What do you want, Jason?"

"Where are you, Miz Lizbeth?"

"On Sweet Gum Road."

Teddy answered. "Yes, Mother Dearest."

"Where are you, Teddy?" Pam asked.

"With Miz Lizbeth, headed south on Sweet Gum Road."

"You need to come home immediately," Pam answered. Miz Lizbeth moved her free hand across her throat indicating Teddy should disconnect. "Mom, Jason is talking with Miz Lizbeth about whatever concerns you. I'll call back in a minute."

"What are you two doing on Sweet Gum Road?" Jason asked his mother.

"Enjoying a fine ride."

"How fast are you going?"

Miz Lizbeth looked at the speedometer. "A sedate forty-five. Teddy's a fine driver."

"You've been going faster, haven't you?"

"I wanted to give this truck a good test run."

"How fast?"

"Fast enough. We don't want to alarm Pam."

"You must come home immediately."

"Why?"

"Look at the sky to the north," Jason said. "What do you see?"

Miz Lizbeth leaned to her right side to look behind the truck in in the outside mirror. "I declare. Black swirling clouds."

"Are you headed south?"

"We are."

"Have Teddy turn around and get back to the Big House with all deliberate haste."

"Why? We're enjoying our time together."

"The National Weather Service has issued a tornado warning for this area. The TV stations show really bad weather heading this way."

"Tornadoes generally stay to the north of our property."

"Not always. Please come home immediately or seek shelter somewhere else."

"We'll be there soon. Please have our people move to the Big House. We'll want them to have a safe place to stay."

"Martin and Jackson have already started that process, and I've made sure our generator is ready for action." He paused briefly. "Change of plans. Please come home at flank speed rather than with deliberate haste."

"The forecast has deteriorated?"

"Quickly, Mother, please!"

"Teddy," Miz Lizbeth directed, "please turn around and take us home like my son said, as fast as you can drive safely. Seems as if we're under a tornado warning. After you turn around, I'll call Pam on your cell phone to tell her we're on the way, and that she shouldn't worry. We'll be back at the Big House in a flash . . . I have every confidence in your driving ability."

CHAPTER 9

Winds blew relentlessly across the Andrews property. Hail beat a disorganized rhythm on the metal roof of the Big House, the intensity changing from minute to minute. The electricity flickered and failed seconds after a huge lightning flash followed by a devil's roar of thunder that shook the house. Jason spoke to the family assembled in the den.

"Martin and I will start the generator once we're sure the power grid has been knocked out."

"Jackson, please assure the people in the basement that we'll have power and lights in a few minutes," Miz Lizbeth said. Jackson left on his mission.

"How long will the generator supply power?" Teddy asked.

"We'll have sufficient power for lights, the refrigerator, and freezer for days, if we don't overload the generator capacity. We can also run the AC at low levels," Jason replied.

"What about cooking?" Pam asked.

"We cook with gas," Miz Lizbeth said.

"Where is the generator?"

"In the garage. If the power grid stays out for several hours, Martin or I will refill the diesel fuel tank. We have a large supple of fuel," Jason said.

Martin grinned at Shanna. "Don't worry about your daily shower and hair wash. The hot water heater is gas-fired."

The sky was pitch dark, casting gloom inside as the howling wind buffeted the outside. Jackson returned.

"I've set up some battery-powered lanterns and flashlights in the basement, and a battery-powered radio will let our people know what's happening in the outside world."

Teddy looked up from her cell phone. "The Weather Underground radar map shows a tornado is very near."

Jackson went to the front porch and returned seconds later, almost soaked from the horizontal rain. "Miz Lizbeth, best all of us get to the basement," Jackson said,

"That bad?" Miz Lizbeth asked. Jackson nodded in confirmation. "Jason and Martin, please help Shanna down the stairs. We don't want her stumbling in the gloom. Jackson, please light the way for them with that flashlight you're holding."

In a few minutes, Martin and Jason returned to the first floor to stand by Miz Lizbeth. Jackson turned the flashlight beam up the stairs from the basement. "Do your thing," Miz Lizbeth told her sons.

Martin and Jason, one in front and the other in the rear, lifted Miz Lizbeth in the wheelchair and cautiously began to descend the stairs as a roar filled the house. "Here we all are, snug as bugs in a rug," Miz Lizbeth said when she came into the basement. As the minutes ticked by, she reassured them all. "No need to be afraid. My husband built the Big House to survive worse weather than we're having now."

"I don't know if we've survived a tornado, but whatever it was has moved on. I'm going upstairs for a look outside," Jackson said.

"May I come with you?" Teddy asked.

"Don't go off the porch, and follow Mr. Jackson's directions," Pam said.

After several minutes, Jackson and Teddy returned to the basement. "The worst of the storm has passed by," Jackson said.

Pam, who had Teddy's cell phone, confirmed the observation. "That's what the radar map shows."

"Martin and I will start the generator now," Jason said. "Jackson, once our people can safely move around the property, please ask some of the men to make a quick assessment of the damage we've suffered." The two brothers left for the barn.

The lights soon came back on, much to everyone's relief. Jason and Martin returned to the Big House and went to the basement. "Miz Lizbeth, we can move everyone out of the basement, and our people can go back to their homes. If anyone's home has been damaged, they can come back to the Big House," Martin said.

***

Jackson stood behind the bar in the den preparing drinks for the family when Jason's cell phone chimed. "Yes?" He listened carefully before replying. "Martin and I will be there soon to help." After disconnecting, Jason spoke to the assembled family.

"Some large trees, mainly pines, fell across the front and back entry roads. We need to get them out of the way in case we need an emergency egress or ingress."

"My brother means we must rid the road of obstructions in case we need to get out or someone needs to get into the property. We'll fire up the chain saws and take care of the problem." Martin looked to Shanna. "You all right?"

"I'm going to the bathroom." Shanna stood. "Damn!"

"What's wrong?" Martin asked, concern evident in his voice.

"My water broke."

Pam jumped into action. "Miz Lizbeth, we need to get Shanna to a bed. Teddy, get my doctor's bag." Pam took a deep breath. "We don't have an emergency. Shanna most likely will give birth in a reasonably normal fashion . . . Shanna, I've delivered many babies. You and the baby will be fine, even if the delivery takes place here."

"Jason, let's walk Shanna to our bedroom. Might as well birth the boy-child there," Martin said. The two men, one on each side, helped Shanna out of the den and into the corridor leading to the west wing.

Teddy, carrying Pam's bag, rushed back into the den. "Teddy, how would you like to see a baby born?" Pam asked,

"You want me to assist?"

"I do, unless Miz Lizbeth has someone else on the property knowledgeable about childbirth."

"Several ladies have given birth, although I wouldn't classify any of them as midwives," Miz Lizbeth said.

"Then it's you and I, Teddy." Pam beckoned Teddy to follow her to Martin and Shanna's bedroom.

Twenty minutes later, Pam came back into the den. "Miz Lizbeth, Shanna's baby may come a lot sooner than expected for a first birth."

"I suspect she and Martin, not to mention the rest of us, will be grateful," Miz Lisbeth said. "How can we help?"

"Jason, can you speed up the process of clearing one of the roads in case we need EMS?"

"I'll do the best I can. Should I take Martin with me to get his mind off the birth?"

"Not unless you need him. He might like to see his son born, and he's doing a great job comforting Shanna," Pam said.

"If he gets in the way, send him out here," Miz Lizbeth said.

"We need warm towels and soap. Hot water from the in-house plumbing should be adequate," Pam said. "I want to wash Shanna's lower body. We'll need to clean the baby after he's delivered and keep him warm."

"Will you do an episiotomy?"

"Not unless I have to. If I perform an episiotomy, I'll give

Shanna an injection of the broad-spectrum antibiotic I keep in my doctor's bag. We're not birthing this baby under sterile conditions." Pam grinned. "Shanna, supermodel that she may be, has rather wide hips. She definitely isn't anorexic."

"Shanna has been in the forefront of convincing the fashion industry to eschew the starvation look for models," Miz Lizbeth said.

"That's great." Pam looked at her watch. "Miz Lizbeth, Jason, I'll feel a lot better once the road is open." Pam left the room.

"Do you think we have a problem?" Jason asked his mother.

"I don't know. Pam may simply be exercising appropriate caution, or she may be worried and reluctant to show any uncertainty. No matter. Open a damn road!"

"On the way. Jackson, how many men are working on the road?"

"Four."

"Please see if you can recruit more unless they're needed with their own families." Jason rushed out of the den.

"Jackson, please call Sally and Ann to come back to the Big House," Miz Lizbeth said. "Tell them about the towels. And ask them to prepare something for us eat."

"I'll put some towels in the dryer to carry us until Sally and Ann arrive."

"Before you go, will you please prepare me one of your special martinis? My nerves can no longer take this level of anxiety."

"You haven't lost your nerves of steel. You simply want a drink."

"Make it a double."

"That's what I thought you'd want."

***

Teddy, flushed with excitement, returned to the den an hour later where Miz Lizbeth and Jackson waited for news. "Miz Lizbeth, is the road passable?"

"Jason called a few minutes ago to say the crew should have the road open in a couple of hours," Jackson said.

"That's what Mom was afraid of. She expects the baby's head to crown very soon. I'll tell her we're on our own." Teddy started to leave but stopped in mid-stride. "My mom's in her element. I've never seen her this way," Teddy said as she left the den.

"Jackson," Miz Lizbeth said, "please open the door to Martin and Shanna's wing, and push me into the hallway. I want to hear the baby's first cries."

"Do you want another martini while we wait?"

"Not until we celebrate. Pour yourself whatever you want and bring a chair to sit by me."

"I'm with Martin, Wild Turkey on the rocks for me." Jackson brought his drink and a chair to sit beside Miz Lizbeth. She reached out her hand for him to hold. Jackson took the proffered hand and held it firmly.

"Our time passes, Jackson."

He squeezed her hand. "We'll have a few more good years, and the family will thrive."

"What can we do to focus Jason's mind on Pam?"

Jackson raised his glass in a toast. "From the way Jason looks at her, he's already interested. So, we should let nature take its course. If necessary, I'll speak to them." He laughed. "Or I'll have Miss Theodora speak to them."

"She's a strong young lady."

"As strong as you are, Elizabeth." Jackson kissed her on the cheek.

***

Thirty minutes passed before Miz Lizbeth and Jackson heard the first lusty cries of the newborn baby boy. A shout of joy sounded. "That'll be Martin rejoicing over the birth of his son," Jackson said.

Teddy emerged from the bedroom and saw Miz Lizbeth and Jackson in the hall. "Mom says the baby's perfect. Shanna's doing well. From the way he cries so loudly, Martin says the baby sounds like Jason when he's whipping him on the tennis court."

Miz Lizbeth smiled. "Teddy, please ask when we can see the baby."

"Now," Martin announced, coming into the hall with the baby wrapped in a clean towel. "I have the distinct honor of presenting Jason Jackson Andrews to you." Martin showed the baby to Miz Lizbeth and Jackson. "I think we should call him JJ." Martin placed the baby in Miz Lizbeth's arms.

"A fine young man. I'm honored he has my name. Thank you," Jackson said.

"Miz Lizbeth is my mother and you are my father. As soon as we have a girl-child, we'll name her 'Elizabeth.'"

"Don't rush Shanna," Miz Lizbeth said.

"I won't." Martin took JJ, holding him securely. "Sure would be nice to have Pam deliver the next baby, especially in a hospital."

Once Miz Lizbeth and Jackson were alone in the hall, he kissed Miz Lizbeth full on the lips. "See, the family will continue."

"Praise God," Miz Lizbeth answered, tears of joy streaming down her cheeks.

CHAPTER 10

Teddy, dressed in shorts, T-shirt, and running shoes, came onto the front porch the next morning and stopped when she saw Jason and Martin sitting together drinking coffee. "Teddy, do you want to join us?" Jason asked.

"I thought I might go for a jog around the perimeter road."

"Not a good idea," Jason said.

"Why?"

"We don't want you out of our sight."

"We could jog together, unless you think you can't keep up with me."

"Teddy, we face a critical situation. While Martin and I think the probability of Kendal and his goons getting onto this property undetected remains low, we can't let you jog alone, and we want to be available in case we're needed."

Martin clapped. "I have an idea that might satisfy all of our needs for exercise and a little excitement."

"Please enlighten us," Jason said.

"Teddy, why don't Jason and I introduce you to the finer points of power tennis. Would you like the benefit of our excellent instruction?" Martin asked.

"I don't have my tennis rackets," Teddy said.

Jason held out his right hand with two fingers extended. "Hold my fingers as if they were the handle on a tennis racket." Teddy's grip easily encompassed the two fingers. "How about three fingers?" Teddy managed to get her hand around the extended fingers. "Good. You can play with one of my rackets."

"Jason," Martin said, "we should take Teddy to town later this morning and purchase two or three rackets sized for her."

"You're serious?" Teddy asked.

"We are. If you're to play with us, you'll need the best equipment," Martin said.

"I'll bring our rackets and balls to the court," Jason said.

Teddy went with Martin to the court. "Teddy, you first need to learn how to deal with Jason's serve. If you can't return his serve, you won't be able to play anywhere near his level."

"I've seen his serve. What's the trick to returning it?"

"Don't simply try to block his serve. He'll pound the ball out of your reach even if you manage to get the ball over the net."

"So?"

"You gotta hit the damn ball back at him as hard as he serves. You might drive your return into the net or out of bounds. No matter. He'll win the point unless you learn to drive the ball back to him."

Jason came onto the court and handed Teddy a racket. "Best I can do."

"You serve, Jason. I'll coach Teddy. Start with a three-quarters cannonball, no twist."

Jason served to Teddy's forehand. She drove the ball into the net. "Same thing, Jason, but give me time to instruct Teddy." Martin told Teddy, "Don't overthink what you're doing. Empty your mind and react, nothing more."

Jason's serve once again came to Teddy's forehand. She drove the ball down the line into Jason's backcourt. He easily blasted the ball out of her reach.

"All we're doing now is learning how to return Jason's service." Martin shouted to his brother, "Serve to her backhand."

The ball hit the left corner of Teddy's service box. She managed a two-handed backhand drive deep into Jason's backcourt. His forehand return stunned Teddy.

"Don't worry, Teddy, we got his attention. Full speed cannonball, no twist, wherever you wish, Jason." Martin put a hand on Teddy's shoulder. "React, don't think. For this lesson, you only want to learn how to return Jason's serve."

Jason served and Teddy attempted to return for the next thirty minutes. She became increasingly adept and confident. "Jason, no holds barred, let Teddy see that twisting full-throttle blast of yours."

Jason's serve, the ball twisting wickedly, came to Teddy's forehand. Her return went into the net. "Damn," she said.

"One final serve for today's lesson. Jason, same thing but to her backhand."

Teddy, alerted to where the ball would come, managed a two-hand backhand to drive the ball into Jason's backcourt. He cut the ball out of play.

"You tired?" Martin asked Teddy.

"Damn right," Teddy said.

Jason jumped over the net. "Well, Teddy, you've done quite well, although we need to increase your stamina."

"That's right. Think how you'd be sucking wind if you were actually playing Jason in a match," Martin said.

"You told me I can't jog around the perimeter road. What should I do instead?" Teddy asked.

"I'll jog with you," Jason said.

"May I jog with you?" Pam put a hand on Teddy's shoulder.

"Shall we jog tomorrow morning before breakfast?"

"Yes," Jason said. "Pam?"

"I'm in," Pam said.

"What about when school starts?" Teddy asked.

"We'll still jog early, before breakfast. We'll continue the tennis lessons in the afternoons and weekends provided you complete your homework," Jason said.

Teddy shook her head. "There's always a price, isn't there?"

"In this instance, the price is not unbearable, and you'll probably win the state championship next spring without breaking a sweat," Pam said. "Jason, Martin. While Teddy cleans up, may we talk in private?"

"Any chance I can join the conversation?" Teddy asked.

"Adults only," Pam said. "We'll be on the front porch for at least half an hour, Daughter Dearest, so make yourself scarce somewhere else."

"I'm gone but not forgotten."

Pam, Jason, and Martin settled on the front porch with fresh cups of coffee in hand.

"We need the disks or whatever media Thompson used to record Teddy," Pam said. "I think the safe in Thompson's study is the most likely place to find the videos. Do you have a plan for retrieving them?"

"We do," Martin said.

"We want to get the disks or thumb drives without Thompson's knowledge or interference," Jason added.

"Getting into the house shouldn't be a problem. We'll simply find a time when Thompson's away for a couple of hours," Pam said.

Jason cocked an eyebrow. "What's with this 'we'? Martin and I don't want to involve you in something illegal."

"I own the house. I brought it into the marriage, and I insisted that we kept the house in my name. I can legally go into my house whenever I wish," Pam declared.

"We sashay right into the front door, in full daylight?" Martin asked.

"Why not? The three of us can pick a time when Thompson's in court or otherwise occupied. We go to Atlanta and legally enter the house. No problem, as long as Thompson isn't there." Pam laughed wryly. "Even if he were there, I don't think we'd face an insurmountable problem."

"You're offering to be a coconspirator with Martin and me?" Jason asked.

"What's the conspiracy? I'm entitled to enter the house with whomever I want as guests," Pam said. "We shouldn't even have a legal problem removing items from the safe; it's in my house."

"Teddy indicated she didn't have the safe combination. Do you?" Martin asked.

"No. Do you have any ideas about how we might get the combination?"

"Teddy told you about Hack, our computer wizard?" Jason asked.

"I overheard your conversation with Teddy. Can this Hack get us the combination?"

"Hack says he needs time to acquire the requisite equipment and software from the dark web."

"Dark web?" Pam asked.

"Apparently, all of the best hackers utilize the dark or black web, where you can get many items and services of questionable legality, like what we need to crack the safe electronically."

"Hack says the job would be easier if we knew the name of the company that manufactured the wall safe. Do you know?" Martin asked.

"I don't. Teddy might know." Pam held up a hand to forestall any comments from Jason and Martin. "You two have become our champions, but we're all in this fight together. Our major problem will be Teddy wanting to go with us on this expedition."

"You'll exercise parental authority?" Jason asked.

"I will."

"And I'll help," Miz Lizbeth said, maneuvering her wheelchair to join the group.

"Miz Lizbeth, you have that wheelchair in stealth mode. We weren't aware you were eavesdropping," Martin said

"Pam saw me come onto the porch. You were too involved with your nefarious schemes in the defense of our family and friends to notice my arrival."

"Well, please feel free to join us," Jason said.

"I already have. Martin, Jason, only two requirements: First, don't get Hack involved to such an extent that he runs afoul of the law."

"Agreed. What's the second of your requirements?" Jason asked.

"Don't get caught."

"We'll do our best with subterfuge, misdirection, and laying down smoke."

"See that you do."

"Pam, does your home have a security system?" Jason asked.

"Top of the line, according to Thompson."

"Do you think he's changed the code since you left?"

"I don't know. What if he has?"

"Hack will get us what we need to circumvent the alarm."

"Be better, though, if the asshole hasn't changed the code," Martin said.

"Thompson's so arrogant that I doubt he has any idea that I'll want to come back into the house. When do we go on our righteous mission?"

"As soon as Hack has what he needs." Jason looked as his mother. "Hack is excited to be back in the game, as he calls it."

"Remember what I told you regarding Hack," Miz Lizbeth admonished.

"Haven't I always remembered what you've pronounced in your august wisdom?"

"Pam, if I were able to get up from this chair, I'd smack Jason upside his head," Miz Lizbeth said.

"I have a better idea," Pam said. She kissed Jason's cheek. "All will be well, Elizabeth. I'll make sure we insulate Hack."

Teddy, who had been listening from inside the front doorway, came onto the porch. "How 'bout I come with you on this righteous mission? At a minimum, I could serve as a lookout."

Pam gave a small negative shake of her head. "Teddy," Miz Lizbeth said, "I'd like for you to stay with me, help me deal with my worries until our family members return."

"Martin and I, as well as your mother, would be grateful, Teddy, if you keep Miz Lizbeth company," Jason said. "We don't want her to worry too much,"

"I thought Mr. Jackson could provide that support."

"He can, and he does; however, I'd like the pleasure of your company without any distractions," Miz Lizbeth said.

"I'd love to stay here with you, Miz Lizbeth. Maybe you could tell me more about the poultry business."

"Seems as if we have everything settled, at least for the time being. Let's have lunch," Miz Lizbeth said.

CHAPTER 11

Jackson's cell phone buzzed near the end of breakfast the next morning.

"What's happening? . . . I'll tell the family."

"Trouble?" asked Jason.

"A black Suburban with three men followed by a state patrol car; one trooper."

"Let's get to the front porch."

"I'll let Martin know we have a situation." Jackson left the room.

"Take me to the porch," Miz Lizbeth directed.

Teddy pushed Miz Lizbeth out of the dining room. Pam and Jason followed. Martin burst through the front door as the two vehicles stopped in front of the house. Jackson lingered by the door.

Giovanni, Alberto, and another man got out of the Suburban. The state trooper waved a piece of paper. "I have a court order to bring Theodora Nelson back to Atlanta and return her to the care of her father, Mr. L. Thompson Kendal, Esq." The trooper pointed to the third man stepping from the Suburban.

"No way," Teddy shouted. Pam glared at her husband.

Jason and Martin immediately interposed themselves between the trooper and the other people on the front porch.

"Let's all calm down for a minute. Who signed this alleged order?" Miz Lizbeth asked the trooper.

"It's a real order, ma'am, signed by Judge Asa M. Albright, Superior Court, Fulton County," the trooper said.

"Let me have the paper," Miz Lizbeth directed. Jason passed the court order to his mother. Miz Lizbeth looked briefly at the order. "Seems legitimate to me, although I must consult with a legal authority." She gave her cell phone to Teddy. "Theodora, go to the contacts on my phone and call Tucker Morgan." The trooper looked perplexed.

In a few moments, Teddy handed the phone back to Miz Lizbeth. "It's ringing now."

Miz Lizbeth smiled and spoke forcibly into the phone. "Mrs. Elizabeth Andrews in Alexander County for Colonel Morgan." She frowned. "Miss, I don't care if the good colonel is sitting on the toilet. Put him on this line immediately or there will be severe consequences for you and for Colonel Morgan's political career." Miz Lizbeth activated the speaker function on the phone and turned the volume to maximum.

"Miz Lizbeth," a strong voice came through the speaker. "To what do I owe this great pleasure?"

"One of your young troopers stands before me with a court order stating we must turn over Miss Theodora Nelson to an L. Thompson Kendal. Theodora and her mother, Dr. Pamela Kendal, are our guests and under our protection. We expect our lawyer to help us bring charges of sexual assault of a minor against this L. Thompson Kendal. We aren't giving up Theodora or Pamela; do you hear me, Tucker?"

"I do. Let me speak to the trooper." Miz Lizbeth beckoned the trooper to the front porch.

"Son, what's your name?" asked Col. Morgan.

"Trooper Jack Smith, sir."

"How long have you been one of our troopers?"

"On active duty for almost a year, sir."

Col. Morgan sighed. "Son, who signed this order?"

"Judge Asa M. Albright of—"

"I damn well know that sorry excuse for a judge."

"May I speak to Colonel Morgan?" Kendal asked in a loud voice.

"No, you may not, Counselor," Col. Morgan spat out. "I damn well know who you are and who you represent. Trooper Smith!"

"Yes, sir," the trooper replied.

"What county are you in right now. Do you know?"

"Alexander Country, sir."

"Well, Judge Albright has no authority in Alexander County."

"He does! You're violating the law!" Kendal shouted.

"Not half as much as you and Judge Albright do every chance you get. Counselor, you can shut up and sue me later. I've waited a long time for the opportunity to deal with you, your client, and the judge. Trooper Lane!"

"Sir?"

"Where's your barracks?"

"Fulton Country, Colonel."

"Well, you go back to your barracks and I'll deal with you later. Leave now, if not sooner."

"Yes, sir." The trooper handed the court order to Kendal and rushed to the patrol car. He sped away.

"Miz Lizbeth, do you need anything else from me right now?" Col. Morgan asked.

"Thank you, Tucker. You've done admirably well."

"Watch yourself. You're dealing with godawful people."

"Warned and prepared," Miz Lizbeth said. She disconnected the phone.

Kendal went on the offensive. "Pam, Teddy comes back to

Atlanta with me. I'm instituting a suit to have you declared an unfit mother. Teddy belongs with me."

Miz Lizbeth shook her head at Teddy. Pam said, in a strong voice, "We're serious about bringing you up on child molestation charges."

"You have no proof."

"I'll testify," Teddy said.

"And I'll destroy your testimony as coming from a child with an overactive imagination."

"See you first in court, Thompson, and then in handcuffs as you're led to prison," Pam said.

Kendal looked to Giovanni and Alberto. "Now's the time."

Jason and Martin had their pistols aimed before Giovanni and Alberto could withdraw their weapons. Martin laughed without mirth.

"These two idiots still don't understand the tactical situation."

"Perhaps they're slow learners," Jason said. "Giovanni, you and Alberto know the drill. Remove the pistols from your waist and ankle holsters, slowly with you thumbs and forefingers. Don't try anything stupid or you'll be dead. Keep in mind you three are trespassing."

The two men complied. "Cover me, Martin," Jason said while he collected the firearms and gave them to Jackson.

"Please let me have one of the pistols, Mr. Jackson," Teddy requested.

"Teddy, you'll have your day. Right now, you shouldn't interfere with the adult business," Miz Lizbeth said.

"I'm involved."

"You most definitely are. Please hold your peace for a little while longer."

Teddy flipped a middle finger to Kendal.

"Very eloquent, very eloquent, Teddy, but you're coming home with me," he said.

"No, she is not," Jason said.

"You know, Jason, I'm getting tired of these two apes trying to shoot us. I have a proposal," Martin said.

"Let's hear it."

"You and I will give our pistols to Jackson. Then, if these three excuses for real men think they're up to the task, they can fight us. If they win, Teddy goes with the shyster. If we win, as we most certainly will, he and his minions drag their tails back to Atlanta or to whatever hole they call home."

"You mean a challenge to fisticuffs?" Jason asked.

"More or less."

"I doubt these three really know how to fight. We probably won't break out into a sweat before they go down for the count. How do you see the matches?"

"We could simply fight these three assholes in a free-for-all."

"I'm not sharing. I want L. Thompson Kendal all to myself," Jason said.

"You want me to take on Giovanni and Alberto by myself?"

"We can make this fight a two-stage affair. I'll take on Alberto, you can have Giovanni, and when we finish, I'll beat L. Thompson Kendal's arse into the ground."

"That means you get to have twice the fun as I do."

"You two quit arguing," Miz Lizbeth said. "Martin, you can have Giovanni and Alberto. Jason, L. Thompson Kendal is yours."

Jackson held the Browning shotgun that he kept inside the front door. "Gentlemen, this fine old shotgun does not have a magazine plug. I have five shells loaded with double-ought buckshot to blast anyone who gets out of line into hell and beyond." He looked at Kendal. "If you have a weapon, best you bring it to me now."

Kendal raised his hands. "My hands are all the weapons I need."

"Like I told you, Martin, Giovanni and Alberto are yours," Miz Lizbeth said.

"Miz Lizbeth, that's not fair, two against one," Teddy insisted.

"You're right. It's not fair for Giovanni and Alberto. Get on with it, Martin."

Martin charged his two opponents before they could prepare themselves. His forearm strike broke Giovanni's jaw and the man fell gasping to the ground. Martin pivoted to meet Alberto's headlong charge and stepped aside to trip him. Alberto went sprawling. Martin straddled the fallen man and hit his face until he was unconscious. Martin stood upright.

"Seems as if they truly don't know how to fight." He looked to Jason. "Before you devastate L. Thompson Kendal, I have some things to do." Martin seized Alberto's right hand and twisted it backward until the wrist bones snapped audibly. Before anyone could object, he repeated the process with Alberto's left hand.

"Anybody got a problem?" Martin asked. Receiving no answer, he broke both of Giovanni's wrists, eliciting screams from the still conscious man. Martin spoke to Jason. "Your turn."

"Jason, Thompson has a black belt in martial arts!" Pam shouted from the front porch.

Jason adopted a defensive posture as Kendal moved to an offensive position.

"To hell with you," Kendal shouted as he launched a vicious spinning kick aimed at Jason's head.

Jason easily dodged the attack. "Can't you do any better than that?"

Kendal charged, his hands furiously in motion, trying to hit Jason in a weak spot. Jason fended off Kendal's blows, retreating steadily and never going on the offense. Kendal continued his barrage and Jason his strategic defense, as if toying with his opponent.

"What's wrong with Jason? Why isn't he fighting back?" Teddy asked Miz Lizbeth.

"Be patient. Jason's hiding his real martial arts skills."

"What?"

"He intends to humiliate Kendal."

"Mr. Jason isn't even breathing hard, and Thompson is sucking air," Teddy said.

"Keep watching. This uneven fight will soon be over."

Jason dropped his hands to his sides. "Come on, Kendal. I thought you had a black belt. You fight like an amateur."

Kendal rushed forward and launched himself into the air, feet first with the aim of killing Jason with the double strike to his head.

Jason used both hands to flip Kendal onto his back and then put his knees on both of Kendal's arms, slapping him several times in the face with each hand. Jason then put a forearm on Kendal's throat. "You understand the tactical situation? Don't start something you can't finish." Jason stood and kicked Kendal in the stomach. Kendal turned on his side, retching.

"You're a sorry excuse for a man," Jason said.

Teddy rushed from the front porch and reared her leg to kick her stepfather. Jason grabbed and restrained her.

"Calm down, young one. He's not worth it."

Thompson rolled onto his back. "Teddy, return to Atlanta with me. You know that you want me as much as I want you."

"Kendal, you're one sick bastard," Jason said and turned to Teddy. "Do you know any martial arts?"

"A little."

"One blow, not fatal. You understand?"

Teddy reared her leg and kicked Kendal in his testicles. "Maybe not fatal, but painful."

Kendal drew both legs up to his chest and turned his head to the side to keep from choking. Teddy walked reluctantly back to the porch.

"Be thankful women are present or I would piss on your face, Kendal," Jason said.

"What now?" Martin asked.

Jason raised his palm to strike Kendal's nose.

"Don't kill him, Jason," Miz Lizbeth ordered.

"I reserve the right to do so in the future," Jason responded.

Pam slowly walked off the porch and stood over the barely conscious Kendal.

"My turn, Thompson."

She leaned over to slap her husband and to spit in his face.

"I hope never to see you again, you pervert, except in court and on your way to prison. I wish I had never met you." She took a huge breath. "Someone should call 911 for an EMS bus to take these seriously wounded men to your local hospital. We don't want their deaths on our hands."

"I do," Teddy said.

"Not today," Jason said. "Jackson, please call the EMS. I have one more thing to do." Jason watched Kendal shakily trying to regain his feet and kicked him in his right knee. Teddy and her mother gasped at the sound of Thompson's knee joint snapping. Screaming in agony, he fell again to the ground. Jason stood over the fallen man.

"Try to stand again and I'll destroy your other knee. You don't deserve to walk on two legs like a man."

"Please, please, no more," Kendal groaned.

"Then shut your mouth until the EMS arrives. And remember, I can always find you."

CHAPTER 12

A fter lunch the next day, Jackson's cell phone chimed to announce an Alexander County patrol car driving onto the property. Martin went to the front porch to welcome Captain Bruce Covington. "Welcome, Deputy Dog. Are you here about the fracas yesterday?"

"I am. I don't suppose you and Jason suffered any damage?"

"Not at all. Come into the house and we'll fill you in on what happened. We have several witnesses."

Captain Covington laughed and followed Martin into the dining room.

"Welcome, Bruce," Miz Lizbeth said. "What can we offer you?"

"A cup of black coffee would be nice." Jackson poured strong black coffee into a mug, which he placed in front of the captain. "Thanks, Mr. Jackson."

"You're here on official business?" Miz Lizbeth asked.

"I am. As you know, late yesterday afternoon an EMS bus transported three seriously injured men to the City-County Hospital from this property. The men claim they suffered an unprovoked vicious assault resulting in their grievous bodily harm." Captain Covington grinned at Martin and Jason. "What really happened?"

"The three men were trespassing. The large No Trespassing sign stands in plain view at the main gate to our property," Miz Lizbeth said.

"I know," Captain Covington said.

"The three men, one of whom was Pam's estranged husband and Teddy's stepfather, had a court order directing us to surrender Teddy to her stepfather, L. Thompson Kendal. I called Colonel Morgan of the state police, who said the court order lacked standing here in Alexander County. He ordered the state trooper escorting the three men to leave, which he did. The three men refused to leave without Teddy, so we showed them the error of their ways."

"With the A-Team?"

"Yes, Bruce, with my sons, and with some assistance from Pam and Teddy."

Captain Covington laughed. "From the looks of the three men, the fight was a rout."

"They chose to fight, and they got their asses beat after they tried to pull their weapons," Pamela said.

"Mom! Language!" Teddy jested.

Captain Covington's arm swept the group at the table. "All of you will testify to what Dr. Kendal and Miz Lizbeth said occurred?"

"Of course we will," Pam said.

"I don't think anything legally will come of this affair," Captain Covington said.

"I agree with your assessment, Bruce. We'll wait and see while remaining vigilant," Miz Lizbeth said.

"A-Team, did you even work up a sweat?" Captain Covington asked.

"They did not, not at all," Teddy said.

"Bruce, we need the three men kept out of circulation for three or four more days," Jason said.

"May I ask why?"

"Better that you don't."

"We want time to make certain arrangements to bring this unfortunate affair to an equitable conclusion," Miz Lizbeth said.

"From what the hospital staff have told me, the men won't be released from medical care until day after tomorrow," Captain Covington said. "When they leave the hospital, we'll arrest them. Giovanni and Alberto obviously have violated the terms of their previous release on bail. From what I'm hearing, this Thompson Kendal fella provoked an assault. I'll need one of you to swear out a warrant to that effect. We probably can keep the guys in our jail until the end of the week, maybe until next week." Captain Covington laughed. "I'll suggest to Judge Watkins that he spend another long weekend on the lake. Will that timeframe suit you?"

"It will. I'll go with you to swear out the warrant," Jason said.

Captain Covington sat back in his chair. "My official business is over. Miz Lizbeth, may I have a generous portion of that good Scotch you keep? I have a powerful thirst."

"Jackson, please make it so. We can't let the fine captain drink alone. Please pour everyone what they want," Miz Lizbeth said.

***

Miz Lizbeth spoke to the assembled group after Captain Covington left. "Let's review the bidding."

"Miz Lizbeth, do you play bridge?" Teddy asked.

"I do, if I can find worthy opponents."

"I'll be your partner, if you can find someone who will give us a good game."

Pam looked at Jason, who shook his head in mock disbelief. "Pam and I will be your opponents as soon as we can make time."

"Later. First, is Hack ready?" Miz Lizbeth asked.

"He is," Martin said.

"We can make the incursion tomorrow," Jason acknowledged.

"Do it," Miz Lizbeth commanded. "Teddy?"

"Yes, ma'am."

"We'll need to pass the time tomorrow constructively. You may, if you're willing, drive me around the property again."

"In one of the trucks?"

"No, in Jason's Porsche."

"I can do that."

"Teddy, no matter what my mother says, keep to the speed limit. You hear me?" Jason said.

"I'll let Miz Lizbeth determine our course of action," Teddy said.

"Theodora!" Pam exclaimed.

"I got it, Mother Dearest. Sedate, slow, and steady."

"Humph!" Miz Lizbeth said.

CHAPTER 13

The next day at mid-morning, Martin brought Jason's Accord to the driveway at the front of the Big House. The front passenger seat had been moved as far forward as possible. Martin said, "Pam, please sit behind me; Jason, you sit beside Pam."

"You're chauffeuring us?" Jason asked.

"That is my firm intention."

Jason followed Martin's instructions, and Pam smiled warmly at him. Jason reached for her right hand, which she allowed him to hold. "Do I need to turn down the temperature in this fine car in order to keep the windows from fogging up?" Martin asked.

Pam laughed. "Not immediately." The three occupants of the car waved goodbye to Miz Lizbeth, Jackson, and Teddy on the front porch.

Martin drove sedately until he had maneuvered the Accord onto Sweet Gum Road and then headed south on I-85. "Here we go," Martin said, depressing the accelerator until he had reached a speed of eighty miles per hour, ten miles above the limit.

"I thought Hack would be coming with us," Pam said.

Martin looked in the rearview mirror. "Hack's behind us.

Once we get to your house, he'll be driving around the area in case we need him."

Jason felt a slight tremor in Pam's hand. "Are you nervous?"

"A little."

"Always better to feel a little edgy going into a contest or difficult situation—keeps your senses on high alert."

Pam took a deep breath. "Is that how you felt going into combat when you were flying jets?"

"The tension began with being catapulted off the carriers."

"And ended when?"

"Back in the ready rooms, after the missions. The carrier landings were the most difficult."

"Do you miss the epinephrine rushes?" Pam asked.

"At times." Jason held Pam's eyes. "You must feel the same rush, as an emergency room doc."

"Sometimes, although no one has ever shot at me."

"Like me, you've learned to handle the tension, haven't you?"

"The ER is far removed from what we're doing today."

"If anyone tries to shoot at us today, you'll be safe."

"I know. I'm with my champions."

***

That afternoon near the cocktail hour, Martin brought the Accord to a stop at the Big House. He pushed the lever near his left foot to open the trunk. Teddy, watching from the front porch, let out a cry of joy when she saw her tennis rackets.

"Thanks for bringing my weapons," she said, removing the rackets from the trunk. "I'm ready for combat with you guys." Jason and Martin retrieved the laptop and electronic equipment Hack had provided from the trunk.

Jackson held open the front door. "You all come into the house. Miz Lizbeth, Shanna, and JJ are in the den. I hope you have good news for us."

"The best," Pam said. Teddy took the rackets to her bedroom. When Teddy returned, Miz Lizbeth motioned for the girl to sit beside her. Jason and Martin placed the computer and equipment on a small table near the wet bar. Jason sat beside Pam, and Martin took his seat next to Shanna, who placed the infant JJ in his father's lap.

"Should I fix drinks before or after we hear your news?" Jackson asked.

"I need a little tranquilization now, please," Pam said. "I hope we won't need any more adventures like today. I was concerned Thompson might have asked Frank Gordon for some of his men to watch the house."

"You didn't need to worry; your own gunslingers were with you," Shanna said.

"I didn't want to deal with a lot of blood in the house, blood from Frank's men. I wanted"—she grinned at Jason—"a quick ingress and a quick egress."

"We all have our areas of expertise," Jason said.

"We do," Miz Lizbeth said. "Pam, all of us would be willing to have you treat us, in or out of an emergency room setting. Look what you've already done for this family by taking such good care of Shanna and JJ. My sons simply returned the favor. Now let's have the details." Miz Lizbeth raised her martini glass to her sons.

"No matter that Pam says she was nervous, she's cool under pressure. When we arrived at her house, she got out of the car to retrieve the mail in her mailbox. A neighbor lady came over to ask what was going on," Martin said.

"Mrs. Listborn, the neighborhood snoop?" Teddy asked.

"The one and only," Pam said.

"Pam lied to the neighbor that Thompson was hospitalized after an auto accident near Vickery, and that she and Teddy were staying with family friends in the area in order to tend to him,"

Martin said. "Pam, cool under fire, pointed to Jason and me. According to her, our mother sent us with Pam to collect a few things Kendal needed."

"Did the noisy neighbor buy the explanation?" Miz Lizbeth asked.

"She seemed to. In any event, the lady didn't call the cops," Jason said.

"Had Thompson changed the entry code on the security system?" Teddy asked.

"Still the same. We entered the house without any problem," Pam said.

"What about the wall safe?" Teddy asked.

"With Hack's super special device, we gained entry to the safe in fifteen minutes. Hack, genius that he is, professed great disappointment the task took that long," Jason said.

"What we need was in the safe?" Miz Lizbeth asked.

"The laptop and several disks.

Miz Lizbeth pursed her lips. "You didn't need Hack in the house?"

"He provided backup from his car."

Teddy clapped her hands. "Enough minutia! Did you get the videos?"

"We made copies. Hack gave us a high-speed copying device that we attached to our laptop. We were careful to put the discs, after we copied them, back into the safe in the same order as they were before we removed them," Jason said. "Also, we copied relevant files from Thompson's laptop to ours. His laptop had the file showing the assault."

Teddy pumped her right fist into the air. "You're telling us that, other than Mrs. Listborn, there's no trace of what you did?"

"If a forensic team made a detailed examination of the house, they might find some evidence like fibers, but no fingerprints, no DNA," Martin said.

"Like I've been saying, such evidence wouldn't matter. I own the house and I'm entitled to bring anyone I wish into it and remove what I want," Pam said.

"That's correct, Pam. We simply prefer that Kendal have no idea what we've done until we reveal the recordings in court or another setting," Jason said.

"You'll give copies to Allison?" Miz Lizbeth asked.

"Tomorrow. We made the appointment on our way back here," Jason replied.

"Well done. Teddy drove me around the property and about the county without seriously breaking the speed limit in the Porsche," Miz Lizbeth said.

"Praise the Lord, if I were willing to believe you. Anyway, you're home safe, hopefully without any law enforcement encounters that would negatively impact Teddy's forthcoming driver's license," Jason said.

"Why must I continually remind everyone we're in Alexander County?"

Jackson addressed the group. "If you all want refills, say so now. Dinner will be ready within a half hour."

"Dare we ask what's on the menu?" Miz Lizbeth asked.

"I'm reasonably informed we're having mystery meat and sundry vegetables."

"Pam, Teddy, we're having Sally's famous pot roast with potatoes, carrots, onions, and whatever else she's put into the crockpot throughout the afternoon," Miz Lizbeth explained.

When everyone had finished their drinks and Jackson led the family into the dining room, Miz Lizbeth asked her sons to linger. "Quickly now. What do you two have planned beyond giving copies of the discs to Allison?"

"Who says we have something more planned?" Martin asked.

"Please, you two, don't try to fool me."

"We think Frank Gordon should be given the opportunity to

view what's on the critical disk," Jason said.

"What the—?" Miz Lizbeth started to speak before realization came to her. "Do it," she said.

"We might not need to go to court," Martin said.

"Let's hope not." Miz Lizbeth gave a thumbs-up. She spoke to Jason. "I think we can all have some confidence in predicting Teddy's reaction to what you hope to set in motion. How do you think Pam will react?"

"I think her actions when Jason beat down Kendal should give us a clue: She probably couldn't care less about Thompson's well-being," Martin said.

"Even so, Pam may not want to see her husband harmed any more than he has been," Jason said.

"Jason, do you intend to let Pam know what you two have planned?" Miz Lizbeth asked.

"Depends."

"Pam and Teddy will probably figure it out," Martin said.

"I think we'll have a favorable outcome for all interested parties. Let's go to dinner," Miz Lizbeth said.

***

After dinner as everyone left the table, Pam drew close to Jason.

"May we talk in private?"

"Of course. Why don't we meet on the front porch after everyone goes to their bedrooms?"

"I'll make sure Teddy has an early night; if not asleep, at least surfing the Net in her bed."

Not long after, Pam came to the front porch where Jason sat. She took a chair beside him. "Thank God everyone seems to have turned in early."

"What did you tell Teddy?"

"That I wanted to spend quality time with you."

"How did she react?"

"Teddy said she hoped the earth moved for us tonight."

"What did you say in response?"

"That I'd let her know." Pam took a deep breath. "You were a Top Gun fighter pilot, right?"

"I was."

"Accustomed to making quick decisions?"

"Yes."

"Well, why haven't you made a move on me? Unless I've completely misread the signals you've given off, you want to make love to me."

"No, I want to make love *with* you."

"Excellent choice of words. Do you foresee any obstacles?"

Jason left his chair to lean against the front porch railing. "How would you feel if Thompson came to a violent end?"

"At your hands?"

"If necessary."

"I don't give a good goddamn about him any longer. He can go to hell. Three things to keep in mind."

"Let me hear them," Jason said.

"First, while I prefer that Teddy won't need to go to court to testify against Thompson, I nevertheless want him in jail for the rest of his life or"—Pam looked directly in Jason's eyes—"put six feet under the ground." She sat back in her chair, sobbing. "I can't believe I missed all of the signs about him and Teddy."

"What's the second thing?"

"Whatever you have in mind, don't get caught."

Jason sat beside Pam and held her hands. "Teddy will not need to testify if what Martin and I will put into play comes to pass."

Pam took several deep breaths. "I won't ask for details. I will trust you as I already have with our lives."

"Good. What's the third thing?"

"I'll ask you again with your words: Do you want to make love with me?"

"I want a long-term relationship with you, not a one or two-night stand."

"Are you proposing marriage?"

"If you're willing to go there despite the short time we've known each other. I worry that the emotions of the past few days may keep you from making an informed decision."

"Didn't you say you're a Top Gun pilot, accustomed to making quick decisions under pressure?"

"I did."

"Well, neither of us is getting any younger, so we need to reach out for happiness sooner than later."

"True."

"Stand up," Pam ordered.

"What?"

"Please stand up."

Jason got to his feet and Pam came to him, pressing her body into his. He held her tightly. "Like this?" he asked.

"Yes. I love you."

"I love you . . . Whose bedroom?"

"Yours. I don't want to disturb Teddy." Pam smiled.

CHAPTER 14

Teddy came into the dining room the next morning to find the family—minus Jason and Pam—seated at the table eating breakfast.

"Miss Theodora, what would you like for breakfast?"

"Scrambled eggs, lots of bacon, toast with real butter and grape jelly, and an endless cup of coffee, Mr. Jackson."

"I'll tell Sally and Ann. Your food will be here directly."

"I need to be fortified in case Jason or Martin want to do battle on the courts this morning." Teddy turned to Miz Lizbeth and grinned. "By the way, where are my mom and Jason? Her bed looks like she didn't sleep there last night."

"They may have spent the night talking, discussing recent events," Miz Lizbeth replied, struggling to keep a straight face."

"I sincerely hope they didn't simply talk the night away. Do you know where they are?"

"As you must suspect, they're in Jason's bedroom," Shanna said.

Teddy clapped. "Outstanding! How do you all know about this turn of events and I don't?"

Jackson delivered Teddy's food. "Eat up, Miss Theodora. The day is full of promise."

"Earlier this morning, Jackson alerted us to the change in sleeping accommodations," Miz Lizbeth said. "We saw no need to wake you with the information."

"You may need your rest for tennis later today," Martin said.

Teddy took several bites of her food and a gulp of black coffee. "I hope Mom and Jason had a wonderful night making the beast with two backs rather than discussing current events."

"Theodora!" Miz Lizbeth exclaimed.

"It's Shakespeare," Teddy countered, before cramming more food into her mouth.

"The Bard is sometimes too bawdy for the breakfast table."

"Miz Lizbeth, I think Teddy has the appropriate outlook on the situation," Martin said.

"What situation?" Pam asked, sitting at the table. Jason sat beside her. Pam had changed her clothes, applied a small—but tasteful—amount of makeup, and brushed her hair.

"Well, Mom and Jason, Miz Lizbeth doesn't want me to be too bawdy, so I'll simply ask, did the two of you have a restful night?"

Pam drank the orange juice Jackson brought her. "In between several times that the earth moved."

Martin clapped his hands and motioned for the rest of the family to follow his lead. After a minute of applause, in which Jason and Pam participated, Martin motioned for quiet.

"Jason, does Jackson need to get his shotgun in order to make this affair legal?"

"You mean a shotgun wedding?" Teddy asked.

Pam hit her knife against her water glass. "We won't need a shotgun. We simply want to proceed along the present path for a little while. For the record, I love Jason and he professes to love me. We can talk marriage sooner than later."

"You'll be spending the nights in Jason's bedroom?" Teddy asked her mother.

"As Spartan as it is."

"Choose his bedroom or yours," Miz Lizbeth said. "We'll go into town later today to purchase whatever items you want to make you more comfortable. If we can't find anything suitable, we'll motor on to Anderson."

"How about a few items for my bedroom including a small desk and an office-type chair," Teddy said.

"Of course. We'll turn one of the extra rooms in your wing into a study. That way you won't be so cramped when school starts. You might like peace and quiet to study. We want you to keep up your grades," Miz Lizbeth said.

"Do you play chess, Miz Lizbeth?" Teddy asked.

"Why do you ask?"

"You seem to have planned things several moves ahead."

"Let's simply say I am rationally optimistic about our futures."

"While we're talking about the future, I need a place to practice medicine," Pam said.

"In an emergency room?" Miz Lizbeth asked.

"Preferably. Do you think there might be an opening at your new hospital?"

"Now *you* don't understand the tactical situation," Martin said with a grin.

"I guess not. Why don't you enlighten me?"

"I won't steal Miz Lizbeth's thunder other than to point out that when you visit the hospital, you'll see that one of the wings is called the Andrews Family Wing."

"You donated one of the wings at the new hospital?" Pam asked Miz Lizbeth.

"The family did. Allison took care of the details." Miz Lizbeth motioned to Jackson for a fresh cup of coffee. "Pam, after we finish here, I'll call Dr. Ellison, the chief medical officer at the hospital, to let him know you're available." Miz Lizbeth smiled at Pam and then at Teddy. "I don't want you two to think I'm trying to direct your lives. I simply made preparations in case things turned out as they have."

"I'm overwhelmed and thankful," Pam said.

"Dr. Ellison has already told me that he needs someone with your experience in the emergency room. He's understaffed there." Miz Lizbeth looked to Jason. "If Pam signs on, she may need to work some nights and weekends."

"No problem," Jason said.

"Good. I'll set up a time for you to talk with Dr. Ellison." Miz Lizbeth turned to Teddy. "We'll have plenty of time after lunch to do our shopping."

"Pam, why don't you come with me while I take care of JJ? I'd like to give you some background on the family you've joined," Shanna said.

"That would be great."

"Should I contribute anything to this conversation, or are you all regarding me as a stud horse?" Jason asked.

"We all have our parts to play," Miz Lizbeth said.

Pam leaned over to kiss Jason. "Finish eating your food in order to replenish your strength for tonight. Doctor's orders."

"Tennis, anyone?" Teddy asked.

"I'll meet you on the court in a few minutes. I need to make a telephone call," Jason said.

"I'll be more than ready now that I have my own rackets. Your day of reckoning approaches," Teddy said.

"Teddy, don't engage in sports trash talk unless you're sure you can back up what you say," Pam said.

"She needs to keep up her enthusiasm. Besides, in about twenty years when Jason and I grow old, and Teddy reaches her maturity, she may have a small chance with us on the court," Martin teased.

CHAPTER 15

After Shanna fed JJ and put the infant to bed, Pam asked if they could speak privately. "I'm intrigued by the Andrews family history, Shanna. They seem to have a lot of secrets."

"Subjects the family won't talk about unless questioned directly," Shanna said.

"You have my full attention," Pam said.

"You're sitting on one of the last surviving intact land grants in northeast Georgia that the government provided to officers who served in the American Revolution."

"The Andrews family goes that far back?"

"Even further," Shanna said. "The Andrews managed to keep the majority of their land after Reconstruction following the Civil War and after the Great Depression."

"How much land are we talking about?"

"About ten thousand acres, mostly around this house."

"How did the Andrews manage to retain their property during those difficult times?" Pam pressed.

"After the American Revolution, and Andrew Jackson running the Cherokees from the land, the settlers grew a lot of corn and other crops. The roads in this area were non-existent or in terrible shape. The settlers needed a way to get their crops to market."

"I'm guessing they turned to making moonshine?"

"That's right. The Andrews never considered making moonshine anything other than a good business practice important for their survival. This whole area, Sweet Gum, once had the distinction, or the notoriety, of being the moonshine and bootlegging capital of northeast Georgia. Moonshining and bootlegging died out after the national repeal of Prohibition coupled with local option county sales of recreational alcohol."

"How does this history of illegal alcohol relate to the present-day status of the Andrews family?" Pam asked.

"Alexander Poultry Industries traces its origins to illegal alcohol. Jason Andrews Sr.—Miz Lizbeth's husband—moonshined and bootlegged in his younger days in order to provide cash, primarily to pay taxes on the land, at least initially. Jason was ten years older than Miz Lizbeth and, like her, intellectually way above average. He also was lucky that law enforcement never caught him, although he probably knew the right people to pay off. He foresaw the arrival of local option in Alexander County."

"I suppose he used his money and political influence to encourage the county to vote against legalizing alcohol sales?" Pam guessed.

"No, quite the opposite."

"Seems counterintuitive, if he was so adept in his illegal activities."

"Like I said, he saw the future. He and Miz Lizbeth studied pamphlets about the poultry industry that they obtained from the state agricultural office, the Farm Bureau, county extension agents, and agricultural schools. They also traveled to interview poultry farmers in other states."

"Sounds like they did their homework," Pam said.

"They did."

"Jason Sr. and Miz Lizbeth used the money he made from illegal alcohol to start Alexander Poultry Industries?" Pam asked.

"That's right. At the time they began, the poultry industry was almost non-existent in northeast Georgia. Currently, Alexander County is the leading poultry producer in Georgia as a direct result of Andrews Poultry Industries."

"What a story," Pam said.

"There's more. Early on, and continuing to this day, Andrews Poultry Industries contracted with local farmers to raise chickens, and for a while turkeys, for the company. In the beginning, the Andrews loaned the farmers the funds needed to construct grow houses. Vickery Bank and Trust provides the financing now. The company furnished the chicks and feed; the farmers took care of the chickens and turkeys. When the birds reached the proper weight, Jason Sr. collected and sold them to a processing plant in Gainesville.

"Later, he and Miz Lizbeth built their own feed mill in Vickery, right by the downtown railroad tracks. The company also has its own grow houses located on this and other properties in the county. The Andrews used the profits to form their construction company, which built—and still builds—many of the grow houses you see around here.

"Jason Sr. and Miz Lizbeth were busy building the business, which probably accounted for the fact they were childless for a while. A year after Jason's birth, a terrible automobile accident late one night killed Jason Sr., and Miz Lizbeth ended up in her wheelchair."

"Miz Lizbeth told Teddy and me some of these details. Any idea who drove the second car?"

"Rumors suggest Stuart Whitfield caused the wreck. He tried to compete against the Andrews in the local poultry industry. Bad blood existed between them, and the two families remain personal and economic rivals, although recently the Andrews have thoroughly gained the upper hand."

"What happened to Stuart?"

"A local court declared Stuart legally dead seven years after he disappeared."

"He disappeared?"

"A sheriff's patrol car found Stuart's pickup truck abandoned on a back road in the woods deep into Sweet Gum," Shanna said.

"No signs of foul play?"

"The truck had no fingerprints other than those belonging to Stuart, and no footprints or tire prints appeared on the ground surrounding the abandoned car."

"When did Stuart disappear?"

"Shortly after Jason and Martin, the fearsome A-Team, turned eighteen."

Pam took a few moments to absorb this information. "No one knows what happened to Stuart Whitfield?"

"He may have fed the chickens," Shanna said.

Pam shook her head. "I understand the allusion to the *Godfather* movies, feeding the fish, but feeding the chickens?"

"Stuart may have been turned into chicken feed," Shanna laughed.

"You're telling me someone processed Stuart's body into chicken feed at the mill?"

"A rumor only, maybe a conspiracy theory. Law enforcement never seemed interested in pursuing the matter."

"Miz Lizbeth, if involved, could not have acted on her own to get rid of Stuart."

"True."

"Jason and Martin?" Pam asked.

"Who knows? Some people around here say Stuart received justice, albeit delayed."

Several moments of silence ensued before Pam spoke.

"Thank you, Shanna, for telling me this history, which doesn't change my opinion of your husband and, I hope, my husband-to-be. My interpretation would be that Jason and Martin continue to exact justice when the legal system either cannot or will not."

"They are heroes."

"Champions."

"Anyway, Miz Lizbeth brought her own resources into the marriage; her family had people and land, not a lot of money."

"Cash poor but land rich?"

"That's right. Miz Lizbeth brought many of her family's workers with her when she and Jason Sr. married. In the early days of the marriage, she and Jason Sr. couldn't pay a lot of money to people who came with her. In compensation, Jason Sr. and Miz Lizbeth provided comfortable places for the people to live and allowed them to keep all the crops they grew, except for what was needed here in the Big House. As time went by, the Andrews began to pay the workers on the place with real money."

"What about now?"

"Pretty much the same arrangement. The people who work the property are sharecroppers, except they keep maybe 90 percent of what they grow and produce, as well as receiving salaries. Many of the people also help with the poultry business."

"The workers must be tremendously loyal."

"That they are," Shanna said.

"Jackson and Miz Lizbeth, exactly what is their relationship?"

"I'm not sure. Ever since Miz Lizbeth came home from the hospital after the accident, Jackson has slept in the bedroom adjacent to hers. He's intimately involved in her care, down to the nitty-gritty. I think Miz Lizbeth and Jackson are emotionally close."

"She's both urinary and bowel incontinent?"

"That's my understanding."

"Does anyone help Jackson with the nitty-gritty of Miz Lizbeth's personal hygiene?"

"Sally and Ann, plus other women on the property. Jackson basically runs this place under Miz Lizbeth's direction and provides her primary care."

"What's Jackson's relation to Jason and Martin?"

"For all practical purposes, Jackson has been Jason and Martin's father. I'm led to believe Jackson was a loving and strict disciplinarian, which Jason and Martin needed."

"To your knowledge, has Miz Lizbeth been evaluated medically in the past few years?"

"You'll need to ask her or Jackson. Why do you ask?"

"A lot of progress has been made with spinal cord injuries." Pam held up a hand to caution Shanna. "Nothing we should mention until I've had a chance to make some assessments."

"You're like the boys; you never admit defeat, do you?"

"I came close when I found out about Teddy and Thompson."

Shanna reached out to embrace Pam. "Yet, here you are, alive and kicking, with vengeance in your mind, if not in your heart."

Pam looked long and directly into Shanna's eyes. "Maybe I'm not that different from Jason and Martin."

"Welcome to the Andrews family."

CHAPTER 16

The Andrews family, including Pam and Teddy, walked down the central aisle of the Ebenezer at Aldersgate United Methodist Church in Vickery a few minutes before eleven o'clock on Sunday. Sections had been removed from the first two pews on the right side of the sanctuary to accommodate Miz Lizbeth's wheelchair while leaving the central aisle unobstructed. As soon as Jackson and Miz Lizbeth took their places, the organist and pianist began the prelude to open the worship service.

Pam and Teddy looked at each other in wonderment at the performance when the choir, under the direction of John Carver, began the choral introit. The minister of music held himself erect despite his advanced age. Teddy whispered in Jackson's right ear, "How old is he?"

"At least eighty years young."

The music ended, and John Carver turned to face the congregation composed of approximately equal numbers of black and white persons with a smaller number of Hispanics.

"Let those who are able and willing stand to join together in singing one of our greatest hymns, number 154 in your hymnals—'All Hail the Power of Jesus' Name.'" The congregation stood and sang lustily with the first verse.

All hail the power of Jesus' name! Let angels prostrate fall;
bring forth the royal diadem, and crown him Lord of all.
Bring forth the royal diadem, and crown him Lord of all.

Teddy remained silent. Jackson spoke commandingly in her ear. "Miss Theodora, you cannot remain silent in this service. Sing out!"

As the second verse began, Teddy joined the congregation and choir:

Ye chosen seed of Israel's race, ye ransomed from the fall,
hail him who saves you by his grace, and crown him Lord
of all.
Hail him who saves you by his grace, and crown him Lord
of all.

On the third verse, Teddy's voice grew even stronger in keeping with her position as lead soprano in her high school chorus:

Sinners, whose love can ne'er forget the wormwood
and the gall,
go spread your trophies at his feet, and crown him
Lord of all.
Go spread your trophies at his feet, and crown him
Lord of all.

John Carver, ever vigilant for persons who could sing, walked several feet away from the choir loft in order to be closer to Teddy as she sang on the fourth verse:

Let every kindred, every tribe on this terrestrial ball,

Facing Teddy, John Carver motioned behind his back for the choir to be silent. Teddy and most of the congregation continued to sing.

to him all majesty ascribe, and crown him Lord of all.

John Carver moved even closer to Teddy, who seemed unaware of his movements.

To him all majesty ascribe, and crown him Lord of all.

The organist realized what John Carver wanted done and began a joyful riff to transition between the third and fourth verses. John Carver motioned for the congregation to remain silent.

At the start of the fifth verse, Teddy realized that only she and John Carver were singing while the organist and pianist continued to play softly. She looked at the minister of music, who motioned for her to sing out. His still firm baritone voice provided a foundation for her soaring soprano, which seemed to grow stronger as she and John Carver sang.

*Crown him, ye martyrs of your God, who from his
altar call;
extol the Stem of Jesse's Rod, and crown him
Lord of all.
Extol the Stem of Jesse's Rod, and crown him
Lord of all.*

The organist and pianist began another even more joyful riff before the last verse. With a grand gesture, John Carver directed the choir and congregation to join him and Teddy.

*O that with yonder sacred throng we at his feet may fall!
We'll join the everlasting song, and crown him Lord of
all*

The music from the two instruments and the singing from
the choir and congregation pulsated through the sanctuary.

*We'll join the everlasting song, and crown him Lord of
all.*

When the hymn ended, the sanctuary erupted into sustained
applause, and shouts of "Amen" and "Praise God." Reverend
Beatrice Parker, a dark-skinned African American woman in her
late forties who projected an aura of immense gravitas, stood
behind the Gospel pulpit to the congregation's right.

"The Holy Spirit truly has descended upon us and rocked
this sanctuary!" More applause and acclamations greeted this
announcement. Rev. Parker waited until the noise subsided
before speaking again. "John Carver, I think you may have a
new soprano for our choir, a young lady God has blessed with
an immense talent." The congregants applauded. Rev. Parker
looked intently at Teddy. "Miss Theodora Nelson, I believe?"

"Yes, ma'am," Teddy answered in a strong voice.

"Our choir practices from seven to about nine o'clock on
Thursday evenings here in the sanctuary. If you would care to
join the choir, you'll be home before too late on school nights."

John Carver stood. "Miss Nelson, we'd love to have you sing
with us."

Rev. Parker pointed to JJ sleeping in Shanna's lap.

"I note that young Jason Jackson rests quietly for the present.
We should go forward with his baptism and welcome him into
this community of believers. Will the candidate, his family and
friends please come forward."

Jackson pushed Miz Lizbeth to the altar rail. Martin and Shanna, who held JJ, joined Miz Lizbeth on her right. Teddy stood on Miz Lizbeth's left while Jason and Pam placed themselves behind the infant and his parents.

"Brothers and sisters in Christ," Rev. Parker began the centuries-old ritual, "through the Sacrament of Baptism, we are initiated in Christ's holy church. We are incorporated into God's mighty acts of salvation and given new birth through water and the Spirit. All this is God's gift, offered to us without price. Who comes now to be baptized?" Rev. Parker asked.

Miz Lizbeth's response carried easily to the balcony at the rear of the sanctuary. "I present my grandson, Jason Jackson Andrews, for baptism."

JJ awoke at the sound of his grandmother's voice. Rev. Parker asked, "Who will be godparents for Jason Jackson?"

"I will be godfather to Jason Jackson," Jason said.

Pam took Jason's hand. "And I will be godmother to Jason Jackson."

JJ made no objection to the proceedings at which he was the center of attention until Rev. Parker placed holy water on his head with the pronouncement "Jason Jackson Andrews, I baptize you in the name of the Father, and of the Son, and of the Holy Spirit." Jason Jackson unleashed strong cries of surprised outrage.

Shanna and Martin put the baby in Miz Lizbeth's lap. Miz Lizbeth held the baby with one arm and placed a hand on JJ's head. The mother and father put their hands on top of Miz Lizbeth's hand. The rest of the family reached out to put hands on top of Martin and Shanna's hands. The laying on of hands quieted JJ.

"The Holy Spirit work within you, that being born through water and the Spirit, you may be a faithful disciple of Jesus Christ," Rev. Parker said.

The congregation responded, "Amen."

Rev. Parker took JJ from Miz Lizbeth and held him in the crook of one arm. "It is my great pleasure to introduce the newest member of our congregation." Rev. Parker used both hands to lift JJ high above her head. The infant seemed to be surveilling the congregation.

The congregation made the traditional response. "Through baptism you are incorporated by the Holy Spirit into God's new creation and to share in Christ's royal priesthood. We are all one in Christ Jesus. With joy and thanksgiving, we welcome you as a member of the family of Christ."

Returning JJ to the crook of her right arm, Rev. Parker motioned to the young assistant pastor to come to her side with a container of holy water. The two ministers walked down the central aisle to the back of the sanctuary. The assistant minister sprinkled holy water on congregants to his left and right while Rev. Parker repeatedly pronounced, "Remember your own baptism." The two ministers followed the same procedure as they returned to the front of the sanctuary.

Rev. Parker shouted, "Hallelujah, thine be the glory!" before returning JJ to Shanna. Once the family resettled in the pews, JJ promptly reached for his mother's breast. Shanna looked inquiringly to Martin, who whispered, "Feed the beast here."

The assistant minister read the Scripture lesson from the epistle pulpit to the congregation's left, trying to keep his eyes off Shanna and JJ. "Hear, now, the word of God, from the sixth chapter of St. Paul's epistle to the church at Rome:

> Do you not know that all of us who have been baptized into Christ Jesus were baptized into his death? Therefore, we have been buried with him by baptism into death, so that, just as Christ was raised from the dead by the glory of the Father, so we too might walk in newness of life.

For if we have been united with him in a death like his, we will certainly be united with him in a resurrection like his. We know that our old self was crucified with him so that the body of sin might be destroyed, and we might no longer be enslaved to sin. For whoever has died is freed from sin. But if we have died with Christ, we believe that we will also live with him. We know that Christ, being raised from the dead, will never die again; death no longer has dominion over him. The death he died, he died to sin, once for all; but the life he lives, he lives to God. So you also must consider yourselves dead to sin and alive to God in Christ Jesus.

Rev. Parker stood in the center of the chancel in front of the altar.

"You might ask what does this Scripture have to do with young Jason Jackson? The Scripture means that he has been united with Christ, our Lord and Savior. Through the symbolism and reality of baptism, Jason Jackson has been freed from the clutches of sin; he is free from sin through the sacrificial life and death, and resurrection of Jesus Christ."

Someone at the rear of the sanctuary shouted, "Thanks be to Jesus Christ!" Murmurs of praise coursed through the sanctuary.

Rev. Parker fixed her eyes upon Teddy and continued speaking, never breaking eye contact with the young woman.

"What about the rest of us, those who have been baptized into Christ? What is the take-home message; no, rather, the life-affirming message for us?" Still keeping eye contact with Teddy, Rev. Parker raised both hands toward the ceiling of the sanctuary. "Hear now, my brothers and sisters in Christ, what we must incorporate into our hearts for ourselves and for each other."

The organist produced another ascending riff through the scale. "Through Christ Jesus' life, death, and resurrection, all of our sins—past, present, and future—have already been forgiven. We are free, thank God, we are free from sin!"

More shouts of praise rang throughout the sanctuary. Rev. Parker waited for the noise to subside before continuing.

"We don't need to try to parse our sins—whether we were in some manner forced into them, whether we enjoyed them, whether we resisted against the force of evil, whether we had thoughts of revenge we might wreak because of sins against us. No, all of our sins in their entirety have already been forgiven." Rev. Parker, before breaking eye contact with Teddy, nodded and paraphrased verses nine and ten from the fourth chapter of First Timothy.

"What I have told you is sure and worthy of full acceptance. We have our hope set on the living God, who is the Savior of all people, especially those who believe."

***

The rest of the Andrews family waited until the sanctuary had almost emptied before leaving their pew. At the church doors, the entire family came together. Teddy walked beside Jackson, who pushed Miz Lizbeth's wheelchair. Rev. Parker held out her hand to Teddy and leaned closer to the young woman.

"Perhaps you would like to talk with me? I know I would like to talk with you."

"I'll give you a call during the week when someone from the Big House can bring me to your office."

"Would you like for me to come to the Big House?"

"No, ma'am, we might have a hard time finding some privacy to talk."

"You're probably right. Call me. I'll make myself available whenever you're free."

"Thanks."

Once the family had assembled on the sidewalk, Jackson

opened the large passenger's side door of the Honda Odyssey modified for wheelchair access and pushed Miz Lizbeth up the ramp into the open middle of the minivan. He secured her in place and sat in the driver's seat.

"Would you like to ride with us, Theodora?" Miz Lizbeth asked.

"Yes, ma'am." Teddy sat in the front passenger seat. The Odyssey led the Andrews caravan to the Sweet Gum Barbecue and Fish Lodge restaurant. "Elizabeth, did you tell Reverend Parker about me?" Teddy asked.

"In what respect?"

"Did you tell her about my history with Thompson?"

"I did not. I told Beatrice that I hoped you would become a formal member of our family."

"What else?"

"I told her that things had happened to you in the past, things beyond your control to prevent, and that you have shown remarkable courage in the face of those difficulties."

"From what she said to me on our way out of church, I think you must have told her more."

"What exactly did Beatrice say?"

"She asked if I would like to talk with her."

"Would you?"

"I told her I'd ask someone from the Big House to bring me to her office next week," Teddy said.

"I'll make the arrangements," Jackson said.

"Thanks. Elizabeth, did you orchestrate the sermon today?"

"Why do you ask? Are you upset?"

"Not at all. I would like to talk with someone outside the family about some feelings I have, feelings I'm having trouble putting into a proper context."

"Beatrice will be a good person to start with. She's eminently trustworthy. You'll enjoy talking with her."

"Great. You still haven't answered my question."

"Which one?"

"To what extent did you orchestrate the sermon?"

"I merely told Beatrice that the baptismal ceremony for Jason Jackson would be a good lead-in to discuss transforming events in our lives."

"Do you think I somehow sinned to induce Thompson to try to rape me?"

Jackson broke in. "Miss Theodora, neither Elizabeth nor anyone else in this family believes your sins caused you to be assaulted." He turned into the driveway to the restaurant. "Even so, from your comments, you have some questions, questions that Reverend Parker may be best suited to answer."

"Maybe so." Teddy filed away the observation that Jackson had used "Elizabeth" rather than "Miz Lizbeth."

"Teddy, you do know that you can talk to anyone in the Andrews family and to your own mother if something bothers you?" Miz Lizbeth asked.

"I think a neutral observer might be best."

"As early as tomorrow with Beatrice, then."

CHAPTER 17

Jason stopped his Accord in front of the Ebenezer at Aldersgate church the next day.

"Teddy, after your mom and I pick up her car from Rufus's garage, she'll go to the hospital for her interview. I'll wait at Jean's Coffee Shop until you call me to get you."

"I'll probably need some exercise when I finish here. Why don't I walk over to the coffee shop?"

"That's a plan."

"Isn't Mom's position at the hospital a done deal?"

"I want to see the facility and meet some of the staff before making up my mind about working there. When I'm finished at the hospital, I'll drive my car back to the Big House and we can all have lunch together," Pam said.

"See you guys later." Teddy left the car and walked determinedly toward the door to the right of the sanctuary. Jason waited at the curb until Teddy opened the door and waved.

"Miss Theodora Nelson?" asked the church secretary when Teddy walked into the church office.

"Yes, ma'am," Teddy said.

Rev. Parker came out of her adjoining office. "Good to see you this fine morning, Ms. Nelson. Please come in."

"Thank you for meeting with me on such short notice, Reverend Parker."

"My pleasure. Why don't you take a seat on the couch and I'll sit in the chair in front of you?" After they were seated she said, "I hope you're serious about joining our choir. You have a wonderful voice. Do you sing in your school choir?"

"Since grammar school, and in our church youth choir."

"Which church?"

"We were members of the Episcopalian Cathedral of St. Philip in Buckhead," Teddy said.

"That's high church."

"We lived on West Paces Ferry Road, near the governor's mansion. My stepfather thought the church and neighborhood enhanced his law practice," Teddy said.

"Will you and your mom be staying with the Andrews family, at least for the foreseeable future?"

"I'm hoping so."

"Then you can sing in our choir and the choir at the high school. Both choirs will benefit."

"As will I," Teddy said.

"If I'm out of line with my next questions, please don't hesitate to tell me."

"You want to know if Jason and my mom will marry?"

"Yes."

"I hope so. Because Mom and Jason developed a strong and immediate attraction for each other, they decided to wait for a while before making the commitment to marry. In the interim, we're living together as a family."

"You are an exceptionally well-spoken young woman."

"Thank you."

"You want them to marry?"

"The sooner the better after Mom obtains a divorce."

"Will a divorce be difficult?"

"My stepfather may resist. He's a criminal defense lawyer."

"Teddy, Miz Lizbeth has only told me that you and your mom have been going through a difficult time. She gave me no other details, although she suggested my sermon might have been appropriate for you and your mom."

"It was."

"Something's on your mind, a topic you'd like to talk with me about in reference to the sermon?"

"I do."

"Where would you like to start?"

Teddy looked unblinkingly into the minister's eyes. "What we discuss here is confidential?"

"Absolutely, unless I have reason to believe you're going to harm yourself or someone else."

"I have no intention of harming myself and there's no longer any need for me to contemplate harming anyone."

"I'm glad to hear that. You want coffee, tea, a soft drink, water?"

"Black coffee would be great," Teddy answered.

Rev. Parker opened her office door. "Mary, we'd like two cups of the Keurig coffee, black for Ms. Nelson, my usual for me."

"I'll bring the coffee as soon as it's ready," the church secretary said.

Rev. Parker shut the door to the office and returned to her seat. "Mary will knock on the door when she brings the coffee. How do you like living at the Big House?"

"Very much. I feel like one of the family."

"I'm grateful to have the Andrews family in the pews each Sunday. Do you think Shanna will remain here or return to the West Coast and her modeling career?"

"Shanna seems totally involved with JJ. I think the plan is, once she loses her pregnancy weight, she'll take on selective modeling jobs."

"And your mother, what do you think she will do if you and she remain at the Big House?"

"As we speak, Mom's talking with the medical director at your hospital about a position in the ER."

"Do you foresee any difficulties in her working there?"

"You're aware of whose name is on one of the wings of the hospital?"

Rev. Parker let out a great belly laugh. "I am."

The coffee was served.

"Teddy, where would you like to start?"

Teddy related her story, beginning with Thompson's secret viewing of her masturbating, progressing to his assault, the flight from Atlanta, and the rescue by Jason and Martin. Mindful of Miz Lizbeth's advice, Teddy did not mention her desire to kill Thompson, nor did she reveal how Jason and Martin had removed incriminating evidence from the Kendal home.

"You've told the story of your assault to your family?" Rev. Parker asked.

"The first afternoon we were at the Big House, after Jason and Martin rescued us. Mom, of course, knew all the details because she was directly involved in the aftermath of the assault. She had no idea of Thompson's perversion."

"Your mother must have an admirable ability to compartmentalize events surrounding her. I'm amazed that she was able to take care of your needs, physical and emotional, after the attempted rape."

"Mom is formidable and a great doctor, but I don't think the trauma for either of us will soon fade away."

"Have you considered therapy?" Rev. Parker asked.

"I'm not against formal therapy; however, being with the Andrews family is cathartic."

"Are you willing to tell me the reaction from the Andrews?"

"Jason and Martin were—are—angry and wish to see Thompson brought to justice."

"From what you told me about the fight Jason and Martin had with your stepfather and his associates, the path to justice has already begun."

"But probably not finished," Teddy said.

"What about Miz Lizbeth?"

"Miz Lizbeth said I've been thrust into a terrible situation to which I reacted with bravery and resourcefulness."

"She is a shrewd judge of character."

"I think Miz Lizbeth sometimes keeps her cards close to her chest as she plans several moves in advance. I'm confident she supports Jason and Martin's desire to see Thompson brought to justice."

"Presumably through the legal system?" Rev. Parker asked.

"We've already talked with Counselor Allison Jameson."

Teddy did not want to disclose what she knew and inferred about the plans to bring Thompson to justice, through the courts or otherwise.

"So, Teddy, what has really brought you here today?"

"I'm worried that I may always live with the specter of Thompson on a loop in my mind. The tape has already begun playing," Teddy said.

"I can only imagine," Rev. Parker said. "I'll tell you how you may find some relief."

"Please do."

"Teddy, many of us have such recordings playing in our minds. Even so, you don't have to act upon what you hear and see in your mind. I am supremely confident that a strong-willed person like you can figure out how to hear and see but not act upon or be negatively influenced by the memories of the assault and its aftermath."

"Listen but not act?"

"Indeed." Rev. Parker tented her fingers. "I think you face a difficult choice."

"What's that?"

"I think you should refrain from all sexual relations for a time."

"Why?"

"To avoid the temptation of trying to use sex to submerge the trauma of what has happened to you."

"I hadn't thought of that outcome," Teddy said.

"From what I've already ascertained about your character, you need to determine what you want out of sex."

"Please explain," Teddy said.

"Do you want to find a partner you can dominate or a partner with whom you can be an equal?"

"Is there a right or wrong choice?"

"Not as long as you make an informed decision. And you might find that vigorous exercise will take your mind off of your sex drive, at least for a time."

"Sublimation?"

"Yes."

"Do you think I'm weird, on the basis of this conversation?"

"You're a smart and determined young woman who's had an extraordinarily difficult time, which easily could have developed into something much worse. You'll get through this period in your life with the help of your family. I'm also available to talk with you."

"Reverend Parker, I'll probably be back many times to talk."

"My door is always open for you, and I'm a good listener."

"That you are. Thanks."

"Keep the faith. You're well on the way to recovering from your trauma."

CHAPTER 18

L ate the following Saturday afternoon, Teddy, Martin, and Jason, still flushed from their jog around the property, came into the den as the other members of the family gathered for pre-dinner cocktails.

"Miss Theodora, I'd greatly appreciate your help," Jackson said. Teddy distributed the drinks as he prepared them. When she finished, Jackson handed her a tall glass filled with club soda, a lime slice, and crushed ice. Teddy took a sip from the club soda.

"Mr. Jackson, can I have some of the single malt Scotch?"

"When your mother says you can have some."

"Not tonight, Teddy," Pam interjected.

"I have an offer for you, Miss Theodora," Jackson said.

"One I can't refuse?"

"I suspect you won't refuse this offer."

"I'm listening," Teddy said.

"You'll soon be starting school."

"That's the plan." Teddy looked to her mother for confirmation. Pam gave an affirmative nod.

"Well then, with your mother's consent, I'll give you three drinks of an alcoholic beverage of your choice for each A and one drink for each B on your report card at the end of the grading periods." Jackson smiled. "Only one drink per day."

"What about Cs?"

"Cs are not acceptable in this family.

"I agree," Teddy said. "Mom?"

"Eminently sensible. Teddy's a straight A student so she'll have adequate opportunities to indulge her penchant for alcohol."

"Mr. Jackson, did you make the same bargain with Jason and Martin when they were in high school?" Teddy asked.

"I did."

Teddy looked in turn at Jason and Martin before asking Jackson, "Did they keep their end of the bargain?" Miz Lizbeth sat her drink on the table by her wheelchair before laughing. Jason and Martin shook their heads.

"I'm confident they managed to find alcoholic beverages on their own away from home," Jackson said.

"We plead the Fifth," Jason said.

"What makes you think I'll adhere to my side of the bargain and not do like Jason and Martin?" Teddy asked Jackson.

"Miss Theodora, you have more sense at your age than"— Jackson pointed at the two brothers—"these two miscreants combined when they were in high school."

"Hey, we turned out all right," Martin said over the laughter in the den.

"Getting there involved a lot of parental worries for Jackson and me," Miz Lizbeth said.

Teddy took her glass of club soda from the bar and sat next to Miz Lizbeth. "Now that we've settled my drinking problem, I'd like to discuss another topic, Miz Lizbeth."

"Which is?"

"The basketball goal near the tennis court."

"Please continue."

"I understand Mr. Jackson grew tired of cleaning up the

blood when Martin and Jason played one-on-one, so you had the basket removed from the backboard."

"There was more blood on my sons than on the court," Miz Lizbeth said.

"I think everyone here knows I plan to play on the high school tennis team this spring, and that I'll probably win the state championship thanks to the excellent coaching from Martin and Jason."

"What does that laudable objective have to do with basketball?" Miz Lizbeth asked.

"I intend to play on the high school basketball team, like I did in Atlanta."

"You want to practice free throws and your moves here?" Jason asked.

"If you and Martin are willing, I'd like you to coach me."

"How do you propose keeping my sons from engaging in mortal combat?" Miz Lizbeth asked.

"They could take turns coaching me. You could also issue a command that they not play each other."

"No command necessary," Jason said. "Martin and I will accept your proposal."

"Agreed," Martin said.

"May we start tomorrow?"

"If he has no other plans, Martin can return the basket to the backboard and begin the coaching tomorrow," Jason said. "I have an appointment in Atlanta."

"I'm available except when Shanna needs help with the wild child. What position do you play?" Martin asked.

"I had to be the center."

"You were the tallest person on your team?"

"That's right," said Teddy, who stood five foot, ten inches.

"You may be the tallest person on the Alexander County High School team," Jason said.

"We'll see when practice begins. What positions did you and Martin play?"

"Forward. A friend played center. He was almost six and a half feet tall. No one could block his hook shot."

"We have the athletics out of the way for the evening," Jackson said. "Dinner should be ready by the time we gather in the dining room."

CHAPTER 19

Jason, carrying his laptop computer, opened the door to the office suite at ten o'clock for his appointment with Frank Gordon.

"Jason Andrews, to see Mr. Frank Gordon," he said to the stunningly attractive secretary.

The secretary walked toward the door to the inner office. "Mr. Gordon expects you." She opened the door. "Mr. Gordon, Mr. Jason Andrews to see you."

Frank Gordon, some six inches shorter and fifty pounds lighter than Jason, pointed to a chair. "You can sit there."

"Thank you for seeing me, Mr. Gordon."

"I wanted to meet one of the men who did such damage to my associates."

"You should hire better bodyguards, ones who know how to fight."

Gordon made a wry face. "They're apparently better with firearms than with their fists."

"They aren't very fast on the draw."

"They aren't all that fast with their minds either, although they do what I tell them."

"Did you tell them to try to kidnap Dr. Kendal and her daughter on I-85, and from our home in Alexander County?"

Gordon shrugged. "Not directly. My lawyer said he needed their help."

"L. Thompson Kendal?"

"That's right. I believe you've met him."

"I hope he's better in the courtroom than with hand-to-hand combat."

"He's quite good, as long as he stays where he belongs."

"Mr. Gordon, my family has no direct quarrel with you. Thompson Kendal is the reason I asked to see you."

"Presumably, you don't want to hire him as your lawyer?"

"We have adequate legal representation . . . There is something I need to show you regarding your attorney."

Jason opened the laptop and brought up the video of Kendal assaulting Teddy.

"I think you will be interested in this video." Jason placed the laptop with the screen facing Gordon. "Please hit the return key to start the video."

"I hope you're not wasting my time."

"See for yourself."

With the first images on the screen, Gordon sat back in his chair, his face impassive, although his eyes hardened. He watched the video to the end.

"Where did you get this?"

"Let's say Kendal needs a better security system at his home."

"What do you want from me?"

"We plan to release copies of this video to the *Atlanta Journal-Constitution* and to law enforcement."

"Why should I care?"

"The nature of your business should lead you to disassociate yourself from Kendal before he's brought to justice for the attempted rape of Theodora, his own stepdaughter."

"What do you know about my business?"

"Please hold down the command and shift keys. Then depress the option key," Jason instructed.

Gordon looked intently at the screen, stood up, and then sat again in his chair.

"What the hell? How did you hack into my accounts?"

"You need better security on your computers."

"What did you mean by disassociating myself from Thompson?"

"I leave the manner of the disassociation to your discretion."

"How do you know I won't disassociate you and your brother rather than Thompson?"

"Please depress the delete key."

"Goddamn it, I'm tired of these games," Gordon blustered.

"Even so, the delete key, please."

Gordon leapt from his chair as each entry on the screen disappeared, line-by-line.

"What the hell's going on?"

"We planted a worm in your system. The worm methodically erases all the entries in this account before moving on to your several other accounts. The worm also has been placed in your backup files." Jason paused as Gordon returned to his chair. "Also, the worm will make its way into the accounts linked to your accounts. That is, the worm will destroy the accounts of the people in the larger organization to which you belong."

"I for goddamn sure am going to whack you."

"Please depress the F7 key."

Gordon watched as the account was rebuilt, line-by-line.

"I'm still going to whack you."

Jason looked hard into Gordon's eyes. "You mean you'll have someone in your organization try to whack me."

"Makes no difference. You're a dead man walking."

"My brother and I already demonstrated what we can do

to your minions. Bring on more of them, unless you're brave enough to try, as you so elegantly put it, to whack me yourself."

"You don't have any idea who you're talking to."

"I have a firm idea that you don't know how to hire effective people. Unless someone at a specific time each day issues a command to stop the worm, it will eat through you accounts. I don't have the command, nor does anyone in my family. If you harm anyone in my family or me, the worm will still do its job."

"How do you know two things?"

"Which are?" Jason asked.

"That I won't have my or the organization's techies remove the worm?"

"And?"

"What if I whack the guy who must be your techie?"

"I'll answer the first question. You may be able to remove the worm, but another will be inserted. You can't hide your accounts from my techie."

"Like I said, what if I whack him, whoever the hell he is?"

"He has friends alerted to what's happening. You might as well give up the idea. Your accounts are in peril, a circumstance people above you in your organization will view with extreme prejudice."

Gordon smiled. "Bottom line: You want me to take care of your problem with Kendal." Jason did not answer. "I get it. You've fallen for Pamela and don't want to do the dirty work of eliminating Kendal yourself. She might resent that."

"I'm certain you will do the right thing."

"Let's say I 'do the right thing' with Kendal."

"It would be in your best interests."

"I did some background research on you and your family. Perhaps we could work an agreeable arrangement beneficial to both of our interests."

"In what way?" Jason asked.

"Your company trucks would be a great help in moving my product north on I-85. Also, you could exert your family's political influence by instructing law enforcement agencies to stop their drug interdiction tactics along I-85. Work with us and your family could receive hundreds of thousands, maybe even millions, of dollars."

Jason retrieved the laptop and stood.

"Let me be perfectly clear, Mr. Gordon. I have no designs on your territory; however, if you try to expand your interests into Alexander County, you will not become a dead man walking, you will be dead."

"Brave words."

"Take care of Thompson Kendal in whatever manner you wish. And stay out of Alexander County." Jason nodded toward Gordon and walked out of the office.

Gordon sat still for a few minutes. He depressed a key on the office intercom. "JoAnne, please call Rafe Butler and tell him to come here. I have a job for him."

"Of course, Mr. Gordon."

CHAPTER 20

Jackson answered the family's landline several days later.

"Andrews residence." He listened for a few moments. "Please hold, Detective." Jackson took the telephone to the front porch where Miz Lizbeth watched Teddy, Jason, and Martin compete in shooting free throws on the reconstituted basketball goal.

"Elizabeth, you should handle this call," Jackson said.

"Who is it?"

"Sam Turner, a detective in the Atlanta Police Department."

Miz Lizbeth took the telephone and activated the speaker function.

"This is Mrs. Elizabeth Andrews, Detective. How may I help you?"

"Are Dr. Pamela Kendal and Miss Theodora Nelson staying with you?"

"They're part of the Andrews family. Why do you ask?"

"May I please speak with Dr. Kendal?"

"She's on duty at our local hospital emergency room. What is the purpose of your call?"

"When will Dr. Kendal return?"

"She'll be on duty at the hospital until Monday morning. Again, why do you want to speak to her?"

"I have sad news to relate, and I wish to interview her."

"Please tell me the news and I'll inform Dr. Kendal."

"I'll call Dr. Kendal at the hospital," the detective replied.

"I'd prefer that you tell me what's going on before bothering Dr. Kendal."

"Earlier this morning, we found Dr. Kendal's husband, L. Thompson Kendal, and two other men shot dead in his home."

"How unfortunate!"

"I need to interview Dr. Kendal."

"Detective, I can assure you that Dr. Kendal has been with us continuously for the past several weeks. She went on duty at the hospital early this morning," Miz Lizbeth said.

"Even so, I must interview her. What about her daughter?"

"With us."

Miz Lizbeth covered the mouthpiece of the telephone and spoke to Jackson.

"Call Pam on your devil's contraption and tell her not to speak with the detective until she hears from us." Jackson went into the house to make the call.

"Mrs. Andrews, are you still there?"

"I am, Detective. I will make arrangements for you to interview Dr. Kendal and Miss Nelson at our lawyer's office Monday afternoon."

"Why involve a lawyer unless you all have something to hide?"

"I resent your implication. I simply know better than to allow you to interview members of my family in the absence of our lawyer, Ms. Allison Jameson." Miz Lizbeth gave Allison's contact information to the detective. "Unless you have ironclad evidence of Dr. Kendal's involvement in this crime and intend to arrest her, the interview will take place Monday afternoon. Do you understand?"

"We have no reason to suspect Dr. Kendal or Miss Nelson of any crime. We simply want to gather as much information as we can."

"Monday afternoon, then." Miz Lizbeth disconnected the call. "Jackson, get Allison on the phone. And please summon my sons and Theodora."

Once Jackson, Jason, Martin, and Teddy were seated on the front porch, Miz Lizbeth said, "Theodora, I have some news that you and Pam should hear as soon as possible. Please call your mother and see if she can talk with us."

Teddy activated the speaker function on her cell phone when Pam came on the line.

"I have news we need to consider," Miz Lizbeth said. "A detective from the Atlanta Police Department called a few minutes ago to inform us that Thompson Kendal and two other men were found dead earlier today."

"Where?" Pam asked stoically.

"At your Atlanta home."

"Cause of death?"

"Gunshots."

Teddy smiled. "The two men with Thompson most likely were Giovanni and Alberto."

"I'm sure we'll soon learn their identities. Pam and Theodora, the detective wants to interview you. Apparently, you're not suspects. The detective says he only wants information. I've arranged the interview to take place in Allison's office Monday afternoon. In the meantime, no one should talk to anyone about this affair outside the family except for Allison."

"What if the detective shows up at the hospital?" Pam asked.

"Tell him you're on duty and will talk Monday. He can't make you talk before then, and he doesn't have sufficient evidence, if any, to arrest you. Furthermore, I doubt the Atlanta detective has any legal powers in Alexander County."

"Please hold on for a minute," Pam said. A few moments later she said, "I need to get back to work. EMS brought two accident victims into the ER."

"Take care of them, and don't worry about repercussions," Miz Lizbeth said.

"Well, may I say I'm relieved?"

"Inside the family," Miz Lizbeth answered.

Teddy terminated the call. "I'll get my laptop and check for information about what happened." She left the porch.

"Jason, Martin, what do you think occurred?" Miz Lizbeth asked.

"Someone did our dirty work for us," Jason said.

"Did you have anything to do with it?"

"Not directly, and let's stop the conversation here."

"Even so, can you be implicated in the murders?"

"No."

"Pam or Teddy?" Miz Lizbeth demanded.

"No way. They had no involvement whatsoever."

Teddy rushed onto the front porch carrying her laptop computer. "You guys need to hear this!"

"Pray enlighten us," Miz Lizbeth said

"The bastard really is dead." Teddy pointed to the computer screen. "According to this report from the *Atlanta Journal-Constitution* website, the police found Thompson, Giovanni, and Alberto dead in Thompson's study. They were shot in the head with small caliber bullets. I'll print out the article if you'd like to see a hard copy," Teddy offered.

"I would very much like that. How were Kendal and his associates found?"

"Someone in Thompson's office called the police when he didn't show up for work after Tuesday and wasn't answering his home or cell phones. The police broke into our house and found the three dead bodies. The police won't comment more

about the circumstances. The reporter who wrote this article"—
Teddy pointed to her laptop—"speculated that robbery may have
precipitated the homicides: A safe in the study was left open
without any contents inside."

"That's a convenient cover story," Jason said.

"Do you think Frank Gordon had them killed?" Teddy asked.

"Such speculation stays within our family, Theodora," Miz
Lizbeth cautioned.

"I know, I know. Gordon must have had some reason.
Maybe he learned about the video of Thompson and me. If that
video were made public, Gordon might have been implicated
in knowing what Thompson did to me." Teddy smiled at Jason.

Jason remained stoic. "Once again, Teddy, be conscious of
plausible deniability and for damn sure don't engage in that kind
of speculation when the detective interviews you and your mom,"
he said.

"I thoroughly understand. I'm sure Allison will cut him off at
the pass if he broaches that subject," Teddy said.

"Unless the Atlanta Police Department and Detective Turner
are incompetent, they've already concluded that a simple robbery
gone bad was not the precipitating factor in the murders," Miz
Lizbeth said.

"I'm sure law enforcement in Atlanta highly resented
Thompson's alliance with Gordon. Detective Turner most likely
wants information that will give him a reason to more than
suspect something other than robbery as a motive in the deaths,"
Jason said.

"Well, he won't get that information from Mom and me."
Teddy clapped her hands. "I'm supposed to believe that a miracle
occurred that allowed Gordon to learn about the video and how
Thompson used Giovanni and Alberto to facilitate my abuse?"

"Let me quote the prophet Hosea," Miz Lizbeth said. "'The
ways of the Lord are right, and the just shall walk in them; but

the transgressors shall fall therein.'"

Teddy looked in turn at Jason and Martin. "May I be assured that one day all will be revealed?"

"I think you've already figured out the main themes," Martin said.

"I'd like to know the details."

"Let's leave things at this point," Jason said.

"One last question, for now," Teddy countered.

"Ask away," Jason said.

"Do we have anything to fear from Gordon?"

"If he tries to act against this family, we have him boxed in," Jason assured Teddy.

***

Late Monday afternoon, Pam and Teddy walked into the den where the family had gathered for the daily cocktail ritual.

"Mr. Jackson, I'd like one of your super martinis," Pam said.

"Miss Theodora, would you prefer the single malt?" Jackson asked.

"I would, Mr. Jackson. You should probably make Mom's martini a double."

"Did you have a difficult time with the detective?" Miz Lizbeth asked.

"Not really, despite his insistence. Thankfully, Allison was able to steer him away from the truly sensitive topics," Pam said.

"Surely he didn't suspect you and Teddy of foul play?"

"He tried to determine if we had hired Frank Gordon to kill Thompson and his partners in crime," Pam said.

"When he had no luck with that line of questioning, the detective moved on to asking what we know about Gordon," Teddy said.

Pam sipped her martini. "Allison thinks the entire interview was designed to elicit any information we might have about

Gordon's criminal activities."

"I'm not surprised," Jason said. "It's public knowledge that Frank Gordon is a mob boss."

"The Atlanta police probably would like to pin something on Gordon in view of all the times Kendal managed to keep Gordon out of jail," Pam said.

"You gave the detective no meaningful information about Gordon?" Miz Lizbeth asked.

"Not one thing. The detective was persistent. He kept asking the same questions in several different ways until Allison ended the interview. She said the detective was harassing her clients," Teddy said.

"What did Allison say once the detective left?" Jason asked.

"For us not to worry; Gordon was the actual subject of the interview. Allison also said the detective wasn't at all sorry about the three deaths, only that he found no linkage from us to incriminate Gordon," Pam said.

Miz Lizbeth motioned to Jackson for a refill of her martini. "Does Allison think the detective will be back to harass the family again?"

"Not unless he can find evidence of the family's involvement in the murders, directly or indirectly," Teddy said.

"Like I keep instructing, this affair stays within the family, including Allison. She'll fend off any further attempts from the Atlanta police," Miz Lizbeth said.

"Miz Lizbeth, you're preaching to the choir," Martin laughed.

"All of us know the stakes involved and will be silent," Pam said.

Teddy drew a thumb and forefinger across her lips. "Zipped tight." She continued to sip her Scotch. "Can we go for a long jog in the morning? I feel the need for exercise."

"I'll meet you on the front porch an hour before breakfast," Jason said.

"If the wild child doesn't interfere and if Shanna doesn't need me, I'll join you," Martin said.

"I think the exercise will do you good. You're too restless, so burn off some excess energy," Shanna told her husband. When Martin grinned, Shanna instructed, "Vigorous exercise, my dear husband, to redirect your mind."

CHAPTER 21

Pam, Teddy and attorney Henry Anderson were seated in Allison Jameson's conference room one month later. The lawyer from Atlanta opened the proceedings.

"First, let me thank all of you for this meeting. Counselor Jameson, based upon our telephone conversation late last week, I understand you represent Dr. Pamela Nelson Kendal and Miss Theodora Nelson."

"I represent them individually and as part of the Andrews family," Alison said.

"What is your relationship to the Andrews family?" Anderson asked Pam.

"Jason Andrews is my fiancé," Pam replied.

Anderson removed a packet of papers from his thin briefcase.

"As I've already informed Counselor Jameson, I represent the estate of your late husband, L. Thompson Kendal, Esq., and on that basis, I requested this meeting."

"Are you a member of Thompson's firm?" Pam asked.

"I work for another firm. We specialize in estate planning, and associated activities. Your husband engaged my services to handle his estate and to ensure that his, shall we say, final documents are in order. I'm here to carry out both a sad and pleasant duty." Anderson kept his eyes on Pam. "Do you have any knowledge about the contents of your husband's estate?"

"Not really. We kept our estates separate at my insistence."

Anderson turned to Teddy. "Miss Nelson, have you any knowledge about Mr. Kendal's estate?"

"Nothing definite other than I suppose his estate has considerable value."

"He was, as a matter of public knowledge, very successful, and his estate reflects that fact." Anderson handed the packet of legal documents to Allison. "Counselor, Mr. Kendal's will has passed through probate. You have certified copies of the relevant documents . . . I don't anticipate any challenges to Mr. Kendal's will."

"Will you please summarize the distribution of the estate for us?" Allison asked.

Anderson kept his eyes on Teddy. "Simply put, Mr. Kendal left his entire estate, currently valued at ten million after taxes, to Miss Theodora Nelson with Dr. Kendal as executrix of the estate until Miss Nelson reaches eighteen years of age."

"It doesn't cover the—" Teddy began.

Allison cut her off. "I'm sure Teddy means her inheritance doesn't compensate adequately for the loss of her stepfather, as no amount of money could."

"Well said. Even so, Miss Nelson, you are now a very wealthy young woman. I'm sure your mother and Counselor Jameson will properly advise you on the financial implications of your inheritance."

"I'm sure they will, and I don't expect any problems," Teddy said.

"When was Mr. Kendal's will put in force?" Allison asked Anderson.

"Well over a year ago. He recently set up an appointment with me to discuss some alterations in his will; however, Mr. Kendal was killed before we had time to meet."

"Do you have any idea about the alterations?"

"None whatsoever. In any event, such alterations are now moot, as you know, Counselor." Anderson closed his briefcase. "Counselor Jameson, please don't hesitate to call me if you have legal questions about the will and/or associated issues. I'm confident everything has been handled properly. Before I go, one last question. To what account would you like the funds transferred?"

"If my clients agree, please wire the money to my corporate account at the Vickery Bank and Trust here in this city. We'll need a short time to set up a separate account for the estate."

"Perfectly acceptable to me," Pam said. "Teddy?"

"Fine with me."

Allison removed a blank check from her checkbook. She wrote *Void* on the check and handed it to Anderson, who said, "If the abominable afternoon traffic on I-85 and in Atlanta permits, I'll have the funds wired to your account this afternoon. If not, first thing in the morning. I'll have someone in my office call you upon initiation of the transfer. I'll have no claims for my services; Mr. Kendal has already paid me generously."

"We thank you for what you've done," Pam said.

"My pleasure. With that said, I'll take my leave and journey back to Atlanta." He shook hands with everyone and left Allison's office.

When Anderson was out of earshot, Teddy exclaimed, "Holy shit!"

"Theodora, once again, your language does not reflect ladylike behavior." Pam grinned. "I will, however, confirm what you just said: holy shit indeed!"

"Of course, ten million dollars does not begin to compensate me for the abuse I suffered from Thompson," Teddy said.

"The money you've inherited is amoral. Spend it as you think best," Allison said.

"I for damn sure won't erect any monuments to the pervert."

***

Pam and Teddy joined Miz Lizbeth on the front porch of the Big House.

"How was the session with Allison?" Miz Lizbeth asked.

Teddy smiled. "Thompson left his entire estate of ten million dollars to me with Mom as executrix until I'm eighteen."

"He might have felt some guilt over his voyeurism and what he planned to do to you. The money may represent a plea for forgiveness or an attempt at absolution on his part."

"He was a pervert and never gave any indication to me that he felt guilty of anything. Although I'm taking his money, I won't give him any thanks, much less any credit for good intentions."

Pam patted Teddy on her shoulder. "I don't care to psychoanalyze Thompson other than to accept what Teddy just said. We'll move on, like we've already begun."

"Mom, I have a request for some of the money now," Teddy said.

"What do you want, a new and better computer?"

"Maybe later. As you know, I'll soon turn sixteen and get my driver's license."

"Let me guess. You want to buy a car for yourself."

"I'll let you drive it."

"What kind of car?"

"A Mercedes-Benz SL550. It's a cross between a true sports car and a touring sedan without a back seat."

"How much does this vehicle cost?" Pam asked.

"Fully loaded with all the bells, whistles, and safety features—about $110,000. The cost will hardly dent my new fortune."

Jason walked onto the front porch. "What's this about your new fortune?"

"Teddy has become a very rich young woman. She can tell you the details," Miz Lizbeth said.

After Teddy summarized the meeting with the lawyers, Jason asked, "Teddy, do you have any readily accessible information on the car you wish to buy?"

"On my laptop. I'll be back in a few minutes to show you." Teddy left to retrieve her laptop.

"Are you at all familiar with the car she wants to buy?" Pam asked Jason.

"A little. I wanted an opportunity to prepare a united front."

"I assume this Mercedes will go very fast?"

"It will."

"Can Rufus install a governor to keep her from speeding?" Pam asked.

"I'd advise against it."

"Why?"

"Teddy might encounter legitimate reasons to speed."

Martin stepped onto porch. "You could always buy her a tank. That would slow her down and provide a lot of protection." He smirked.

Teddy returned with her laptop. "You want me to buy a tank instead of the Mercedes?"

"Not really. Please show us what you have on the car you want," Pam said.

Teddy showed the group the material on her laptop. "You have good taste, although I worry about your proclivity for speed," Pam said.

Teddy looked to Pam. "I promise not to drive recklessly."

"We probably need to agree on the term *recklessly*," Jason said.

Jackson joined the group. "From my perspective, Miss Theodora, as I've already mentioned, has more sense and self-control than Jason and Martin combined when they were her age."

"Let me add a word or two of grandmotherly or matriarchal advice," Miz Lizbeth proposed.

"Please do," Jason said.

"Amen," Martin confirmed.

"I think Theodora can be trusted, if we treat her as an adult. Jackson and I decided on that approach with Jason and Martin, fully realizing we couldn't protect the two of them from all sources of potential harm, self-generated or external."

"I've got too much planned for my life to be reckless," Teddy said.

"I think we'd all like to hear your life plans, Teddy," Pam said.

"Later, please. I have two suggestions for the present."

"Let's hear them," Jason said.

"First let me buy the car. Jason and Martin have been instructing me on the finer points of competitive tennis and basketball. They can, if they agree, give me the benefit of their driving experience."

"I'm sure Jason and I can help you," Martin said.

"Imparting some wisdom along with knowledge would be pertinent," Jackson said.

"Agreed, if Pam agrees," Jason said.

"I agree, under the terms specified," Pam said.

"Can we go to the Anderson Mercedes dealership tomorrow and look at the car?" Teddy asked.

"How do you know the dealership has an SL550?" Pam asked.

"I checked in my room when I went to get my laptop."

"I'm free tomorrow," Pam said. "Are you, Jason?"

"I am, and I'll be glad to accompany you two."

"Teddy, did we just respond to your two-part first suggestion or your two suggestions in total?" Martin asked.

"First suggestion. You want to hear my second suggestion?"

"With baited breath," Pam said.

Teddy looked at Pam and then at Jason. "You two should

hurry up and marry. There're no impediments and I'd like a real father to be with my mother."

Miz Lizbeth clapped her hands and was soon joined in applause by everyone on the porch. "Hear! Hear! Wisdom from the mouth of a young woman."

Jason left his chair and kneeled before Pam. "I love you. Will you marry me?"

"Of course, my love. When?"

"As soon as possible."

"Sooner," Teddy said.

"I'll call the good Reverend Parker to begin the preparations, if the two of you want to be married in a church," Miz Lizbeth said.

"We do," Pam said.

"The whole-nine-yards wedding?" Teddy asked.

"The whole megillah," Jason confirmed.

"Celebratory drinks are in order, Jackson. Let's move into the den. Praise God almighty, two grandchildren within a short time," Miz Lizbeth said.

"What a day! Mom, will I be your maid of honor and give you away as well?"

"I think you should give me away. If she agrees, Shanna can be my matron of honor." Pam spread her arms wide. "I want the whole family surrounding Jason and me during the ceremony."

CHAPTER 22

Captain Bruce Covington, seated as usual near the front window of Jean's Coffee Shop, watched a black Cadillac Escalade maneuver into an open parking space. He noticed the Fulton County license plate. The tall and lanky driver opened the door for the shorter, compact passenger, who quickly looked up and down the sidewalk before moving to the door of the coffee shop. The two men glanced at the uniformed Captain Covington and took seats at a table in the rear of the coffee shop. Captain Covington shook his head at Jean when she started to his table with his bill.

Captain Covington smiled as he approached the two men. "Welcome to Vickery, gentlemen."

"Thank you, Officer," the passenger said, also smiling.

"Are you passing through our fair city or staying a while?"

"We'll be here for a few hours."

"Are you visiting anyone?"

"We're exploring business opportunities," the driver said.

Captain Covington pointed toward the old train depot that had been converted to provide offices for the chamber of commerce.

"Mrs. Susan Clark at the chamber of commerce will be happy to provide you with a lot of information on Vickery and Alexander County. We welcome legitimate businesspeople."

"We plan to stop by the chamber as soon as we finish our lunch."

"Good idea. What kind of business are you interested in?"

"Whatever looks good and remunerative to us. We understand the Andrews family plays a major role in the poultry business around here," the passenger said.

"Along with a lot of other commercial concerns."

"We won't be in competition with them."

"A wise choice. Let me know if I can be of help to you."

Once Captain Covington was outside the coffee shop, he passed by the Escalade and memorized the license plate number. He drove his patrol car across the square and parked on a side street.

"Dispatch," Captain Covington said into the handset of his car radio.

"Dispatch here, Captain."

"I want you to run a license plate number for me." Captain Covington gave the dispatcher the the plate number.

A few minutes later, the dispatcher said, "Captain, the car belongs to a corporation in Atlanta, Gordon Enterprises, Inc."

The two men piqued Captain Covington's law enforcement sensibilities. He would not be able to provide a rational explanation for his unease, yet his long experience suggested the men were not necessarily upstanding citizens. The fact that the Escalade was registered to Gordon Enterprises troubled him even more. He spoke again into his radio.

"Dispatch. Do a quick Google search for Gordon Enterprises. I want to confirm that one Frank Gordon owns the business.

"Hang on, Captain . . . Affirmative. Frank Gordon owns Gordon Enterprises. Same Frank Gordon with mob ties, Captain?"

"Looks that way. Atlanta and Georgia state law enforcement have been trying to pin something on him for years."

"An interesting morning, Captain."

"That's right. Signing off but watching." Captain Covington pondered the situation for a few minutes. Although highly interested in what the two men in the Escalade were up to, he would not be able to follow the Escalade without them noticing his patrol car. A solution came to him.

"Dispatch."

"Captain, you're quick on the draw today. What can I do for you this time?"

"Please patch me through to Sergeant Willis."

"What's happening, Captain?" the sergeant asked when he was connected.

"I want you to launch the drone for observation purposes."

"Anyone specific you want to observe?"

"Two men in a black Escalade, Fulton County license plates." Captain Covington gave the license plate number to Willis.

"Where's the vehicle?"

"In front of Jean's Coffee Shop in Vickery. The two men may go over to the Vickery Chamber of Commerce building when they leave Jean's. One of them said they're in town looking for business opportunities."

"You figure the two guys aren't legitimate businessmen?"

"Their car is registered to Frank Gordon Enterprises."

"The Frank Gordon?"

"Yes, the one and the same," Captain Covington said.

"Can you keep the car under observation until I get Snoopy in range?" the sergeant asked.

"From a distance. I don't want the guys to know we're watching them."

"I'll bring Snoopy nearer Vickery and launch him when you give me info about the location of the car."

"I'll let Chief Holderfield know what's going on. We're on his turf."

Captain Covington called the Vickery police chief. After completion of the usual pleasantries, the captain recounted the morning events.

"We'll have the car under surveillance, most of which probably will be in the county, not within the Vickery city limits."

"Thanks for the update. Do you want or need something from us?" Chief Holderfield asked.

"Help with the surveillance without spooking the occupants of the Escalade."

"We'll be glad to assist, Bruce."

"Thanks, Chief." Captain Covington disconnected the connection with the Vickery police headquarters.

"Snoopy and I are on the way, Captain," Sergeant Willis announced over the radio.

"Good. Covington over and out."

Captain Covington maintained his position, watching the two men leave the coffee shop and walk across the town square to the chamber of commerce. After thirty minutes, the two men walked back to the Escalade, the driver carrying a large manila folder that Captain Covington inferred contained materials about Vickery and Alexander County. The driver carefully backed out of the parking space and headed north toward Sweet Gum Road. Captain Covington spoke into the radio handset.

"Dispatch, Sergeant Willis's location?"

"A few minutes ago, he was almost at the south Vickery city limit."

"Please patch me through to him."

"Snoopy and I are in range. Where's the car?" Sergeant Willis asked.

"Going north on Sweet Gum Road."

"I'll pull over and launch Snoopy. Deputy Rogers rides with

me and he can control Snoopy while I drive. We'll take a chance and send Snoopy a few miles north of Vickery."

"Good. Keep him high."

"Will do."

Captain Covington drove a short distance north on Sweet Gum Road before parking on a side road.

"Sergeant Wills, do you have the Escalade in sight?"

"We got it. The car has stopped at the south entrance to the Andrews property. Looks like the passenger may be taking photos or a video. Now the car is moving on north. The Escalade has turned left, looks like it's going toward the back entrance to the Andrews property. Yes, the passenger took more photos or video."

A few minutes later, Willis said, "They turned around, coming back toward you."

"Keep them in sight."

"Will do, as long as Snoopy has gas."

Captain Covington saw the Escalade pass his position. Once the Escalade was well out of sight, he drove south on Sweet Gum Road. When he approached Vickery, he radioed Sergeant Willis. "Where are they?"

"On the road to the high school."

"I'm coming closer. Let me know if they reverse direction so I can get out of the way," Captain Covington said.

"They're headed south, maybe to I-85," Sergeant Willis said several minutes later.

"As soon as you're sure they've left our county, call in Snoopy and close down the operation. You've given us what I wanted."

"Yes, sir. How do you want me to write up the report?"

"As a training exercise."

"I can do that. What do you think is going on?"

"I'm not sure," Captain Covington said. "I'll put my considerable investigative skills to work on the problem."

"Too bad we can't keep Snoopy in the air 24/7/365."

"Even so, we may soon need him again."

"Over and out, ready and willing."

***

Captain Covington used his cell phone to call the Big House.

"Good afternoon, Mr. Jackson. Is Jason available?"

"No, Captain Covington. He's at the bank with Miz Lizbeth."

"I'm on the square of our great metropolis. I'll see if I can meet with him at the bank."

"I'll alert Jason you're on the way."

"Thanks. I'm off." Captain Covington parked in front of the Vickery Bank and Trust. The pretty young receptionist greeted him.

"Captain, are you here to make a huge deposit or withdraw a small sum?"

"Hey, Gabby. How are your parents?"

"Doing well for eighty years of age."

"I'm sure you're responsible for their good health."

"If they get any ornerier, my health will go to hell."

"Keep the faith. I'm told Jason Andrews is here."

"He's with Miz Lizbeth in her office. I'm to take you back there."

Gabby escorted Captain Covington into the depths of the bank. She knocked on the double doors leading to Miz Lizbeth's office and stood aside as he entered the office.

"Miz Lizbeth, Mr. Jason. Captain Bruce Covington to see you."

"Bruce, great to see you," Jason said. The two men shook hands. "Do you want coffee or something else to drink?"

"No, thank you."

"Bruce, are you here on official business?" Miz Lizbeth asked.

"Semi-official, Miz Lizbeth." He looked at Jason.

"It's OK, Bruce. Mother will find out everything anyway," Jason said.

"Do you have any idea why two men, who probably work for Frank Gordon, would be scouting our area?" Captain Covington asked.

"When?"

"Earlier this afternoon, after they ate lunch at Jean's."

"Where exactly did they go?" Jason asked.

"They first stopped to take photos at the main entrance to your property. They then went to the back entrance for more photos."

"Was that all?" Jason asked.

"They traveled slowly by the high school before leaving the county, heading south on I-85."

"You managed to follow the two men without being detected?" Miz Lizbeth asked.

"From a safe distance. We had time to launch our observation drone to follow the car the guys were in, a black Cadillac Escalade. We ran a trace on the Fulton County license plates. The Escalade is registered to Frank Gordon Enterprises."

"Were you eating lunch at Jean's when the two men were there?" Jason asked.

"I had finished when they walked in. We had a brief conversation. They claimed to be exploring business opportunities in Vickery and Alexander County. I directed them to the chamber of commerce, and they came back to their car with a large packet of materials."

"What made you think the two men were up to no good?" Miz Lizbeth asked.

"My lawman's sensitivity. The guys would have been better off not stopping at Jean's."

"Maybe they were hungry," Jason said.

"Something about them worried me. Once we determined the vehicle registration, my sensitivities were even more activated."

"Why?" Miz Lizbeth asked.

"When the A-Team and I first encountered Dr. Kendal and her daughter, we learned the husband and stepfather was Thompson Kendal, a lawyer for Frank Gordon. Seems as if law enforcement in the Atlanta area has been interested in Gordon for many years without being able to pin anything on him."

"What do you think we should do next?" Jason asked.

"I've already given Chief Brockman a heads-up. After we finish here, I'll talk in more detail with him. At a minimum, the Vickery police and the sheriff's department should be alert for more incursions on our turf. The Andrews family should be equally alert."

Jason shook his head at Miz Lizbeth. "I think Frank Gordon will have his men create some kind of disturbances at the entrances to our property while another group attempts to kidnap Teddy."

"I will not have my granddaughter harmed!" Miz Lizbeth declared.

"We'll prevent any harm to her. The kidnapping, if that's the plan, would have to take place on the roads between your home and the school, unless Teddy is at another other location for some reason," Captain Covington said.

"Basketball practice has begun and she goes to choir practice most Thursday nights at our church," Miz Lizbeth said.

"From what I know about the young lady, she would be hard to catch in that new car of hers," Captain Covington said.

"She could be blocked in by two or three vehicles," Jason said.

"Do you plan to tell Theodora and Pam about what's going on?" Miz Lizbeth asked Jason.

"Let's cogitate about that," Jason said.

"Why would Frank Gordon want to snatch Teddy?" Captain Covington asked.

"I possess something of great value, maybe potentially lethal, to him. He'll probably want to make a trade—Teddy for what I have."

"Are you going to tell me what you're talking about?" Captain Covington asked.

"After you and I meet with Counselor Jameson."

"When will that meeting take place?"

"I have an appointment with her this afternoon to discuss some business matters. You and I can go to her office now." Jason stood.

"Are we going to discuss anything illegal, unethical, or unsafe?" Captain Covington asked.

"Depends on the definitions," Jason said.

"You're not going to tell me what you have in mind, Jason?" Miz Lizbeth asked.

"Not now."

"We're back at plausible deniability?" Miz Lizbeth huffed.

"For the time being. Bruce, let's leave before mother invokes parental privilege. We'll consult with Allison and then make some plans."

"I tell you one more time: I will not have my granddaughter harmed!" Miz Lizbeth insisted.

"What about me?" Jason grinned.

"You can take of yourself. You, Martin, and Bruce had damn well better protect my granddaughter and her mother."

Jason and Captain Covington left the office.

CHAPTER 23

Jackson sat beside Miz Lizbeth on the front porch where the family had gathered.

"Do you know what's going on?" she asked.

"Jason and Martin filled me in. That's why I'm sitting next to you, to give you moral support."

"All right, Jason, let's have it," she said calmly.

Jason recounted the day's events and his speculation about Frank Gordon's motives.

"We have a plan to combat him."

"Does this plan include protection for Pam and Teddy?" Miz Lizbeth asked.

"You may have some reservations."

"If Gordon intends to have me kidnapped, you probably want me to be bait," Teddy said.

"Have you already talked with Teddy?" Miz Lizbeth asked Jason.

"No, Miz Lizbeth. She's a smart young woman and made the correct interpretation."

"Jason, if you think Gordon wants to trade Teddy for the videos from Thompson's safe, why not simply forward them to the appropriate authorities?" Pam asked.

"Good question. If we can get evidence that Gordon ordered the kidnapping, law enforcement will gain additional ammunition to convict and send him to prison for a long time," Martin said.

Teddy held up her hand. "What else do you have on Gordon besides the video of Kendal abusing me?"

"What makes you think something more exists?" Jason asked Teddy.

"With Thompson dead, Gordon should have no motive to kidnap me for a trade involving the"—she laughed wryly—"sex video."

"Let's suppose we have financial information about the extent of his illegal activities along with links to his associates or bosses," Jason said.

"You have more, don't you?" Miz Lizbeth asked.

"We can wipe out all traces of his many accounts, thereby depriving him and his bosses of a great deal of money. If everything works out, law enforcement can apply the information about the accounts to bring RICO charges against Gordon and his bosses."

"RICO?" Pam asked.

"Racketeer Influenced and Corrupt Organizations Act. Did Allison suggest a RICO charge?" Miz Lizbeth asked.

"Among several others," Jason said.

"The only way you could have obtained this type of information is with Hack's help," Miz Lizbeth said.

"I promised you we'd protect Hack . . . and we have," Jason said.

"Hack for damn sure enjoyed helping us. He was a willing participant," Martin said.

"Before we get to the specifics of your diabolical plan, what's Bruce's involvement?" Miz Lizbeth asked.

"He'll confidentially pass on the relevant information to his law enforcement colleagues in Atlanta," Jason said.

"Before or after Hack destroys the information about Gordon's accounts?" Miz Lizbeth asked.

"Simultaneously, although Bruce will alert his colleagues to watch for Gordon attempting to run and hide."

Shanna handed JJ to Martin. "Are you sure this Frank Gordon only wants Teddy?" she asked.

Jason stood and walked behind Pam's chair. "He might also want Pam."

"I'm to be bait along with Teddy?" Pam asked.

"We'll have you covered at all times. Chief Brockman will assign additional security to the hospital. Martin or I will accompany you to and from the hospital."

"I am greatly comforted." Pam turned her head up for a kiss from Jason. "We'll trust you."

"What about me?" Teddy asked.

"We want you to continue with your normal activities. Bruce will have a conversation with the principal at the high school to remind her that only a family member or a designated member of our staff can take you away. Bruce also will talk with the school safety officer, one of the sheriff's deputies. She'll also be forewarned."

"What about my traveling to and from school, and to choir practice? If someone tries to accost me on the roads, do I have permission to outrun them? Let's see how fast that fancy car will go."

"Hopefully there'll be no need for that. Bruce and Chief Brockman will mobilize unmarked cars to travel behind you," Jason said. "We don't want you speeding away from them. Snoopy, the county drone, will be overhead whenever you're on the road. "

"What will I do if I'm attacked on the road?"

"Keep your cell phone activated and on hands-free status at all times. You'll get instructions. You may have the opportunity to blow past any attacker," Jason said.

"What about choir practice?" Miz Lizbeth asked.

"Jason or I will accompany Teddy. Chief Brockman will have police cars cruising the area," Martin said.

"A reasonable person could easily infer that you showed the sex video to Gordon. He wouldn't want to be tainted with a lawyer involved in such activities and therefore had Thompson killed," Pam said.

"Not that I give a goddamn," Teddy said.

Pam chose not to make an issue of Teddy's language. "Why destroy and reveal Gordon's financial wheeling and dealing?"

"Retribution," Miz Lizbeth preempted Jason's reply.

"What do you mean?" Pam asked.

"Gordon must have had some idea of what Kendal was doing to Theodora. Let's not forget that Gordon assigned two of his men to help Kendal," Miz Lizbeth said.

"Although Giovanni and Alberto were not in my bedroom with Kendal and me, there's no way they didn't know what was going on," Teddy said.

"There's an additional reason," Jason said.

"Which is?" Miz Lizbeth asked.

"At the end of our conversation, Gordon proposed an alliance between his organization and our family."

"To what purpose?"

"To help him move his products. I guess he thought we could package his illicit drugs along with our chickens when we shipped them out of Alexander County."

"What did you tell him?"

"That he would be dead if his organization ever tried to move into our county."

"Excellent. I have one more question before we succumb to the Hunger Monster," Miz Lizbeth said.

"Ask away."

"Allison must have told you that the information about

Gordon's finances was obtained illegally and couldn't be used in a court of law. The information would be considered fruit from a poisoned tree in legal terms," Miz Lizbeth said.

"That point could be argued, Allison said. We can always send the information to *The Atlanta Journal-Constitution*. Gordon's organization would suffer if the information were made public even without a RICO charge."

"I'm in with the plan," Teddy said.

"So am I," Pam said.

"Miz Lizbeth, what about you?" Jason asked.

"You already know my restrictions—no harm to Pam, Theodora, or Hack, and no legal consequences to him."

"Agreed," Jason said.

"There's one more thing."

"Which is?"

"Don't you and Martin put yourselves in unnecessary peril while you two bring this unfortunate affair to a successful conclusion."

"I hear you," Jason said.

"As do I," Martin said.

CHAPTER 24

Jackson answered the house phone Monday afternoon.

"Thanks, George. I'll tell Martin. Hold on."

"What's up?" Martin asked.

"Car stopped at the back entrance." Jackson held up a hand. "Got it. Stay connected and out of the line of fire."

"Time for Jason and me to move?" Martin asked.

"Go, Martin," Jackson said. He listened to the phone. "The men at the back are using bolt cutters to remove the locks and chains at the gate."

Martin left the house and drove one of the Ford trucks toward the back gate. Jackson turned to Jason.

"Another car with four men at the front gate. They're trying to come on the property. The chains and locks are slowing them down."

Jason also left the house. He drove a second truck toward the front entrance. When he came to a curve in the road 200 yards away from the Big House, he parked the truck across the road, blocking further access. Jason left the truck's cab and stood behind the rear wheel with a Heckler & Koch MP5 pointed in the direction the intruders would come once they burst through the front gate. Jason's shooting vest held several magazines in addition to the one loaded in the MP5. Each magazine contained thirty 9 x 19 mm cartridges. He checked to make sure the firing selector on the MP5 was on automatic. Satisfied with his preparations, Jason called Martin.

"I'm in position, waiting for the fun to begin," Martin answered.

"Same here. Sure was nice of Bruce to supply us with these MP5s."

"I guess that makes it legal. Hold on, I have an incoming call."

"Same here. Signing off and good shooting to you."

"Piece of cake."

Jason listened to the call on his cell phone.

"I'm ready. Stay in the woods. One of Captain Covington's patrol cars will move into position to block the guys from getting back onto Sweet Gum Road." Jason took the safety off the MP5.

A black Escalade came around the curve in the road leading to the Big House and slowed when the driver saw the Ford truck twenty-five yards ahead. Jason stood up and emptied a full magazine into the front windshield of the Escalade. He quickly reloaded and continued firing into the Escalade through the destroyed windshield. Jason inserted a third magazine into the MP5 and waited for signs of activity within the vehicle. After several minutes passed, he cautiously approached the vehicle. The MP5 in his right hand, Jason opened the back door on the driver's side of the Escalade. Four men, their bodies bullet-ridden and bloody, were slumped in their seats. He detected no pulse in the carotid arteries of the men. Jason removed the men's weapons—four AR-15 assault rifles and various handguns.

Jason called Martin, realizing he would not answer if engaged in a firefight.

"Hey, bro," Martin answered. "Your work done?"

"Yes. Yours?"

"Four men dead, AR-15s and pistols confiscated. Unassailable case of trespass with murderous intent. How 'bout you?"

"The same. Bruce's men arrived at your site?" Martin asked.

"Coming on the scene now."

Jason saw a patrol car approaching his position. A deputy, holding a shotgun, met Jason at the shot-up Escalade. "Any need for EMS, Mr. Andrews?"

"Just a meat wagon."

"I'll call for one as soon as our crime scene investigators finish. Captain Covington tells me you have a dashboard camera in your truck?"

"I do. It should have captured the entire episode."

"If you don't mind, I'll tell CSI to get the camera for evidence."

"Be my guest. That's why we wanted the camera in place." Jason's cell phone chimed. "Hey, Martin. You finished?"

"I am. The deputies and crime scene investigators have made the scene."

"Any survivors?"

"Only me. You want to meet at the Big House?"

"Let's do that. I'm sure Miz Lizbeth and Pam will be relieved."

"You hear anything from Bruce?"

"Not yet. If Gordon's men planned a coordinated attack, they should be ready to make an attempt on Teddy."

***

"Captain Covington, dispatch here."

"Go ahead."

"Snoopy shows two Escalades still parked on Reynolds Road, about a mile ahead of Miss Nelson on her way home. You're following her?"

"Discreetly."

"You figure the bad guys intend to block her in, front and back?"

"That plan won't work." Bruce called Teddy's cell phone. "Are you buckled in securely?"

"I am."

"When I give you the word, floor that Mercedes with all due caution."

"Hot damn dog!"

When Teddy was within fifty yards of the Reynolds Road intersection, Captain Covington said, "Teddy, let it all hang out until you get to the Vickery city limits. Wait for us at Counselor Jameson's office."

Teddy pressed the accelerator and the car bolted, reaching 110 miles per hour in seconds, faster than the men in the Escalades could react. Captain Covington, following Teddy, pulled into Reynolds Road. More patrol cars came from behind the Escalades to block them from turning around. Deputies carrying AR-15s approached the two Escalades.

"Come out immediately, hands in the air, and we won't kill you," Captain Covington ordered over the loudspeaker in his patrol car.

Eight men, hands in the air, left the Escalades. The deputies disarmed the men from the Escalades while Captain Covington watched with his 10-guage shotgun from the road. "Line 'em up," he commanded the deputies.

Once the men from the Escalade were lined up along the side of the road, Covington stood in front of the first man. "Who's leading this misbegotten adventure?"

No one answered. Captain Covington used the butt of his shotgun to hit the first man with a powerful blow to the solar plexus, which drove him to the ground, gasping for air. After a few minutes, the man tried to regain his feet. Captain Covington kicked the man in the face, and he fell, whimpering, back to the ground. Covington moved to the next man in line. "Who's your leader?"

The second man glared at Covington, whose shotgun butt struck the man in his face, breaking his nose and teeth. He collapsed unconscious. Captain Covington moved to the next man in line.

"Are you going to tell me what I want to know?"

The man quivered, his voice trembling. "Mr. Rafe Butler."

"Point him out."

The man turned and pointed to another man further down the line. Captain Covington moved to stand in front of Butler, one of the two men the captain had encountered in Jean's Coffee Shop.

"Why did Frank Gordon order you to kidnap Theodora Nelson?"

"Screw you."

"I'll deal with this bastard," the captain told his deputies. "Take the rest of these criminals to the county jail."

Once the deputies left with the other men, Captain Covington told Butler, "We can do this the hard or the easy way."

"Like I said, screw you."

Captain Covington kicked Butler's testicles. The man fell to the ground in agony. "You want more, asshole?"

"Screw you."

"You have two knees and two arms I can break at the elbow. Then, I'll start on other areas. How long can you hold out?"

"Screw you."

Captain Covington used the butt of his shotgun to strike Butler in the face. Butler screamed as blood gushed out of his nose.

"Pitiful sight you are, asshole," the captain laughed. "Which elbow do you want broken first?"

"Go to hell. I won't talk."

Captain Covington twisted Butler's left arm until the bones broke. Butler screamed, nearly fainting. Captain Covington grabbed Butler's right arm and began to twist.

"Stop, no more. I'll talk," Butler wheezed.

"A delayed but excellent decision." Captain Covington pulled Butler into a sitting position, ignoring his screams. "Speak up. You have one chance." Captain Covington put his cell phone in front of Butler's face. "What is your name?"

"Rafe Butler."

"Who ordered you to kidnap Theodora Nelson?"

"Frank Gordon."

"Why?"

"He wanted to trade her."

"We're making progress. In exchange for what?"

"To keep Jason Andrews from wiping out Gordon's financial accounts."

"Did you organize the attacks at the Andrews property and this kidnaping attempt?"

"I did what Gordon ordered me to do." Butler collapsed fully onto the ground.

"Where were you to meet Gordon once you had Teddy?"

"At his office."

"Have a short rest," Captain Covington said and spoke into his cell phone. "You guys in Atlanta heard Butler's true confession?"

"Perfectly and recorded," Colonel Tucker Morgan answered.

"You're going after Frank Gordon now?"

"My troopers have his office building surrounded, waiting for me to arrive and arrest him."

"Enjoy."

"I will, immensely. Thanks for your help," Morgan said.

"My pleasure." Captain Covington next called the sheriff's department. "Send an EMS bus here to pick up a criminal who resisted arrest."

Captain Covington then called Jason. "Everything Alpha Sierra at the Andrews property?"

"All intruders neutralized."

"Any of them still alive?"

"No."

"Teddy should be at the counselor's office by now. You want me to bring her home?"

"That would be great."

"I'll ride with her to the Big House. One of my men can pick me up later."

Jason called Hack. "Clean him out."

"Will do."

CHAPTER 25

Teddy drove the Mercedes to her usual parking spot Wednesday afternoon when she arrived at the Big House after school. She sat beside Jason and Pam on the front porch.

"I checked my cell phone before I left the parking lot at the high school. Seems as if the fecal matter has hit the fan for Frank Gordon."

"That's right, according to reports on the Atlanta TV stations," Jason said.

"On what charge?"

"Several, conspiring to kidnap you being the major one at this time."

"Did you check the Net?"

"We did. The *Atlanta Journal-Constitution* website suggests further charges are pending," Pam said.

"Too bad the pervert's not available to get Gordon out of jail," Teddy said.

"He'll find other legal representation. He has significant financial resources." Jason did not add that Hack had compromised Gordon's accounts.

"What would be the further charges?" Teddy asked.

"Time will tell."

"What about you and Martin? Any possibility you two will face legal consequences?" Teddy asked.

"No, we have documentary evidence that Martin and I stopped an intended home invasion and assault. We, along with two of our men, are the only survivors who can testify. The moment those guys cut the chains on the gates and came onto our land, Martin and I had the right to shoot them in order to protect our family and property. The cache of weapons the men had with them solidified our right to protect the family and property."

"I guess someone could argue you trapped the men and killed them without offering a chance to surrender," Teddy said.

"Teddy, what county are we in?" Pam laughed.

"Alexander County." Teddy pumped a fist into the air.

"No other law enforcement agency—Georgia Bureau of Investigation, FBI, state police—will come after Martin and me. We did them a favor," Jason said.

"You gave them Frank Gordon."

"That's right. Even with a spirited defense, he's facing prison for a long time when this affair concludes."

"What about the men who were after me? What will happen to them?" Teddy asked.

"They were arraigned earlier today. You, Martin and I will be testifying in their subsequent trials, if they take place."

"Why wouldn't there be a trial?" Pam asked.

"The guys are guilty as sin. The county attorney might be willing to offer a plea deal to avoid the expense and mess of a trial. Also, part of a plea deal would be for the guys to testify against Frank Gordon when the FBI brings him to trial for racketeering as well as conspiring to kidnap you."

"The RICO charge?" Pam asked.

"That route would allow the feds to go after Gordon's criminal organization. Gordon would be the gateway," Jason said.

"You're talking about a Mafia-style criminal organization?" Teddy asked.

"I wouldn't want to be accused of bias toward Italians. Franco Gordano, a.k.a. Frank Gordon, simply occupies the second or third rung on the ladder of a larger organization."

Teddy pursed her lips. "Thinking about my unlamented late stepfather, I'll bet Gordon doesn't have a long life expectancy."

"Unless he agrees to testify against the organization and enters witness protection."

"I'll repeat, I hope one day you'll tell me the details of what you, Martin, and Hack have done."

"Maybe one day." Jason smiled. "How was basketball practice?"

"Intense. The team's coming together. The state championship should be ours."

"You're OK playing forward?"

"Best chance for us to win the state championship. Besides, LaShaun Macky stands a foot taller than me and is an awesome force under the net. I'm going to my room to start on my homework," Teddy said.

CHAPTER 26

Two months after the attempted kidnapping, an exhausted Teddy sat next to Miz Lizbeth in the den of the Big House.

"From what I observed, you had a great match against Martin," Miz Lizbeth said.

"I'm almost holding my own against him, thanks to the training and advice he and Jason have been giving me."

"You'll be doing more than holding your own before too much longer."

"Practice, practice, practice and optimism," Teddy said.

"Also, determination, of which you have an abundance."

"I got a text from Mom this morning."

"How goes the honeymoon?"

"Wonderful. She's really enjoying being on the cruise ship with Jason."

"I'm sure your mother prefers the accommodations on a cruise ship more than the cramped conditions on an aircraft carrier where Jason spent so much of his adult life."

"Mom says he likes going back to sea with no responsibilities other than being with her."

"He definitely has a romantic streak, even if it doesn't always show."

"The idea of an around-the-world cruise seems very romantic," Teddy said.

"The cruise gives your mother and my son ample time to get to know each other without the distraction of helping with the family businesses and practicing medicine."

"Maybe they'll come back with an announcement about enlarging the family."

"Better sooner than later. A pregnancy might be difficult for Pam, although she appears to be in excellent health and great physical shape for her age."

"If having a baby interests Mom, she'll have evaluated all the potentialities."

"I'm sure, to the extent she can. Speaking of potentialities, have you any ideas what career path you might follow?"

"I've been cogitating. Do you have ideas you want me to consider?"

"Consider and evaluate, not dictate."

"I'm all ears, Elizabeth."

"Let me lay the groundwork. You understand that Jackson and I are getting older and that one day we'll need to relinquish control of this house."

"Not for several more years, I hope."

"Agreed, although the time will come."

"The implications for me?"

"Theodora, we will need a new châtelaine of the Big House."

"A what?"

"A lady of power within the castle," Miz Lizabeth said.

"You don't see Shanna as châtelaine?"

"I think Shanna will revive her modeling career and probably move into acting. She's also mentioned writing children's books."

"She wants to return to California?" Teddy asked.

"Somewhat reluctantly, but she will go because the Los Angeles Chargers want Martin back as head coach."

"Martin would take the job?"

"If Martin's reasonably confident he's no longer needed here. Martin has never been ecstatic about participating in the family business on a long-term basis."

Miz Lizbeth saw from Teddy's face that the young girl was thinking.

"What about Mom, assuming Jason wants to stay in the business? Couldn't she be mistress of the manor?"

"Don't you think Pam would be happier concentrating on her medical profession and a baby, if one appears?"

"Probably. Does Jason want to stay involved in the family business?"

"Before he and Pam left on their honeymoon, Jason assured me that was his desire."

Teddy chuckled with good humor. "You've been waiting for the right opportunity to broach the subject with me?"

"Like I said, for consideration, not a dictate."

"Elizabeth, you know I'm only sixteen and a sophomore in high school." Teddy made more of a statement than a question.

"I'm planting seeds and giving them time to flower, God willing."

"*Seeds* plural?"

"You could also consider undertaking an increasingly important role in our business endeavors. Jason and I would be your mentors. You could keep the business operating until, if and when, JJ and your potential new sister or brother want to be involved. In some sense, I'm suggesting a normal progression for you into the family business. After all, you've already invested the bulk of your fortune in our bank."

"I'm intrigued. I won't say no to your proposal. I'll start paying more attention to how you're managing the Big House."

"Wonderful. With the time you have left after your studies and sports activities, I'll start showing you the details."

"Let's do it," Teddy said with some understanding of the enormity of the tasks she might undertake and the opportunities the responsibilities would offer her. She had already discarded the law and medicine as careers, and had no desire to be a professional athlete. She also did not want to spend any more time than necessary in high school and college.

CHAPTER 27

LaShaun Macky, the basketball team's center, struggled against two opponents who pushed her back and prevented her from blocking the layup by the Montclair center. Neither referee whistled to call the obvious offensive foul committed against LaShaun. The basket gave Montclair a two-point lead with ten seconds left in the Georgia state AAA championship game. Alexander's coach immediately called for a timeout over the deafening roar from the full-capacity crowd and summoned her team to the bench. Once the team was huddled, the coach looked directly at Teddy, then at her point guard.

"Betty, you take the inbound pass while LaShaun streaks for the goal. Pass the ball to Teddy, who'll be behind the three-point line. Just like we've been doing throughout the game, Teddy will lob the ball high to LaShaun for the layup. Everybody be ready to improvise."

"Coach, what do you want us to do if Montclair guesses what we're planning and blocks LaShaun from the basket?" Teddy asked.

"Teddy, drive to basket for a layup so we can go into overtime, or shoot the three if Montclair closes off the lane to the basket. If you drive for the layup, try and draw a foul."

The ball came to Betty at mid-court. LaShaun ran to the basket, taking three opponents with her, and Betty made the pass to Teddy, standing unguarded.

"Well, here goes the ballgame." Teddy took a classic jump shot. Before the ball left her hand, a Montclair player ran directly into Teddy and the ball went awry. Teddy fell hard to the floor on her butt. She laughed at the player who had committed the obvious shooting foul.

"Idiot! You just lost the championship."

The referee's whistle thankfully announced the three-shot foul. Teddy's coach signaled for a timeout. The players on the floor left for their respective benches.

"Teddy, you all right to go back on the floor?"

"Yes, coach. My butt may be sore tomorrow. Otherwise, I'm ready for fame and glory."

Pam, sitting with Jason behind the Alexander bench, asked, "How can a fall like that not hurt Teddy? She seems unfazed."

"Teddy's on an adrenaline jag and probably feels no pain."

"Epinephrine or not, if she's hurt her back, we may have trouble."

"She's a warrior, Pam. Don't worry."

"Even so, I may take her to the emergency room for an X-ray."

"Watch her. She's not hurt in any serious way. She may have sore muscles tomorrow. You can play doctor then."

"Will she make at least two of these three free throws?" Pam asked.

"Teddy will make all three. Martin has taught her how to concentrate only on the rim and let her muscle memory do the rest, even with me in her face trying to distract her."

"Well, young Martin Jackson just kicked his approval."

"Let's see what he does after the third free throw."

Teddy got into position for the first foul shot, looking only at the rim as Martin and Jason had taught her. She did not hear the crowd noise. A shrill whistle sounded a timeout from Montclair.

"No way. You can't ice the ice woman," Teddy said.

"How many more timeouts does Montclair have?" LaShaun asked when the team returned to the bench.

"One more. They probably won't call it until after Teddy makes the second basket." She spoke to her team, "Ladies, sit back and enjoy the moment. We've already won the game."

Teddy took three dribbles, and a deep breath before the shot. The ball arced toward the hoop with backspin and went directly through the net. The Alexander partisans in the crowd cheered, and the Montclair people jeered. Teddy went through the same routine with the same result on the second throw to tie the game. The Montclair coach called for another timeout.

Rather than going to the bench, Teddy stood behind the foul line. Coach Sparks motioned for the team to stand in a circle around Teddy.

"Why didn't Teddy go to the bench with the team?" Pam asked Jason.

"She's a warrior who doesn't want to leave the field of battle. Staying at the foul line shows her determination to win the game on her own, if necessary."

"What have I raised?" Pam asked.

"A strong, resolute young woman, very much like her mother."

After the successful third foul shot, Montclair had three seconds to make a game-winning goal. Teddy somehow knew who would be targeted for the in-bounds pass. She jumped in front of the player who was to get the ball, took it out of the air, and launched a shot toward the Montclair goal. The crowd went wild as the ball went through the hoop a split second before the final whistle sounded.

The Alexander supporters flooded onto the court and lifted Teddy to their shoulders.

"Was that basket really necessary?" Pam asked with a huge smile.

"What did I tell you? Our warrior wants absolute victory," Jason said.

"Next thing, you'll be quoting General MacArthur to me."

"There is no substitute for victory."

***

The next morning, Teddy walked gingerly into the dining room where the family had assembled for breakfast. She sat carefully in a chair next to Miz Lizbeth.

"A glass of OJ and a never-empty cup of coffee would be helpful, Mr. Jackson," Teddy said.

"On the way," Jackson replied.

"Teddy, are you in pain?" Pam asked.

"The Tylenol I took last night has worn off. I'll take more after breakfast."

"If the pain persists for a couple of days, I'm taking you to the ER for an X-ray," her mother said.

"Mother, my doctor dearest, I fell on my butt, not my coccyx bone. I'm simply muscularly sore, something that will go away in a couple of days."

"Your butt doesn't have a lot of padding," Pam retorted.

"How did the next wild child react to the game?" Teddy changed the subject.

"With a high level of activity, kicking and punching," Pam said.

"He shouldn't have worried. His sister had everything under control."

"Theodora, I think all of us around this table would be comforted if you refrained from any vigorous exercise for a few days," Miz Lizbeth said.

"I agree," Pam said.

"OK, OK. I'll rest and recuperate. I don't want to be incapacitated for the tennis championship in August. If the pain doesn't go away, Mom can play doctor."

"Wise decision. We'll have plenty of time to practice before the tournament begins," Jason said.

Teddy looked at Miz Lizbeth. "While I'm resting, I'd like to come to the bank after school and get an introduction to that part of the family business."

"What exactly do you have in mind, Teddy?" Jason asked.

"I'll let you know after I win the tennis championship. Right now, I want to learn about the bank."

"That's entirely appropriate. You have a lot of money invested with us. We'll talk this afternoon when you get to the bank," Miz Lizbeth said.

"I know your mind, Teddy. You're making plans," Pam said.

"My plans will be revealed after I win the tennis championship." Teddy looked at Jason. "I'd also like a formal introduction to the family's poultry business."

"We'll start Saturday morning when we collect the next batch of full-grown chickens. You'll need to get out bed at 0430. I'll ask Jackson to have the kitchen ladies prepare something for us to eat on the way to the chicken houses."

Jackson had returned to the table. "Breakfast tacos and a large thermos of coffee."

"Count me in for this adventure," Martin said.

"Pam and Shanna, we don't need to get up that early. We'll have our breakfast at a more civilized time," Miz Lizbeth said.

CHAPTER 28

Teddy and her opponent, Joan Matthews—a Valdosta High School junior—completed the warmup exchange of volleys and returned to their respective benches waiting for the call to begin the Class AAA girl's championship match at the Clayton County International Tennis Center in Jonesboro. Teddy had not lost a game in her preceding matches.

"Should Teddy be worried about her opponent?" Pam asked Jason.

"No, Joan Matthews should be beyond apprehensive. Unless lightning or an injury strikes Teddy, she'll win the championship without any problem."

"How can you be so sure?"

"Have you seen how Teddy plays against Martin and me? We've taught her all we know, and she's learned her lessons well."

Pam nodded. "So, I should relax and enjoy Teddy's victory vicariously?"

"That's right. Keep in mind that she's benefiting from your genetic contribution."

When the umpire called "Ladies ready," Teddy and Joan shook hands at the net. Joan won the right for the first serve, a cannonball deep to Teddy's backhand. Teddy hit the ball with vicious topspin deep to Joan's baseline backhand. Teddy rushed the net to intercept the weak return and cut the ball away from Joan for the first point. Joan's next three serves elicited similar responses: blasting returns from Teddy that allowed her to win the first game without losing a point. Teddy's warrior face showed no emotion.

Teddy's first serve to Joan's backhand produced an ace. Applying what she had learned from Jason and Martin, Teddy never served twice in the same manner. She won the second game in straight points, with aces or return faults into the net. Teddy saw the confused look on Joan's face at the unexpected power of Teddy's serve. Teddy won the first the set, 6-0.

The second set proceeded to match point without Joan winning a single game despite her valiant attempts to mount an effective counterattack on Teddy. Again, with an impassive face, Teddy served to Joan's strongest stroke, her forehand. The ball twisted out of Joan's reach to give Teddy the game, set, and match.

Teddy ran toward the net and jumped over it, disregarding the tournament officials' dictate that winners not engage in such theatrics due to the fear of injury. Joan, a shocked and defeated expression on her face, shook hands with Teddy.

"You were great, Teddy. Do you plan to turn pro?"

"This match was my last. I have other goals in mind."

"Well, good luck. Maybe I'll have a better chance at the championship next year with you out of the picture."

"You'll be all right," Teddy leaned forward to hug Joan. "I'm glad I won't need to worry about a rematch."

"Me too," Joan laughed.

Teddy collected her rackets and left the court to meet Pam and Jason for the trip back to the Big House.

***

Showered and wearing one of her better dresses, Teddy came into the den where the family had gathered for pre-dinner cocktails.

"Mr. Jackson, I'll help you distribute the drinks," Teddy said.

"Congratulations, Miss Theodora, on your championship. The family takes great pride in what you've accomplished. Maybe you'd like to rest on your laurels while I give everyone their drinks?" Jackson asked.

"No, sir. Why should this day be any different than any other day?"

"Theodora, it's not every day that a family member wins a state championship, and now you've won your second."

Miz Lizbeth began clapping and motioned for the rest of the family to join her.

"Thanks, everyone. If all goes according to the plan I want you to approve, I won't be winning any more championships in basketball or tennis."

"That sounds momentous, Teddy. Is it time to reveal what you've been planning?" Pam asked.

Teddy served Miz Lizbeth her martini and sat beside the older woman.

"I'll need some Andrews family influence to make my plan work," Teddy began.

Miz Lizbeth motioned for Jackson, who had poured himself a Wild Turkey over ice, to sit on her other side.

"You have the floor, Theodora," Miz Lizbeth said. "Continue."

"First, I want to graduate as soon as I can from Alexander County High School. To make that happen, I won't play on the basketball or tennis teams so that I can increase my class load, and I want to take courses at Christ College during the academic year and in summer sessions that will give me high school and college credits."

Teddy referred to the nearby Christ Is Lord College, frequently referred to as Christ College, which had an Evangelical, Pentecostal foundation. The college had a history of working with Alexander County High School students who wished to secure both high school and college credits.

"I'll also want to graduate from the University of Georgia as quickly as possible."

"The Andrews family influence you mentioned?" Miz Lizbeth asked.

"I've talked with the guidance counselor at the high school. She said my beginning coursework at Christ College this year should not be a problem."

"The Christian fundamentalism of the college doesn't bother you?" Jason asked.

"I won't be taking religion classes and I won't live on the campus. If the schedules work out, I'll accumulate enough high school credits to graduate early, and I want to secure admission to UGA as soon as possible."

"Jock that I am, I nevertheless have some contacts at UGA outside the athletic department. I'll call someone for us meet and discuss what has to be done," Martin said,

"Theodora, may we assume you've revealed only the first part of your plan?" Miz Lizbeth asked.

"Yes, ma'am."

"Before going any further, Teddy, I want to make a couple of observations," Pam said.

"Observe away, Mom."

"You're only sixteen, and if you're able to proceed as you've outlined, you'll be giving up some of the best of your teenage years. I'm worried that you might regret the loss in your social life."

"I'll still be in class with kids my age, and I won't be a social hermit. I want to get on with my adult life as soon as possible."

"What do you think the reaction at the high school will be

when you don't play on the basketball and tennis teams?" Martin asked.

"Some people will be irritated, maybe even hostile. I'll deal with it," Teddy said.

"I'll talk with the coaches so that they don't pressure you to play," Martin said.

"And I'll give the principal a call," Miz Lizbeth said.

"What course of study will you pursue at UGA?" Pam asked.

"Agribusiness," Teddy replied.

"Interesting choice," Jason said.

"Neither law nor medicine interest you?" Pam asked.

"No, Mom. Although I enjoyed helping you when Shanna gave birth to JJ, I don't want to be a physician. I'm even less interested in the law with my personal history." Teddy looked at Miz Lizbeth. "We can always hire excellent physicians and lawyers."

"Why agribusiness?" Pam asked.

"That course of study will help Theodora prepare for a major role in Andrews Poultry Industries and at the Vickery Bank and Trust. I had an idea that was in your mind when you asked to start coming to the bank after school, and also to see how we harvest chickens," Miz Lizbeth said.

"Teddy, do you plan to live on the UGA campus?" Pam asked.

"I'll probably need to, at least some of the time, dependent upon scheduling. I'm not averse to commuting even though a one-way trip will take at least an hour." Teddy grinned. "Yes, I'll drive within the speed limit. I want to find out how much coursework I can get done online, most likely from here, although I'll want a condo to stay in when I have to be on the UGA campus. And there's one more part of the plan," Teddy said.

Miz Lizbeth looked around the group. "I've already asked Theodora to consider becoming the châtelaine of this house when the time comes."

"Is there any other family in Alexander County that knows the meaning of or uses châtelaine in conversation?" Jason asked.

"Maybe the two or three people who took French," Martin said.

"Miss Theodora, assuming you have permission to go forward, I'll begin teaching you what you need to know about running this house," Jackson said.

"Thanks, Mr. Jackson," Teddy said.

"Teddy, you know what you're getting into, don't you?" Pam asked.

"I have a good idea, and there'll be plenty of help available to keep me on the right path."

Shanna spoke for the first time. "I think Teddy's plan has a lot going for it. As all of you know, our branch of the family will return to the West Coast in a few days, and we won't be available to help out here on a consistent basis." Shanna looked at Martin. "Husband?"

"Shanna and I are happy there's a plan to keep the property and business interests running for the foreseeable future," Martin said.

"JJ and Martin Jackson should have the opportunity to join in these activities when they're old enough," Teddy said.

"Jackson, please refresh our drinks. Theodora, do you have more to say?" Miz Lizbeth asked.

"Does what I want to do meet with everyone's approval?"

"Pam, you're her legal guardian. What say you?" Miz Lizbeth asked.

"I say, if everyone else agrees with this plan, let's give it a try. Teddy, I will retain the right for the next two years to exert my parental authority if implementing this plan becomes too much for you."

"I agree. Jason and Mom, will you go with me to the college next week to discuss the coursework?"

"Yes, for me," Jason said. "Pam, can you arrange time off from the hospital?"

"Shouldn't be a problem," Pam said.

"We have a plan, so let's go forward with support for Theodora," Miz Lizbeth said.

"I'm waiting, Miz Lizbeth," Jason said.

"Make it so," Miz Lizbeth ordered.

CHAPTER 29

Two years after she graduated from the University of Georgia, Teddy acquiesced to Pam's request not to work late at the bank and arrived at the Big House shortly before dinner. She parked her Lexus 460L next to a Ford Mustang with Maryland license plates. Teddy joined the adults in her family and a tall, handsome man gathered on the front porch for late-afternoon cocktails. Teddy wondered if the newcomer was one of Pam's so far unsuccessful attempts at matchmaking.

"Have a seat, Teddy, and I'll get you a Glenmorangie," Jason said.

"Thanks," Teddy replied and took a seat across from the visitor.

"Theodora, we're happy you managed to tear yourself away from the bank," Miz Lizbeth said.

"Teddy, I want you to meet Mark Fredericks, an orthopedic surgeon and the newest member of the medical staff at City-County Hospital," Pam said.

Mark, also drinking Glenmorangie, stood, extending his right hand. He was slim and tall.

"I'm pleased to meet you, Ms. Nelson. Your mom has told me a lot about you."

"Mom has always been my strong supporter."

Mark pointed to the tennis court. "Ms. Nelson, do you play tennis?"

"Please, call me Teddy, and yes, we're a tennis family, especially Jason and me. Do you play?"

"I've been too busy recently to spend much time on the courts," Mark said.

"Teddy, I suspect Mark may be sandbagging you. He looks like a tennis player," Jason said.

"We can find out if we play each other," Teddy said to Mark.

"Name the date and time," Mark said.

"This Sunday afternoon after church and lunch. We'll keep you two off the court until mid-afternoon to give your lunches time to settle," Pam said.

"What church?" Mark asked.

"We're Methodist. We attend Ebenezer at Aldersgate in downtown metropolitan Vickery. You're welcome to join us," Jason said.

"My pleasure. I know the location of the church. The worship service begins at eleven?"

"That's right. Don't worry about getting a seat," Miz Lizbeth said.

"Mark, are you—in terms of the local vocabulary—churched?" Teddy asked.

"Born and raised an Episcopalian, although I haven't been a regular attendee lately."

"Too busy with your medical studies?"

"And with the residency I recently completed."

"Where did you go to medical school?" Teddy asked.

"Harvard Medical School. Then I went to Johns Hopkins for my internship and residency."

"That explains the Maryland tags on your Mustang."

"I'm in the process of becoming a Georgia resident."

The front door opened, and Jackson announced, "Dinner is served."

"Thanks, Jackson. We'll move to the dining room now," Jason said.

"Where's the wild child?" Teddy asked.

"I'll get him. He's on FaceTime with JJ," Pam said.

"JJ, or rather, Jason Jackson Andrews, is the son of my uncle, Martin Andrews. Martin's family lives in Oakland," Teddy said.

***

After Mark left later that evening, Teddy sat with Pam and Jason on the front porch.

"Are you playing matchmaker?" Teddy asked Pam.

"I can neither confirm nor deny," Pam said.

"What do you know about Mark other than he's a good conversationalist, and presumably a good physician?" Teddy asked.

"Well-trained, personable, as you know, and comes from a good family in Nashville."

"Is he married?"

"As far as I know he's never been married. You can ask him Sunday."

"I'll Google him. Do you know how good a tennis player he is?" Teddy asked.

"I suspect you'll need to bring your A game to the court Sunday afternoon," Jason said.

"I always do."

"Are you interested in Mark?" Pam asked.

"I could be." Teddy remembered what Rev. Beatrice Parker had told her about choosing a partner.

***

Mark showed up as planned on Sunday, decked in tennis garb and with a bag full of rackets.

"I guess you were sandbagging the other day," Teddy said. "You look like a serious hitter to me."

"Yes, I've played some. Second singles on my college team, but not much since then. Becoming a doctor has kept me busy."

"Shall we?" Teddy said, motioning to the court.

After a brief and cordial warmup, the two went full on, blasting serves and returns in heated exchanges, but smiling with nods of approval and mutual admiration after great shots.

"If this match goes on much longer, I'll ask Jackson to stop play," Miz Lizbeth said.

"How?" Martin Jackson asked.

"When either Uncle Martin or I refused to admit defeat while playing each other, Jackson would fire off a couple of rounds from his shotgun and be ready to shoot the tennis ball out of the air if we didn't stop playing," Jason told his son.

"Did Mr. Jackson ever have to shoot the ball?"

"No, Martin Jackson. My sons knew better than to keep playing after Jackson's warning," Miz Lizbeth said.

"Sweetheart, do you think we'll need Mr. Jackson to stop this match?" Pam smiled at her son.

"Mom, I've asked you a thousand times not to call me sweetheart. I'm a big boy now."

"I know, Martin Jackson, but you'll always be my sweetheart."

"Yetch, retch," the young boy answered, pushing his forefinger into his open mouth.

On the tennis court, Teddy and Mark continued to play aggressively. Each had won one set and the third set was tied at six games each. Mark hit the ball to Teddy's forehand. The ball landed two inches inside the line. Teddy ran to hit a return drive. She uncharacteristically tripped before her racket reached the ball, and she fell hard on her right shoulder.

"That hurt," Teddy said as she sat up.

Mark came to the net. "Are you OK, Teddy?"

"Give me a minute to catch my breath. I've only begun to fight." After a few moments, Teddy got to her feet to serve, having lost the preceding game. She started to raise her right arm in order to serve. Intense pain pulsated down her arm and she dropped the racket.

"What the hell? Am I crippled before I can win this match?"

Alarmed, Miz Lizbeth pushed herself up from the wheelchair with her strong arms and remained standing unassisted. Mark, Pam, and Jason rushed to Teddy.

"Does your shoulder hurt?" Marked asked.

"Damn right; it hurts like hell. What's wrong with me?"

"You may have damaged your rotator cuff, Teddy, when you fell so awkwardly," Mark replied.

"Well, snap the shoulder back in place, and we'll get on with this match."

"Teddy, Mark can't simply snap your shoulder back in place. We need to get you to City-County Hospital as soon as possible," Pam said.

Mark looked at Jason. "We need a sling for Teddy's arm, to keep it from flopping around and doing more damage."

Jason removed his belt and handed it to Mark, who made a loop in the belt and slipped it over Teddy's neck.

"Teddy," Mark instructed, "let me guide your arm into this loop. Breathe deeply and try to relax your arm, even if what I do causes you pain."

"I'll try." Teddy did not cry out as Mark put her arm into the makeshift sling.

"We need ice in a large plastic sack or baggie to chill Teddy's shoulder to prevent as much swelling as we can," Mark said.

"Will you and Jason be able to get Teddy to the Big House, or do you want to wait here until the EMS arrives? I'll call them on my cell phone," Pam said.

"To hell with that. I can walk to the Big House and someone can take me to the emergency room," Teddy insisted.

"Teddy, I think it would be best for you to sit here calmly until the EMS people arrive. Let's do the best we can to prevent further damage to your shoulder," Mark said.

"I have some morphine in my doctor's bag," Pam said. "That'll ease the pain and keep her calm. I'll be back in a couple of minutes with your happy juice and the ice," Pam told Teddy and started walking fast to the Big House. Pam called the EMS and identified herself.

"I need you at the Big House stat. My daughter has most likely damaged her rotator cuff."

After what seemed an inordinate time, the EMS bus arrived to take Teddy to City-County Hospital. Mark rode with her in the bus. Pam refused Martin Jackson's vigorous insistence that he go with Pam and Jason to the hospital. She knew how long the diagnostic procedures would take, and she didn't want the young boy staying up well into the night in a strange place.

"Martin Jackson, I have a mission for you while we're at the hospital," Jason said.

"What?"

"Connect with JJ on FaceTime and tell him what's happened. Let him know I'll call Martin and Shanna as soon as we have more details about Teddy."

"Roger, understood, and will do. Tell Sister Woman I love her."

***

"What's up, Docs?" Teddy asked Mark and Pam when they walked into Teddy's VIP suite in the Andrews family wing at City-County Hospital. Jason waited at Teddy's bedside.

"The MRI—" Mark began.

"Magnetic Resonance Imaging," Pam explained.

"I know what MRI means, Mom. What does it show?"

"Teddy, you managed to tear the supraspinatus tendon that attaches the supraspinatus muscle to your upper-arm bone, the humerus, to be anatomically precise. The supraspinatus, part of your rotator cuff, keeps your humerus in your shoulder socket and allows you raise and rotate your arm. People who fall like you did often tear their supraspinatus."

"Thanks for the anatomy lesson. What now?" Teddy asked.

"You suffered a very bad tear and you need surgery as soon as possible. I reserved an operating room for us tomorrow morning," Mark said.

"Arthroscopic surgery?" Teddy asked.

"Yes. I'll make small incisions in your shoulder and insert what we call an arthroscope, a long, flexible tube about the diameter of a drinking straw. The end of the tube contains a miniature camera, a light source, and surgical tools I can operate from the other end. The camera projects an image on a television screen. I'll find the tear and repair it while you're under general anesthesia."

"A hell of a way for me to get on TV."

"Any other problems in addition to the rotator cuff tear?" Pam asked.

"What we might expect from someone with Teddy's history on the tennis courts. She has some extensive arthritis that needs to be removed."

"I've never felt any pain in my shoulder until today," Teddy said.

"Maybe, being such a fierce competitor, you simply ignored the pain," Mark suggested.

"Whatever." Teddy rolled her eyes. "Must the surgery be tomorrow? I have a busy day scheduled at the bank."

"I'll take care of the business, Teddy. You concentrate on getting well," Jason said.

"Mark, you'd better fix my shoulder. I want to finish our match," Teddy said.

"I'll do the best I can. I've been successful with most of my patients, provided they complete the post-surgical physical therapy regimen."

"How long before we can play again?" Teddy asked Mark.

"You'll need six weeks of rest followed by another six weeks of physical therapy. Then, you shouldn't try to play at your previous level until we're sure your shoulder has recovered its former strength and mobility. We want a healed shoulder, not one that gives chronic difficulties."

"The prospect of a rematch will give me something to aim for."

"A great attitude. I'll be ready when you're ready," Mark said.

"Where did you learn to play so well?" Teddy asked.

"At the University of Tennessee. I won the Southeastern Conference singles title in my sophomore and junior years."

"I told you Mark was sandbagging," Jason said.

"What happened in your senior year?" Teddy asked.

"I graduated in three years. What's your tennis history?"

"I was a pretty good player before I became a member of the Andrews family. Jason and my uncle Martin taught me to play at a much higher level."

"Martin is your brother?" Mark asked Jason.

"Indeed," Jason said.

"Teddy, did you say Martin and his family live on the West Coast?" Mark asked.

"That's right. Uncle Martin, his wife, and son—JJ or Jason Jackson—live in Oakland. Uncle Martin is the head coach of the Los Angeles Chargers. Aunt Shanna is a supermodel."

"Your family sounds fascinating!" Mark exclaimed.

"That's one way of looking at our family," Jason said.

"Teddy can tell you more about us," Pam said.

"I look forward to the experience," Mark said to Teddy.

Teddy chose to ignore the gleam in Pam's eyes.

"In due time, Mark. How about you two doctors arrange to have some food brought into this room? We missed dinner at the Big House."

"Teddy, you're going under general anesthesia in the morning, which means you can't have anything to eat or drink after midnight, and it's almost that time now," Pam said.

"This day continues to deteriorate," Teddy said.

"How's the pain in your shoulder on a scale of zero to ten?" Mark asked.

"I think the morphine Mom gave me has worn off; I'd say about an eight."

"I'll have the nurses give you more morphine now and an additional dose if needed later tonight."

"Do you need something to help you sleep?" Pam asked.

"No. You guys go home and leave me to suffer in silence," Teddy answered.

"I'll see you first thing in the morning," Mark said.

"As will we," Jason said.

"Leave already," Teddy sighed.

CHAPTER 30

Within three days after the surgery, Teddy returned to her work as vice president at the Vickery Bank and Trust, thankful she had Dragon Speak on her computers, although she was not a fan of dictation. Even as Mark and Pam cautioned Teddy against pushing too hard, she relentlessly pursued her recovery over the next several weeks. Mark appeared frequently at the Big House for afternoon cocktails and dinner. Most often he and Teddy sat together on the front porch, usually by themselves, after dinner. They developed a close rapport and spoke easily with each other. A few times they went to movies in nearby Toccoa, or in Anderson, South Carolina. The relationship remained chaste. Mark understood that Teddy was reluctant to have a sexual relationship even though she had begun to care for him. He was patient, letting Teddy make up her own mind about intensifying the relationship.

Soon after Teddy regained limited use of her right arm, Mark appeared at the bank in the mid-afternoon without making an appointment. When Gabby ushered Mark into Teddy's office, Teddy looked up with delight.

"Hey, Mark. What brings you to our metropolis and to this illustrious financial institution?"

"Business, Teddy, and the pleasure of seeing you."

"Nice to see you, too. What business?"

"I'd like to secure a mortgage. I have my eyes on a house I want to buy. I'm wondering if the bank can write a mortgage for me."

"We can issue you a mortgage; however, buying a house might be premature."

"What in the world do you mean?"

"I want to tell you some things about me before you buy a house. You might change your mind about the purchase, I hope. Why don't we go to the Big House and I'll reveal all?"

"You can leave early today?" Mark asked.

"I don't foresee any financial crises on the horizon. Let's go. If an emergency develops, someone can call me. I guess the same thing applies to you?"

"I never know."

"Understood. Let's vacate the premises. We'll take whatever opportunities come our way."

"Carpe diem," Mark said, Latin for "seize the day."

***

Martin Jackson came onto the porch to greet Teddy and Mark.

"Where's Mom?" Teddy asked.

"Still at the hospital."

"Your dad, where's he?"

"Inside, getting ready to go to the free-grow houses."

"Is something wrong?" Teddy asked.

"Dad thinks a temperature sensor is out of whack. He's taking me with him."

Jason came to the porch. "Teddy, Mark. Good to see you so early in the afternoon."

"Mark and I need to talk," Teddy said.

"I hope you're staying for dinner, Mark," Jason said.

"It may depend upon how he reacts to what I have to tell him," Teddy said before Mark could reply.

Jason raised his eyebrows. "I don't think you can scare Mark into leaving, Teddy."

"I hope not."

"I'm most intrigued," Mark said.

"Let's go, Martin Jackson. We'll leave Teddy and Mark to talk. We should be back in plenty of time for dinner," Jason said.

"Can we take one of the trucks?" Martin Jackson asked.

"We will," Jason replied.

"May I drive?"

"Not today, son. We're in a hurry," Jason replied.

"Take your time," Teddy said.

"See, Sister Woman thinks I should drive," Martin Jackson said.

"Thanks, Teddy," Jason said as he and Martin Jackson left the porch.

"Can Martin Jackson really drive one of the trucks?" Mark asked.

"He's not quite tall enough to reach the pedals. He sits in Jason's lap and steers. The way he's growing, he'll be agitating to drive on this property within the next year."

"Not on the outside roads?"

"Jason, with Mom's reluctant acquiescence, will teach Martin Jackson to drive on our property as soon as he can reach the pedals. He won't get onto the county roads until he's fifteen and gets his learner's permit."

"Teddy, now that we have the porch to ourselves, you must know I love you. Will you marry me, as soon as possible?"

Teddy leaned forward to kiss Mark. "Yes, provisionally."

"Why provisionally?"

"You may not want to marry me after I tell you some things about my past."

"I can't imagine anything that would dissuade me from marrying you and spending the rest of our lives together."

"You need to know what I'm bringing into the marriage."

Teddy then related how Thompson Kendal had attempted to rape her, how Jason and Martin rescued her and Pam, and how the two brothers brought the mother and daughter into the Andrews family. Teddy also told Mark about the great support and affection Miz Lizbeth and Jackson Williams provided. Throughout Teddy's monologue, Mark kept his eyes on Teddy's, never flinching from even the most sordid details. Teddy, following Miz Lizbeth's long-ago imperative, did not reveal that she had considered killing Kendal. Teddy paused, not sure how to judge Mark's reactions.

"Is there more, Teddy?" Mark asked,

Teddy fought to contain her tears. "There's more—my own insecurities."

"I don't think insecure is the proper word for you, Teddy."

"I have never had sexual intercourse. I'm not sure how I'll react when you and I make love."

"You've been, for lack of a better word, chaste until now?"

"I've had an ongoing affair with my vibrator, and that worries me. As for me being chaste, a wise woman—the former minister at our church—advised me to be sure what I wanted: a person I can dominate or a person who will be a real partner with me, equals."

"How do you view me? As someone you can dominate or as an equal?"

"We can settle the domination issue for tennis as soon as I get back to fighting form. Otherwise, I figure we're equals."

"Great, my view exactly. Any other thoughts?"

"I'd like for us to live here at the Big House. We can have one of the wings as our private residence and eat meals—especially dinner—with the rest of the family. Pre-dinner cocktails are part of our regular routine, as you know. We take care of a lot of family business at cocktail hour. If you agree, you won't need to buy us a house."

"You have a real attachment to this house?" Mark asked.

"While I was still in high school, Miz Lizbeth asked me to be responsible for the Big House, its operation and maintenance, as well overseeing the staff as time progresses. She said I should be the châtelaine of this house."

"Châtelaine, that's French?"

"It means mistress of the castle, a woman of power," Teddy said.

"The word describes you," Mark said. "I can only admire you for what you've overcome and for what you've become, an indomitable human being."

Mark went to Teddy and pulled her to a standing position before embracing her, holding her tightly without stressing her surgically repaired shoulder.

"Our living in the Big House would simplify working with Jason to take care of the family's various business interests."

"Including Andrews Poultry Industries?" Mark asked.

"There're several more in addition to Andrews Poultry Industries and the Vickery Bank and Trust."

"Are you destined to be president of the bank?" Mark asked.

"I am, as well as head of all the businesses when Jason retires."

"Will you have enough time left over for us?"

"Definitely, and for our children as well. Living at the Big House with its staff will make it easier for us to be together. What about you?"

"Except for the occasional emergencies, I'll keep my schedule sufficiently open for you. You did say children, didn't you?"

"At least two."

"Teddy, when do you envision our getting married?"

"Before the professional football season begins. I want Uncle

Martin, Aunt Shanna, and JJ here for the wedding."

"My parents can probably be here on very short notice," Mark said.

"I have a suggestion," Teddy said.

"I'm listening."

"I see no reason for us to wait any longer to consummate this relationship. While we're making arrangements for the wedding, how about moving in with me? We'd have plenty of privacy. I live in a separate wing of the house."

"Outstanding! What will your family think about our being together before the wedding?"

"Shouldn't be a problem. Mom and Jason established the precedent before they married."

Mark pointed to the two vehicles approaching the Big House. "Did you plan for your parents and Martin Jackson to arrive on schedule, in time for an announcement?"

"No, happenstance only. Let's tell them what's happening."

CHAPTER 31

Teddy evidenced no shyness as she and Mark undressed slowly in her bedroom. Once in the bed, Mark brought Teddy into his arms and kissed her gently. She responded eagerly, albeit with obvious inexperience. Mark continued to kiss Teddy, flicking his tongue across her lips and progressively using his tongue to search for hers. At each intensification, Teddy responded in like manner.

Teddy's hips moved in anticipation of Mark entering her. She lifted her hips to press against Mark.

"Teddy, you get on top," Mark said.

When they turned over, Teddy said, "Interesting. I like it."

Mark grasped Teddy's buttocks with both hands and pulled her closer to him as she continued to ride him. Teddy approached orgasm, but failed to climax.

"Mark, you go ahead and finish. Every time I'm about to orgasm, that bastard's face comes into my mind."

"No," Mark said, "we'll keep going. We have all the time you need." As Teddy again approached orgasm, Mark ordered, "Teddy, open your eyes! Look at me! Only me!"

Teddy followed Mark's instructions. Finally, she tensed and orgasmed, pulsating as her eyes rolled back. She fell temporarily exhausted onto Mark. Once she caught her breath, Teddy exclaimed, "Wow! That was fantastic!"

"Same for me, Teddy my love. Give me a few minutes to recover and we'll have another go."

Teddy put her head on Mark's chest and relaxed, deeply satisfied but not satiated, her sexual feelings aroused as never before.

***

When Teddy and Mark came to the breakfast table the next morning, the family broke into vigorous applause much like on the occasion years earlier when Pam and Jason spent their first night together.

"Mark, I hope this family doesn't overwhelm you," Jason said.

"No, not at all. Like I said, I'm fascinated," Mark replied.

"Welcome to the Andrews family, Mark. Glad to have you with us," Miz Lizbeth said.

Mark looked in turn to Jason and Pam. "I think for formality's sake I should ask your permission to marry Teddy."

"How do you feel about that, Teddy?" Pam asked.

Teddy leaned over to kiss Mark. "Mother Dearest, you did a great job of playing matchmaker. I love Mark; he loves me." She turned to Mark. "Let's do it."

"Do you want to get married in our church?" Miz Lizbeth asked.

"I think that's traditional, isn't it?" Teddy responded.

"Is that acceptable to you, Mark?" Miz Lizbeth asked.

"Of course."

Teddy looked at Miz Lizbeth. "Elizabeth, here's the way I see things going."

"Pray tell, Theodora."

"I'm busy at the bank, Jason has a lot to do with the business, and Mom and Mark are involved with their medical practices."

"I will, of course, be your wedding planner and director for the festivities," Miz Lizbeth said.

"Thank you, Elizabeth. You read my mind, as you often do," Teddy said.

"Can you and I at least go together to select your wedding dress?" Pam asked.

"I wouldn't have it any other way," Teddy said.

"Sister Woman, can I give you away?" Martin Jackson asked.

"Well, let's think about this. Mark, do you have a best man in mind?" Teddy asked.

"My father."

"Do you also have some groomsmen you want with us?"

"I'll contact a few friends when we set the date."

"Any family members besides your father and mother?" Miz Lizbeth asked Mark.

"No, I'm an only child and I'm not really close to my more distant family members," Mark said.

"Long story?" Teddy asked.

"Very long. Mom and Dad have been very successful in academia; both hold tenured professorships at Vanderbilt. Most of my relatives resent the fact that Mom and Dad won't help support them to the level they desire."

"Well, you're marrying into a different kind of family," Teddy said.

"Thank God!" Mark replied. "Martin Jackson, I'd like for you to be one of my groomsmen, if you're willing."

"I can do that," Martin Jackson said.

"What else do you have in store for us, Theodora?" Miz Lizbeth asked.

"I want you, Mom, and Shanna to be my matrons of honor, and I want Mr. Jackson, Jason, and Uncle Martin to give me away."

"The chancel area at the church will accommodate everyone

in the wedding party. Maybe my boys and Jackson can walk three abreast behind you from the front door of the church to the chancel. I'll put my mind to the arrangements," Miz Lizbeth said.

"Teddy, I suspect you and Mark haven't had time to plan a honeymoon. Do you have any thoughts?" Pam asked.

Teddy looked at Mark, who shrugged. "By the time we're officially married, Mark and I won't need a honeymoon to become better acquainted. He and I will discuss what we might do. In the meantime, business as usual, I suppose," Teddy said.

"I also think it would be better to delay the honeymoon in order to give us more time to plan it." Mark turned to Miz Lizbeth. "I assume the wedding will take place soon?"

"Like my naval son might say, 'With all deliberate haste if not flank speed,'" Miz Lizbeth said.

"You two might enjoy an extended cruise, like the one Jason and I went on for our honeymoon," Pam said.

Teddy gave a good-natured laugh. "With the same result as for you and Jason?"

After the laughter around the table subsided, Mark asked, "Same result?"

Teddy pointed to Martin Jackson, who looked puzzled. "Your mom and I will tell you more later, Martin Jackson."

"I get it now. Mom and Dad did the nasty on their cruise," Martin Jackson said.

"Many times," Pam said.

"A cruise sounds fun. I've never been on an ocean. Mark and I will make a joint decision," Teddy said.

"I've also been a landlubber and I might like to be on a cruise ship. Teddy, one thing to think about," Mark said

"What's that?" Teddy asked.

"Probably no tennis courts on a cruise ship."

"You'll be too busy with each other to think about playing tennis," Miz Lizbeth broke in. "Tempus fugit."

"What?" Martin Jackson asked.

"Tempus fugit is Latin for time flies," Pam told her son.

Martin Jackson looked first at Teddy and then Miz Lizbeth.

"Do you want Teddy to have a baby?"

"All in good time," Miz Lizbeth replied.

"Well, at least she didn't say, 'Make it so,'" Jason said.

"On that note, let's all go to work," Teddy said. "Martin Jackson, do you want to come to the bank with me? If you get bored, someone can bring you back to the Big House."

"Make it so, Sister Woman, make it so," Martin Jackson said.

CHAPTER 32

L ater that morning, Mark walked into the emergency suite in City-County Hospital. Pam, who did not appear to be busy for the moment, beckoned him over to her. "Hey, Mark. Long time, no see. Do you have an emergency?"

"I'd like some information about Miz Lizbeth, if we can talk doctor-to-doctor."

"You want details on her medical condition?"

"I do. What happened to put her in the wheelchair?"

"An automobile accident many years—decades—ago. It's a long story. I'll give you the details when we have more time."

"She's urinary and bowel incontinent in addition to being mobility impaired?" Mark asked.

"She is. Jackson takes care of those details."

"She and Jackson are close?"

"Very close since the time of the accident that killed her husband, Jason Andrews Sr."

"To your knowledge, has Miz Lizbeth ever used a walker?"

"I've never seen her with a walker. Why are you asking?"

"Do you remember much about when Teddy hurt herself on the tennis court?" Mark asked.

"I recall being scared out of my mind and equally thankful you were there. Otherwise, not much."

"When I first got to Teddy, I looked up at the front porch to see if you and other family members had seen Teddy fall. I caught a glimpse of Miz Lizbeth pushing herself up from the wheelchair."

"She has very strong arms to complement her exceedingly strong will."

"I think she stood more or less upright for a short time with little help from her arms."

"My lord! Her concern for Teddy somehow overrode the nerve blocks from her accident?"

"I doubt Miz Lizbeth was even conscious of what she'd done."

"We need to talk with Jackson. If anyone has insight into her condition, it's him."

"There's more that I've observed," Mark said. "I've noticed that, probably unconsciously, she can move both feet, like she's tapping them on the floor."

"I've missed those signs," Pam said.

"You're accustomed to her problems; I'm a new observer."

"Where are you going with this conversation?"

"Maybe nowhere, maybe somewhere. When was the last time Miz Lizbeth had a thorough medical examination?" Mark asked.

"I don't know. She seems as healthy as the proverbial horse."

"Then, I'm safe to assume she hasn't had any modern imaging performed on her spine?"

"Ultrasound, CAT and MRI were not developed when she was injured."

"Do you think we could convince her to undergo those and some other procedures?"

"We should try. Soon after I joined the Andrews family, I did some research on possible treatments that might help Miz Lizbeth. I didn't find anything I thought was suitable, and she seems thoroughly accommodated to her difficulties."

"You explored stem cell treatment?"

"The experimental procedures I reviewed didn't seem relevant to Miz Lizbeth."

"Did you come across information on Regenerative Biotechnology?" Mark asked.

"No, not that I remember. Are you telling me that I haven't been a good medical advocate for Miz Lizbeth?"

"Not at all, no way! You're an emergency room doc. You most likely don't follow your patients once they're out of the emergency room."

"Right, I treat the immediate crucial effects," Pam said.

"As an orthopedic surgeon, I often deal with the longer-term effects. A lot has been happening lately in the field of spinal cord nerve regeneration."

"Some form of stem cell treatment might help Miz Lizbeth?"

"A low probability this long after her accident. On the other hand, Miz Lizbeth and the family might be willing to pursue the idea. There's little potential for any adverse effects except spending a good bit of the Andrews fortune."

Pam laughed so hard that other people in the emergency room turned to look at her and Mark. She waved off the onlookers.

"I hope Teddy properly informs you about the family you're marrying into. Even a million dollars spent on Miz Lizbeth wouldn't pose a problem."

"Teddy's given me some details with the promise of more to come," Mark said. "First, we need to ascertain Miz Lizbeth's capabilities. If you'll go along with me at cocktail hour this afternoon, we might get a better idea of how to proceed."

"I'm in. I'll follow your lead."

***

Mark and Pam arrived at the Big House as the rest of the family gathered for the late-afternoon cocktail hour. Mark carried a folded walker, and Pam held a rolled-up gait belt. Miz Lizbeth gave Mark and Pam intense looks.

"What's that contraption for, Mark?" Miz Lizbeth bristled.

"Pam and I want to play doctor with you for a few minutes."

"How so?"

"Please let us do our thing," Pam said.

"As long as I don't have to wait too long for my martini," Miz Lizbeth acquiesced.

"Better that we do our explorations before you have any alcohol. I want to wrap this gait belt around you, Miz Lizbeth, and snug it tight through the buckle," Pam said.

"What in the world for?" Miz Lizbeth asked.

"Go with the flow, please." Pam fitted the gait belt around Miz Lizbeth's waist. "Now, Mr. Jackson, please hold on to the gait belt with both hands." Jackson stood to one side of the wheelchair to comply with Pam's request.

Mark opened the walker and placed it within easy reach of Miz Lizbeth's hands.

"Surely you two don't think I can walk," Miz Lizbeth said as the rest of the family watched intently.

"Let's start first with seeing you stand." Mark locked the wheelchair in place. "Miz Lizbeth, please put your hands on the walker and push yourself upright with your arms. Mr. Jackson will hold on to the gait belt and give you an assist if you need it. He'll also keep you from falling, although I don't think we'll need to worry about that problem for a few minutes."

"I was comfortable in my wheelchair," Miz Lizbeth said.

"Up and at 'em, Mama," Jason said. The rest of the family, except for Mark and Jackson, applauded.

"With all that encouragement, I'll try." As instructed, Miz Lizbeth pushed herself to a standing position. "I'll be damned!" she exclaimed. "What now?"

"Mr. Jackson, please keep holding that gait belt. Miz Lizbeth, we won't let you fall. Please think very hard about taking a small step with your right foot," Mark instructed.

"Are you kidding me? I haven't walked since the accident."

Martin Jackson left his seat to stand in front of Miz Lizbeth.

"Take one step toward me, Miz Lizbeth, and I'll give you a kiss."

"What the hell? Why not?" Miz Lizbeth's face contorted with concentration, and she managed a small step forward. Martin Jackson leaned over the walker to kiss his grandmother.

"Let's have a repeat with your left foot," Mark said.

Miz Lizbeth managed a smaller step, and Martin Jackson kissed her again.

"I'm feeling unsteady," she said.

Pam pushed the wheelchair forward so that the seat touched the back of Miz Lizbeth's legs. "Mr. Jackson, please help Miz Lizbeth sit slowly without flopping."

"What now?" Miz Lizbeth asked once she was seated. Jackson gave Miz Lizbeth her martini.

"Mr. Jackson, were you aware that Miz Lizbeth can move her feet?" Mark asked.

"I've seen her sometimes tap her toes on the floor," Jackson said.

"Miz Lizbeth, do you have any feeling whatsoever in your legs and feet?" Mark asked.

"In the past few weeks, she sometimes complains of tingling in her legs," Jackson said.

"Like fiery needles sticking me," Miz Lizbeth agreed, taking a large sip of her martini.

"Miz Lizbeth, why didn't you tell me?" Pam asked.

"What for? I don't think I'll ever walk again," Miz Lizbeth said.

Mark accepted a Glenmorangie from Jackson. "I don't want you to have any unreasonable hopes, Miz Lizbeth, although something positive seems to be going on with you. One more thing for this afternoon. There may be more to come, but for now

I want you to think very carefully. Do you ever have any signals that you need to urinate or defecate?"

Jackson once again broke in. "She sometimes tells me she feels like she needs to pee or have a bowel movement. Those feelings are very new."

"Where are all of these personal details about me headed?" Miz Lizbeth asked.

"To City-County Hospital tomorrow for some modern imaging on your spine," Pam said. "We've already made the appointment."

"We need the new imaging to help us determine what's happening in your spine," Mark said.

"After all these years?" Miz Lizbeth asked.

"We shouldn't ignore what we've learned today. Let's be neither overly optimistic nor overly pessimistic." Mark raised his glass for a refill. "Let me tell you all a story. If we sever a salamander's spinal cord, the nerves controlling the animal's lower body will regenerate, and there will be no lasting evidence of the injury."

"Miz Lizbeth isn't a lizard," Martin Jackson said.

"No, she isn't. Regeneration or regrowth of damaged nerves in those animals has prompted a lot of research into how we might stimulate nerves to regrow in people with injuries like Miz Lizbeth's."

"You think some of the new research might help Miz Lizbeth?" Jackson asked.

"It depends. The imaging results should tell us the current status of her spinal cord." Mark turned to Miz Lizbeth. "Do you recall being told at what level your spine was damaged?"

"Level?" Miz Lizbeth asked.

"Which nerves were damaged. From your symptoms, I suspect your lumbar spine was impacted."

"I remember now. I was told the damage was at L1."

"That makes sense. All of your functions controlled from L1 down would be paralyzed," Mark said.

"Something really intrigues me, Mark," Pam declared.

"What?"

"The fact that Miz Lizbeth appears to be regaining some sensation suggests that either her spinal cord wasn't severed or we're seeing something really unexpected—regeneration of her spinal nerves."

"There's another possibility," Mark said.

Jackson took Miz Lizbeth's raised martini glass for a refill. "I hope we can turn some of these possibilities into actualities," he said.

"What's your other possibility?" Teddy asked Mark.

"Bone fragments from the accident might have been impinging on the L1 nerves." Mark looked at Pam.

"And have begun after all this time to resorb," Pam finished.

"Could you surgically remove the fragments, if they're the actual problem?" Teddy asked.

"Let's not go further with this discussion until we obtain the imaging," Mark replied.

"Aren't you guys glad Mark's part of our family?" Teddy asked the group.

"You done good, Sister Woman, you done good," Martin Jackson said.

CHAPTER 33

"What's taking so long to get my results, Mark?" Miz Lizbeth asked, fidgeting in the bed of her VIP suite at City-County Hospital.

"I transmitted the MRI and CAT to two highly regarded experts. I didn't want to tell you my interpretation until I heard back from them."

"For goodness sake, what's the result?" Miz Lizbeth asked.

"You have some bone fragments pressing against your spinal nerves. Surgically removing the fragments may help restore some functionality to you," Mark said.

"How long after the surgery would we know if I can walk, much less regain control of my bladder and bowels?"

"We could be talking about a relatively short time or not at all. On a positive note, my expert consultants and I agree that the surgery shouldn't result in more impairment," Mark said.

"When can you do the surgery?" Miz Lizbeth asked.

"I have a proposal. Pam and I think you should consider a rather aggressive approach."

"Pray tell. I'm ready to go home."

"We'll make arrangements to fly you to Shenzhen, China— near Hong Kong—in a medically equipped private aircraft.

A company in Shenzhen called Regenerative Biotechnology specializes in restoring functionality in cases similar to yours. Regenerative will harvest some of your own stem cells and activate them. You'll undergo the surgery in Shenzhen and, while you're on the operating table, your activated stem cells will be infused directly into your spinal cord. Later you'll have what's called an epidural stimulation device implanted that might very well help the stem cells grow into new neural tissue."

"Is this Chinese company reputable?" Miz Lizbeth asked.

"Yes, all politics aside. I've already transmitted your case history to them. I expect to hear back from them in a few days about accepting you for treatment."

"How long would I be in . . . what's the name of the city again?"

"Shenzhen. Probably four to six weeks," Mark said.

"Will you and Pam go with Jackson and me?"

"Mark and I will fly with you to Shenzhen, and once you're settled in we'll probably fly back," Pam said. "We prefer not to be away from City-County Hospital while you're being treated. If you would like, Jason could also stay with you,"

Miz Lizbeth gave one of her uproarious laughs. "I can well imagine the consternation among the Chinese authorities if they put two and two together about Jason."

"Adding up to what?" Mark asked.

"I suspect Jason tangled with the Chinese air force when he served in the Navy," Miz Lizbeth said.

"You really think the Chinese would know of Jason?" Pam asked.

"The Chinese are crafty," Miz Lizbeth said.

"What about you, the mother? The Chinese authorities could hold you for political purposes," Mark said.

"Unlikely. They wouldn't want the political fallout about holding a helpless old woman who came to China with her son for medical help. Also, there's another reason."

"In your words, Miz Lizbeth, 'Pray tell,'" Pam said.

"We do business with them. We sell chicken parts, especially feet, to Chinese companies. When we originally closed the deal, Martin—not Jason—went to China to sign the contract." Miz Lizbeth chuckled. "See, I was paranoid even then."

"Even paranoids can have real enemies," Jackson said.

"One more thing, Mark and Pam," Miz Lizbeth said.

"What's that?" Pam asked.

"Assuming Mark can get everything in place for this experience, I don't want to go to China until after Theodora's wedding. I've been in this damn chair for a long time. Waiting a little longer won't be a burden."

"I understand, Miz Lizbeth." Mark took a deep breath. "I'm new in this family, so please excuse my next question."

"Fire away," Miz Lizbeth said.

"You haven't inquired about the expenses involved."

"It doesn't really matter, Mark. I think the possibility of my regaining some functionality will be worth every penny we may need to spend."

"Totally correct, Miz Lizbeth," Pam said.

"I agree," Jackson said.

"Mark, I know what everyone in the room expects. Make it so," Miz Lizbeth said.

CHAPTER 34

Teddy arrived at the Vickery Bank and Trust on a Monday morning three days after Miz Lizbeth and her group left for China. Hack Lawrence stood up from the chair beside Gabby's desk in the outer office of the executive suite.

"Mrs. Fredericks, I need to see you on an urgent matter," he said.

"Please come into my office, Hack, and we'll talk. You look uncommonly serious. Is something wrong?" Teddy asked.

"I'm afraid so, but I'm handling the problem. Are you the only family member here right now?"

"I'm the only adult. JJ and Martin Jackson are at the Big House, hopefully keeping out of trouble while they play computer games or whatever they find to do."

"JJ?"

"He stayed here after the wedding. The web's full of reports that Martin's days as head coach with the Los Angeles Chargers are numbered. Martin and the new owner of the Chargers don't see eye-to-eye, despite Martin's winning record."

"When do you expect the rest of the family back?" Hack asked.

"My mom and Mark should be home within a week. Miz Lizbeth, Jackson, and Jason will stay in China for the duration of her treatment and initial recovery period."

"So be it. You and I will need to handle things," Hack said.

"What's going on, Hack? I can tell you're worried."

"Much earlier this morning, someone with significant computer skills began trying to hack into our network. The alarms I have in place alerted me to the attempted intrusions. The hacker uses some sophisticated approaches."

"Is this hacker as good as you?"

"Probably not. On the other hand, he appears unrelenting."

"Do you have any idea about the identity of the hacker and what he or she wants?"

"The hacker uses a number of cutouts. I've traced the digital footprints to servers in Poland, Russia, China, the UK, and a few other countries. He's definitely trying to hide."

"How much time do you need to find the originating server?" Teddy asked.

"I don't know. I'm masking my efforts to identify him."

"You think the hacker is a male?"

"Probably."

"Why?"

"Prejudice, I guess."

"Well, the person's gender doesn't matter. How do you propose to keep the person out of our systems?" Teddy asked.

"I've moved us to what I call Defcon 2."

"That's military speak, isn't it?"

"Defense Readiness Condition Level 2 signifies one stage below all-out war at Defcon 1."

"Someone attempting to break in to our information technology systems constitutes an act of war as far as I'm concerned," Teddy said.

"My opinion exactly."

"To continue the military analogy, how have you deployed our defenses?"

"I've written code so that all incoming and outgoing texts, emails, or whatever come to me before the stated recipient sees them. That way, I can help our antiviral and malware programs keep the hacker out of our system."

"What should I do?"

"Issue an order that no one links private cell phones or laptops to our IT systems."

"I'll send a companywide email to that effect when we finish here."

"Unless this hacker operates at a true genius level, the attack should be over soon."

"You said Defcon 2. What will be Defcon 1, if you have to go there?"

"I will take all our systems off the web."

"Damn. Can we go on the offensive?"

"Once I identify the hacker and his server, I'll insert a worm into his system."

"A worm?" Teddy asked.

"A complicated piece of code that will eat its destructive way into all parts of his system, destroying all his files."

Teddy leaned back in her chair. "Did you put a similar worm on Frank Gordon's system, back in the day?"

"An interesting speculation, Mrs. Fredericks."

"I'll assume you did. Does your current worm function as well as the one you used with Frank Gordon?"

"These kinds of worms evolve, as do the defenses. The trick will be for us to stay ahead of the hacker."

"I'm convinced you'll be able to protect us."

"I'll do my best, Mrs. Fredericks."

"I believe someone attempting to hack into the computer systems of a bank is a federal crime," Teddy said.

"It is."

"Should we notify the FBI?"

"Not yet, Mrs. Fredericks. Maybe after we identify and disarm the hacker. The feds would get in my way, maybe close us down."

"I imagine the FBI has access to very powerful systems that could identify the hacker?"

"We'd lose control of the process once the feds became involved. I'd rather present them with an airtight case."

"Makes sense to me as long as you can protect our network while you identify the culprit," Teddy said.

"Do you want to notify Jason about our problem?"

"Not immediately. There's nothing Jason can do until he comes home. Hopefully, by the time he returns, you and I will have taken care of the hacker."

"One more thing, Mrs. Fredericks. Don't let JJ and Martin Jackson have access to the Internet to play games or whatever until this attack ends."

"I'll call the Big House with instructions to disconnect the computers they're using from the Net. They can play on the disconnected computers."

"Great idea. Later this afternoon, I'll bring you a thumb drive loaded with games that should keep the boys busy for some time." Hack stood. "I'll get back to work, Mrs. Fredericks. You'll be the first person I notify if conditions change."

"Thanks, Hack. Let me know if I can help."

"Will do."

***

Later that afternoon after the bank closed for the day and Teddy prepared to leave for the Big House, she heard a knock on her office door. Teddy opened a desk drawer where she kept one of her 9mm Glock 17 pistols. "Come in."

Hack came through the door wearing a huge smile. "Good news, Mrs. Fredericks."

"You've identified the hacker?"

"Ralph Whitfield III. You know him?"

"I do. We were in high school at the same time. I also occasionally saw him around the campus at the University of Georgia while I was there. He tried to date me in high school."

"You didn't go out with him?"

"No way! He seemed a little bit off to me, and I also knew the history between the Andrews and Whitfield families."

"Great decision. Do you know his major at UGA?"

Teddy thought for a few seconds. "Computer science, I think."

"That's right. He went to Stanford for his master's and doctoral degrees."

"Formidable background."

"He returned to Alexander County a few months ago. He now has a position in the Whitfield family business in Mercerville, probably taking care of their IT services."

"With his background, the Whitfield IT requirements should be easy for Ralph."

"Right. He probably doesn't have a lot of IT work to do. The Whitfield family lost a lot of influence and business thanks to the Andrews family, and deservedly so."

A sudden thought came to Teddy. "I thought a lot of the friction between the two families was resolved before I joined the family. Martin and Jason told me some of the background when I began working at the bank, in case some of the younger Whitfields tried to retaliate against the Andrews, which appears to be happening with Ralph's hacking."

"Sounds plausible to me," Hack said.

"Wasn't Ralph's grandfather sentenced to life in prison for killing several people associated with our family?"

"Ralph Sr. died in prison about six months ago. He was a very old man when he died."

"Hack, could you access the prison records to determine if Ralph III ever visited Ralph Senior in prison?"

"More than likely. I'll get on that project when I'm back in my office."

"For the present, let's assume the visit took place and Ralph Senior convinced Ralph III to retaliate against the Andrews. Taking down this bank and our other businesses would be sweet revenge."

"Maybe Ralph III began his hacks because so much of the Andrews family is out of town. He may be thinking we're more vulnerable with only you and me to defend against him."

"In that case, he's an idiot."

"Mrs. Fredericks, it's late. Why don't you go to the Big House and be with JJ and Martin Jackson? I'll work a while. If anything important develops, I'll call you."

"Hack, are you ever going to call me Teddy again?"

"Not as long as you're my boss. Be careful on the way to the Big House. We still don't know what we face."

"What about Anna? Shouldn't you go home to be with her?"

"I have much better computer resources here than at home. Anna's bringing supper from Sweet Gum Barbecue and Fish Lodge for us to share in my office."

"You and Anna should also be careful."

"I'll tell Henry Goodson to be especially vigilant about anyone trying to break into the bank tonight." Hack referred to the night guard. "I'll see you tomorrow, if not sooner."

Teddy left her office and met Henry Goodson as he made his hourly rounds of the bank.

"Hey, Mr. Goodson, everything locked up tightly?"

"Yes, ma'am. I'll escort you to your car."

Teddy accepted the offer and was soon on her way to the Big House.

CHAPTER 35

The next morning Hack again sat with Gabby waiting for Teddy's arrival at the bank. He looked haggard.

"Hey, Hack, did you pull an all-nighter?" Teddy asked.

"I spent a productive night," Hack answered.

"Did Anna stay with you all night?"

"She left around midnight, too sleepy to watch me crawl into my computers."

"Please have a seat." Teddy went to the credenza where she knew a carafe of fresh coffee would be available. "Coffee?"

"No, thanks. I'm overly caffeinated after last night."

Teddy poured herself a mug. "A productive night, you said?"

"I inserted the worm into Ralph Whitfield's computer about an hour ago. The worm should be eating its way through all of the Whitfield systems even as we speak."

"Congrats! Any problems?"

"I had to blast through some formidable and rather advanced firewalls on Whitfield's computer, which took me most of the night, before I could insert the worm."

"Any chance Whitfield will know you inserted the worm?"

"He'll probably deduce that I did the dirty deed—a lot of good it will do him."

"Can he trace the worm back to us?" Teddy asked.

"Only with great difficulty, if at all. I employed many more cutouts than he did. My private computer that I used was not attached to our network."

"Could he identify your computer?"

"Very unlikely. Even if he can penetrate the firewalls, he'll be led to a hacking site in North Korea."

"North Korea? You've penetrated a site in that misbegotten country?" Teddy asked.

Hack rubbed his eyes. "I've been keeping an eye on how the North Koreans try to access the US banking system."

Teddy clapped her hands. "Surely you haven't put your worm in their computers?"

"I haven't tried. I don't want us involved in an international brouhaha that would alert the feds to what I've been doing. The NSA, CIA, and our other spooks have much more powerful technology than I do, should our government decide to launch a cyber-attack on North Korea."

"Hack, have our spooks ever tried to recruit you?"

"I refused their offers a couple of times."

"If you don't mind my asking, why?"

"I wouldn't last long in that environment, and I probably couldn't continue my day-trading activities. Besides, I enjoy working with the Andrews family."

Teddy recalled that Miz Lizbeth had mentioned how the Andrews family kept Hack out of prison for his former illegal hacking activities when he was much younger.

"Hack, you're like part of the family."

"Thanks. I feel that way." Hack stood. "I need to go home for some shut-eye. If any problem develops, the alarms on our system will alert me."

"A great idea. Enjoy your well-deserved rest." Teddy made a mental note to reward Hack with a sizeable bonus, if he would accept it.

***

Later that afternoon, Teddy poured herself another mug of coffee. As she took a first swallow of the strong liquid, her intercom buzzed.

"Yes, Gabby?"

"Mrs. Fredericks, a Mr. Ralph Whitfield demands to see you."

Teddy had barely opened the drawer that held her Glock 17 when the door to her office burst open to admit Whitfield. "You bitch!" he shouted.

Gabby stood at the open door. "Shall I call law enforcement, Mrs. Fredericks?"

"Not now, thank you. Please leave the door open," Teddy said. "Have a seat, Ralph, and tell me what's distressing you. Would you like a cup of coffee before you begin?"

"I only want you and your lying, deceitful family brought to justice for infecting the Whitfield IT system and for other crimes, goddamn you!"

"You really ought to try some of this coffee, Ralph. It's very good."

"If I drank any of your coffee, I'd have to spew it all over you."

"No coffee, then. Please have a seat and we'll have a rational conversation."

Teddy shifted her gaze to Gabby, who pointed to her telephone console. Teddy took another sip of coffee and placed the mug close to her own telephone console to allow her to activate the intercom without Whitfield noticing.

"Well, Ralph, if you don't sit so we can talk, I'll tell Gabby to call the police to get you out of this bank. As far as I'm concerned, you're trespassing."

Whitfield clinched his fists and moved toward Teddy. Keeping her eyes on Whitfield, Teddy made no effort to hide her hand reaching for the Glock 17.

"Ralph, you do realize that Gabby and a couple of other people can see and hear you through the open door?"

"Damned if I care."

Gabby, alarmed, held up her fingers to show the numbers 911.

"Yes," Teddy said, looking at Gabby. "Ralph, you'd better think calmly about what you say and do next." Teddy withdrew the Glock from the desk drawer.

"You don't have the guts to shoot me, bitch."

"Are you sure you want to test me?"

"I intend to bring down all of the Andrews businesses."

"Is that why you're here today?"

"I'm here to tell you that I'll also sue you and Hack Lawrence for destroying my family's IT system."

Teddy smiled. "Can you prove we infected your computers? Surely you have adequate firewalls to protect your system."

"Who else could have done it?"

"You don't have any proof that we infected your system, only inferences. And inferences don't count in a court of law."

"You're going down."

"Ralph, Hack detected your feeble attempts to infect our systems, and we have proof of what you did."

"Hack isn't the smartest expert around here, and I don't respect his intellect. He got lucky," Whitfield said.

"Someone outsmarted you, Ralph, despite your advanced degrees in computer science. Seems to be a continuing fact of life with your family." Teddy saw that two Vickery police officers had come into the outer office. She shook her head, indicating the policemen should stay in the outer office for the time being.

"Maybe your family has a genetic lack of smarts?" Whitfield moved toward Teddy and she aimed her pistol at him. He sat again. "Good choice, Ralph. Just so you know, I don't bluff. Why do you hate the Andrews family so much?"

"Your family started the problem when Jason and his nigger half-brother killed my great-uncle Stuart Whitfield."

"To my knowledge, neither Jason nor Martin were arrested for what you claim."

"Everybody knows what they did. The Andrews used their political influence to suppress all evidence of the crime."

"Ralph, you're mistaken about the chain of events," Teddy said.

"The hell I am."

"You're forgetting that your great-uncle caused the wreck that killed Jason Andrews Sr. and put Miz Lizbeth in her wheelchair."

"That's a damnable lie. No charges were ever brought against Uncle Stuart."

"But, to use your words, everybody knows what Stuart Whitfield did."

"The two events are different."

"Seems they're about the same to me. And I suspect this whole affair began because the Andrews were better competitors than the Whitfields. Stuart probably thought he'd corner the poultry business with Jason Sr. out of the way. By failing to kill Miz Lizbeth in the car wreck, she was able to gain the upper hand on your family."

"That bitch on wheels deserves to die, goddamn her."

"Is that why your grandfather, Ralph Whitfield Sr., tried to kill Miz Lizbeth and other friends of the family? Oh, I forgot, your grandfather was also convicted of killing the judge who presided over the trial in which he was sentenced to life in prison," Teddy said, calmly.

"That entire trial was based on manufactured evidence, as you should know by now! It's past time for justice be done."

"Justice was carried out for your grandfather," Teddy said, noticing that Ralph was once again becoming highly agitated.

"No, no, no!"

"You've appointed yourself an avenging angel?" Teddy pressed.

"Or did your grandfather anoint you for that role when you visited him in prison?"

"He not only wanted justice to be done, he wanted justified revenge against your family. That's my purpose and I will not be deterred from it. I'll destroy your family."

"You're not making much progress."

"There's plenty of time, bitch." Ralph started to get out of his chair.

With her free hand, Teddy beckoned the police officers to come into the office. "Ralph, you must suffer from the same genetic disease as the rest of your family—terminal stupidity."

The two officers grabbed Ralph. "Put your hands behind you, Mr. Whitfield."

"The hell you say! You can't arrest me."

One of the officers pointed his Taser at Ralph. "We can handcuff you the easy or the hard way, Mr. Whitfield. Your choice." Ralph put his hands behind his back, and the other officer put handcuffs on Ralph's wrists. "You're under arrest, Mr. Whitfield, for a terroristic threat, among other charges."

While the first officer read the Miranda warning to Ralph, Teddy put her Glock back into the drawer.

"You heard what I said about terminal stupidity, Ralph." Teddy pointed to Gabby. "We recorded this entire conversation, and these two fine law enforcement officials also heard and witnessed most of the events. I'll definitely press charges against you. Too bad you can't share a cell with your grandfather, but you'll see him again in hell one day."

"Fuck you! Our family lawyer will have me out jail before the end of today."

"I hope your lawyer does better than the one who defended your grandfather."

The two officers manhandled the struggling Ralph out of Teddy's office, through the bank, and to a patrol car.

Teddy went to Gabby. "Are you all right?"

"Yes, ma'am. Are you?"

"I'm fine. You did well." Teddy once again congratulated herself for promoting Gabby from receptionist to administrative assistant.

"Thank you, Mrs. Fredericks. I tried to follow your example."

"Gabby, please come into my office. We both need an adult libation." Teddy saw Hack striding through the outer office, fire in his eyes. "Please join us, Hack. We'll talk over today's events while we drink some great single malt Scotch and chill out."

CHAPTER 36

Teddy left the Ebenezer at Aldersgate United Methodist Church through the back door after choir practice on Thursday night. A Vickery police car was parked beside her Lexus in the well-lighted parking lot. Although Teddy still had her Mercedes-Benz, she thought the Lexus was more suitable for her position with the Vickery Bank and Trust.

As Teddy approached the two vehicles, Chief Brockman exited the police car saying, "Evening, Teddy."

"Same to you, Chief. What has happened to bring you here?"

"Ralph Whitfield was released from jail a couple of hours ago."

"That's surprising. How did Ralph manage to get out?"

"Our new federal judge for this district allowed Ralph to post a $500,000 bail. He has to wear an ankle bracelet and must abide by a restraining order to stay a hundred yards away from you at all times. Needless to say, Sheriff Bruce Covington and I aren't happy about what's happened."

"I guess this new judge ignored or didn't know the background between the Andrews and Whitfield families."

"The county district attorney tried to enlighten the judge to no avail. Ralph's lawyer, Dean Scott, convinced the judge that

Ralph won't flee or pose a danger to anyone. I suspect Counselor Scott will employ a diminished capacity defense when and if Ralph goes to trial," Chief Brockman said.

"I'm sure Mr. Scott will insist that we give him a copy of the recording documenting the interaction between Ralph and me."

"The recording could be a double-edged sword for us."

"You mean the recording demonstrates Ralph breaking the law while at the same time showing his presumptive mental illness?"

"That's right," Chief Brockman confirmed.

"Do you know if the Whitman business activities include anything other than farming, raising cattle, and real estate transactions?" Teddy asked.

"What I'm about to tell you goes no further than between the two of us.

"Agreed."

"Sheriff Covington believes the Whitfields may be engaged in making and selling crystal meth to a cartel."

"A local or South American cartel?"

"Could be one and the same. Sheriff Covington and the Georgia Bureau of Investigation followed the trail of the drug to Atlanta. They're still trying to identify the major players other than the Whitfields."

Teddy thought for a minute. "Doesn't the Whitfield property extend to the Broad River?"

"Probably the location of their meth lab, in that thickly forested area. Although Sheriff Covington has the county drone fly regularly over the suspected area, he's had no luck in finding the meth lab."

"No roads in that area?" Teddy asked.

"None. The Whitfields may be moving supplies in and out through the Broad River. Sheriff Covington will locate the lab eventually."

"Let's hope so. My family has long tried to keep illicit drugs out of Alexander County," Teddy said.

"Do you have a current CCL, a concealed carry license?"

"I do."

"Keep a weapon on you and in your car at all times," Chief Brockman instructed.

"I will."

Teddy saw no need to tell the chief that she was almost always armed following Jason and Martin's lead. In her case, the motivation for being armed was not primarily due to the Whitfields. Rather, she thought Frank Gordon might one day leave witness protection with murderous intent against the Andrews.

"Ralph can't be so dumb that he would try to harm me while he's out on bail."

"Teddy, he hates you with a pure, purple, unadulterated passion, and his mind must not be working correctly, considering how he acted at the bank. He may think that a jury might not convict him on the basis of the recording without your direct testimony."

"Gabby was looking on. She saw and heard what went down in my office. She could testify against Ralph," Teddy said.

"I've warned Gabby to be careful. I have patrol cars watching where she and her husband live with her parents."

"I'll also encourage Gabby to stay alert," Teddy said.

"Anyway, tonight I'll escort you to the county line where a sheriff's deputy will take over to make sure you get home safely."

"Surely you don't mean for me to have a law enforcement escort until Ralph goes to prison or a mental institution?"

"Neither Sheriff Covington nor I have the resources for that. We recommend that you hire some of our off-duty officers to provide extra security at the Big House; maybe two-person teams for daytime and for night."

"Good advice. I'll call you and Sheriff Covington tomorrow. Let's hit the road. Time's a-wasting."

CHAPTER 37

Teddy, JJ, and Martin Jackson left the Big House the next morning before breakfast for a jog around the property. She enjoyed exercising with the two boys and deliberately kept to a slow pace so they could keep up.

"Hey, Auntie Teddy, can't we go faster?" JJ asked.

"We're jogging, not running," Teddy replied.

"Let's jog faster."

"Is that OK with you, Martin Jackson?" Teddy asked the younger of the two boys.

"I feel the need for speed, Sister Woman."

Teddy increased the pace, wondering if the two boys had recently watched the movie *Top Gun*. The boys exhibited no difficulty in keeping up with her. Teddy wondered how long before they would be able to outrun her.

The group jogged in silence for a while. The two boys looked at each other and jogged even faster, forcing Teddy to increase her pace. Teddy, meeting the challenge, jogged ahead of the two boys, who soon caught up with her.

When the group came within a hundred yards of the Big House, Teddy said, "JJ and Martin Jackson, I'll race you full out to the Big House. Think you can keep up with me?"

"You can eat our heel dust, Sister Woman!" Martin Jackson challenged.

Both boys began to run as fast as they could, gaining slightly on Teddy. She then ran at full speed and soon pulled ahead of the boys. Teddy was at the Big House when a Honda Odyssey she didn't recognize entered the circular driveway. A few seconds later, the boys reached Teddy, who had removed a Glock 17 from her fanny pack. She relaxed when Martin Andrews opened the driver's side sliding door.

"Daddy!" JJ shouted and ran to his father.

Martin Jackson went to the passenger's side sliding door and helped the visibly pregnant Shanna out of the car.

"Have you two been racing with Teddy?" Martin asked.

"Sister Woman's fast, but we're gaining on her," Martin Jackson said.

JJ embraced his mother and patted her belly over the baby bump.

"See, I leave you two alone and look what happened."

"The precipitating event happened well before Teddy's wedding," Shanna said.

"Boy-child or girl-child?" Martin Jackson asked.

"Girl-child," Shanna said.

The driver of the Odyssey set Martin and Shanna's luggage on the front porch.

"Will there be anything else, Martin?" the driver asked.

"No thank you, Josh. I'll recruit these two young men to move the luggage inside the house."

The driver tipped his hat to Martin and drove the car toward the front gate. Martin looked at JJ. "Son, you've grown this past month."

"He and JJ are in the midst of a growth spurt. Sally and Ann can hardly cook enough food to keep up with their appetites," Teddy said.

"Shanna, why don't you show these two monsters where to put our luggage," Martin said. "That is, if our quarters are ready for us?"

"Been ready for days, although we didn't expect you until next week," Teddy said.

"Great. Boys, please see if you're strong enough to manhandle the luggage. I want to talk a few minutes with Teddy."

Teddy and Martin walked away from the Big House.

"Why are you here so early, Uncle Martin?" Before he could reply, an answer came to her. "Hack must have called you."

"Not Hack. Bruce and Chief Brockman reached out on a conference call to tell me they would feel better if Shanna and I provided some backup for you, even though you're handling the situation. I called Jason to alert him. We decided he should stay with Miz Lizbeth and Jackson in China. Your mom and your husband will get here as soon as they can arrange transportation. We also decided not to tell Miz Lizbeth what was going on. We don't want an interruption in her therapy."

"Miz Lizbeth will be agitated, even angry, when she finds out."

"We'll give Miz Lizbeth some extra martinis to calm her."

"Sounds good. I'll tell Miz Lizbeth I appreciated your arriving early. Did you and Shanna take a red-eye flight here?"

"Private red-eye flight on a Learjet. We left as soon as everything could be arranged. We flew into the Alexander County Airport, Josh met us, and here we are."

"You know this Josh?"

"Josh Thomas was a freshman in high school when Jason and I were seniors . . . Do I smell bacon?"

"You do. I'll inform Sally and Ann to lay on an even more abundant breakfast, if they don't already know you and Shanna are here."

"Before you go please tell me if you would be willing to work at the Big House rather than going into the bank. You can take care of your important tasks from here."

"Uncle Martin, I don't want the Whitfields to think I'm scared of them. Business as usual, although I'm glad you're here. I planned to hire some off-duty law enforcement personnel when I settled in at the bank this morning. Now that you're here, you can provide security here at the Big House."

"I've already called Bruce and the chief about hiring someone. A couple of officers will arrive within the hour. Once we've finished breakfast and we're sure about the security, I'll go with you to the bank."

Teddy knew she'd have no luck persuading Martin to change his mind. "Suits me just fine."

"Are you still driving your Mercedes-Benz?"

"Primarily for pleasure. I have a Lexus 460L to help me look corporate."

"You're armed?"

"I have Glock 17s on my person, in the Lexus, and in my office at the bank."

"Do you practice often?"

"I do. I hope you don't mind that I've taught JJ and Martin Jackson some rudiments of shooting this past month."

"I don't mind at all. In fact, they're old enough for the training. What pistols are they using?" Martin asked.

"Baby Glocks. The same ones I used when you and Jason taught me to shoot."

"Are they any good?"

"They will be after a few more lessons."

"Let's go to the dining room before the monsters consume all the food. We can leave for the bank when the security detail gets here. If you wish, call the bank and tell . . ."

"You remember Gabby? She's no longer the receptionist for the bank. I promoted her to be my administrative assistant."

"Great move. She's good people. Tell her we'll be late getting to the bank."

"I'll do that. Gabby probably can take care of anything that comes up before we get there."

CHAPTER 38

J J and Martin Jackson left the dining room table while the three adults had a final cup of coffee. A bell sounded three times in quick succession. Martin looked at Teddy, his eyebrows raised.

"The alarm system I had installed after everyone left for China sounds three bells for the front driveway and four bells for the back driveway."

"Probably our new security detail. Let's meet them on the front porch." Martin looked at Shanna.

"I'll wait here," Shanna said.

By the time Teddy and Martin reached the porch, a Chevrolet Silverado 1500 truck had come into the circular driveway and parked in front of the Big House. Two uniformed officers, both carrying AR-15 rifles, came onto the porch. "Mrs. Fredericks, Mr. Andrews: I'm Deputy Ron Johnson from the sheriff's department. Officer Larry Jacobs from the Vickery Police Department will be my partner for this watch."

Martin and Teddy shook hands with the officers. "Let's have a sit-down here on the porch and cogitate for few minutes," Martin said. After everyone took their seats, Martin asked, "What do you have in mind security-wise?"

"Sheriff Covington acquainted us with the general layout of this place. Larry or I will always be on the front porch or somewhere near the Big House. The other one will make continuous circuits on the perimeter road. We'll alternate every couple of hours," Deputy Johnson said.

"Teddy, what do you think?" Martin asked.

"Sounds good to me. Do you want the front and back gates locked?"

"That would be a great help. Anyone who has business at the Big House can call and we'll let them in under supervision. Mr. Andrews, do you and Mrs. Fredericks have keys to the locks at the front and back gates?"

"We do and will call to alert you when we've made the scene."

Teddy explained how the alarm system worked. "If you leave the front windows open, you can hear the alert signals."

Deputy Johnson and Officer Jacobs gave their cards to Martin and Teddy. "You should be able to reach us on our cell phones at any time. If not, you'll know something's wrong," Deputy Johnson said.

"I'll make sure the kitchen ladies keep you supplied with beverages and food," Teddy said.

"You have two young men with you?" Deputy Johnson asked.

"JJ and Martin Jackson. I'll put the fear of God into them that they're not to pester you guys, and if the boys go outside to play, they'll have to stay within sight of the person watching from the porch," Martin said.

"Sounds like a winner," Deputy Johnson said.

Shanna walked onto the porch. "You want me to keep the wild ones from getting into mischief?"

"We all have our roles to play." Martin ducked as Shanna made a half-hearted swing at him.

"We have several people who live and work on the property. We should notify them about the security arrangements." Teddy indicated the direction where the families lived.

"When I make my first circuit, I'll stop by each house and tell your people what's going on. Do your people have children?" Officer Jacobs asked.

"They're grown and no longer live here," Martin said.

"That will make our job easier," Deputy Johnson said.

Martin, Teddy, and Shanna went back into the Big House.

***

Thirty minutes later, Deputy Johnson came to the front door as Martin and Teddy prepared to walk through it.

"Mr. Andrews, we have a problem. We need everyone to stay at the Big House and not go to the garage."

"What's the matter?" Martin asked.

"We found explosives under the driver's compartments on Mrs. Frederick's Mercedes and Lexus. I want you to keep the family inside the house until the bombs are disarmed and removed."

"Well, that sucks," Teddy said.

"Let's convene in the dining room in a few minutes," Martin said. "I'll tell Shanna to stay in our quarters."

Martin soon joined Teddy and Deputy Johnson in the dining room. "You've called for the nearest bomb disposal squad?" Martin asked the deputy.

"We've notified Sheriff Covington. He's setting the wheels in motion."

"We need to let Chief Brockman know what's happened. Gabby's the only other direct witness to Ralph Whitfield's craziness in my office," Teddy said.

"Seems like you will be working at home today after all, Teddy," Martin said.

"I am thoroughly pissed. The Whitfields, what's left of them, have once again attacked our family."

An Alexander County patrol car marked with *Sheriff* sped into the driveway and skidded to a stop. Sheriff Bruce Covington exited the car and quick-marched to where the deputy stood.

"Sitrep, please, Deputy."

"Officer Jacobs is examining the other vehicles in the garage."

"Well done. Now that I'm here you can help him."

"Do you have any idea about the explosive power of the bombs?" Martin asked the deputy.

"Several sticks of what appears to be dynamite, enough to blow the cars and occupants to kingdom come."

"Thanks, Deputy," Sheriff Covington said. "You and Officer Jacobs be careful. We don't need to take any chances. If you can look under the other vehicles without touching them, OK."

"Understood, Sheriff."

Martin and Sheriff Covington located JJ and Martin Jackson and brought them back to the Big House, while Teddy sat in a rocker on the front porch. Martin took the boys to where Shanna rested in her and Martin's quarters.

"Young men," Martin instructed, "I want the two of you to keep Shanna company and be ready to protect her. Stay here regardless of what happens outside. You can play computer games or whatever. Under no circumstances are you to leave Shanna until I come for you. Do you read me?"

"I do," JJ said.

"I hear you, Uncle Martin," Martin Jackson said.

"Good. An important part of being a warrior involves waiting in a ready state for events to develop. I'm trusting you guys to protect Shanna and the baby."

"Can we have the baby Glocks Sister Woman has been teaching us to shoot?" Martin Jackson asked.

"Not now. Stay here and be alert. I'll have Sally or Ann bring you some snacks."

"Pecan pie would be acceptable," JJ said.

"And black coffee," Martin Jackson added.

***

Sheriff Covington, Martin, and Teddy gathered at one end of the large table in the dining room. Sally placed a full pot of freshly brewed coffee and mugs on the table.

"Will there be anything else, Mrs. Fredericks?" she asked.

"Uncle Martin, Sheriff Covington, do you want anything besides coffee?" Teddy asked.

"Not for me," Martin said.

"Nor for me," Sheriff Covington declined.

"Thanks, Sally. You and Ann please stay in the kitchen unless there's a compelling reason for you to leave. I'll keep you informed about what's happening," Teddy said.

"Yes, ma'am." Sally turned to leave the room.

"One more thing, Sally," Teddy said. "Will you and Ann call everyone and tell them to stay well away from the Big House and garage until Sheriff Covington gives the all clear?"

"We'll make sure everyone gets the message, Mrs. Fredericks." Sally left for the kitchen.

"Uncle Martin, what do we tell the rest of family?" Teddy asked.

"Nothing until they get back from China, unless something goes terribly wrong," Martin said.

"Good plan. Jason and the others can't help from China. No reason to worry them unnecessarily," Sheriff Covington said.

"You believe the Whitfields or someone acting on their behalf set the bombs in place?" Martin asked.

"I believe the situation calls for Occam's Razor."

"You mean that among competing hypotheses, the one with the fewest assumptions should be accepted?" Teddy asked.

"Correct. Once we secure this place, I will have a come-to-Jesus conversation with Ralph. I will not tolerate what he's done."

"Is there any way to determine when the bombs were put under my cars?" Teddy asked the sheriff.

"You heard no disturbances on the property last night?"

"No dogs barking, no sounds other than what goes on here normally at night."

"The bomb disposal squad might help us with what you asked, Teddy. If the bombs were set to explode when you turned on the ignition, that might indicate the devices were installed here last night," Sheriff Covington said.

He answered his cell phone on the first ring. "Covington here." He listened for a few seconds. "Good to know. I'll have my deputy stand near where you should land your bird. Covington out."

The sheriff spoke to Martin and Teddy. "The bomb disposal team from the state patrol in Atlanta will be here in about thirty minutes."

"They're traveling by helicopter?" Martin asked.

"Yes." Before the sheriff could continue, his cell phone rang again. "Covington here. What? You and Officer Jacobs get the hell out of the garage right now. Get out! Get out! Get out!"

The sheriff turned to Martin. "Is Mr. Jackson's old shotgun nearby?"

"Teddy?" Martin asked.

"In the gun safe. I didn't want to tempt JJ and Martin Jackson. Do you want me to get it?"

"Immediately, if not sooner. A drone, not the county's, is buzzing the property. I'll get the 10-gauge from my car. We'll shoot the damn thing out of the sky," Sheriff Covington said.

"Teddy, I'm going with you to get the Browning. Bruce and I will blast the drone to hell. You should stay inside," Martin said.

"I'll get one of the other shotguns and help you."

Sheriff Covington spoke into his cell phone as Teddy and Martin left.

"We have a developing situation here. Don't land that bird

near the garage."

Teddy and Martin returned to the front porch in time to see the drone headed toward the Big House.

"I'll bet that drone has a video system, and Ralph can see what's happening," Teddy said.

Sheriff Covington joined Martin and Teddy on the front porch and said, "Let's put the fear of God in him. Open fire!"

The three shotguns fired almost simultaneously, but the drone had quickly started evasive maneuvers. Two quick explosions from the garage knocked Sheriff Covington, Martin, and Teddy up against the front wall and blew window glass into the Big House.

The drone returned to a position that allowed the operator to see the front porch and then flew away.

Sheriff Covington and Martin were the first to stand up. When Teddy tried to push herself up, she exclaimed, "Damn it all to hell, my arm's not working."

"Stay still; don't try to get up," Martin ordered. "Which arm?"

"My right arm. Probably the rotator cuff again."

Sheriff Covington spoke into his cell phone. "Covington here. Send an EMS bus to the Big House forthwith, if not faster. Mrs. Fredericks has a damaged shoulder and needs immediate medical attention. Transfer me to Sergeant Willis ASAP."

The helicopter carrying the bomb disposal squad landed near the tennis court. The squad members raced toward the Big House. Sheriff Covington spoke into his cell phone. "Sergeant Willis, get Snoopy into the air over the Broad River where we've been searching for the Whitfield meth lab. Look for another drone flying into that area. If you see the drone, stay back and follow it to wherever lands."

"How can we be of assistance, Sheriff?" asked the Georgia State Patrol lieutenant who led the bomb disposal squad.

"I've already sent for an EMS bus to take Mrs. Fredericks to the emergency room. The explosions blasted the three of us up against the wall. Mr. Andrews and I are OK, more or less."

Shanna and the two boys came through the damaged front door.

"Martin, are you guys all right?"

"Bruce and I will do for now. We suffered not much more than a hard tackle. The blast reinjured Teddy's right shoulder."

"Teddy, do you want to come into the house with us?" Shanna asked.

"Better for her to rest here until the EMS bus arrives," Martin said. "Shanna, you and the boys should go inside to the back of the house in case Ralph planted any more bombs."

"Come on, boys. We don't want to interfere with the men here," Shanna ordered.

"Sister Woman, you look like fecal matter. Are you all right?" Martin Jackson asked.

"Thank you for your perceptive observation. I've been both better and a lot worse. The doctors at the hospital will take care of me," Teddy said.

Shanna and the boys, with obvious resistance on their young faces, left.

"Sheriff, what do you think? Are more bombs likely?" the lieutenant asked.

"I don't know. We have a good idea about the likely perpetrator. His family and the Andrews have been enemies for a long time. The guy we think responsible for the exploded bombs seems to have a deep hatred for Mrs. Fredericks. He's out on bail for attempting to assault her at the Vickery Bank and Trust a few days ago. From where we're standing, it looks like both of her cars were destroyed along with most of the garage and the other vehicles."

"You think this guy set off the bombs remotely with the drone?" the lieutenant asked.

"Looks that way. He probably wanted to see Mrs. Fredericks blown to hell this morning."

"Your perp must be a sick puppy."

"He's beyond sick," Teddy said.

The lieutenant looked at the garage. "We'll have our work cut out for us determining if more bombs are in that mess, much less defusing them."

"Do whatever you think best, Lieutenant," Martin said.

The lieutenant beckoned to one of his men. "Please bring Hannibal up here, Corporal. Let's see if he can tell us anything useful."

"The residue from the explosions may confuse him."

"Acknowledged. Let's give him a try."

"Hannibal?" Martin asked.

"Our bomb-sniffing beast of a German shepherd. He's got a great nose."

The EMS bus arrived. The crew came onto the porch with a stretcher.

"I can walk to the bus," Teddy said.

"Teddy, let these men do their job. Take her away, men," Martin said.

"Martin, do you want to go to the hospital with them?" Sheriff Covington asked.

"Yes. I'll call Josh to bring me back home. I doubt any of the vehicles in the garage survived the blasts."

"Call me and I'll make arrangements to bring you back here. I'll keep a security detail in place at least for the night. Don't worry."

"Sounds good. Perhaps we can talk about how to bring Ralph to justice."

"Please don't act on your own. We may soon have actionable intelligence on his whereabouts."

"Then you can deputize me, and I'll go with you to apprehend the bastard. Maybe we'll get lucky and he'll try to resist arrest," Martin said.

"Stay cool, Martin. Let my team handle this situation. We'll keep you informed."

"For now, unless Ralph gets in my gun sights and I can put him down."

CHAPTER 39

Teddy struggled to awaken from a drug-induced sleep and reached with her left hand for the Glock 17 she had placed under the bed covers when the hospital staff transferred her from the imaging department into a VIP suite in the Andrews family wing two days earlier. Teddy relaxed when she saw that her husband and mother had entered the room. Both moved to the bedside to kiss Teddy.

"Teddy, I'll fix your shoulder again," Mark said.

"Practice makes perfect," Teddy said.

"The staff says you refused to let anyone other than Mark work on your shoulder," Pam said.

"The head of surgery told me he would have to bring in somebody from the outside to do the surgery. I preferred to wait for Mark to get back. I've had enough painkillers to keep me comfortable, even if groggy most of the time."

"We'll perform the surgery tomorrow morning. The imaging shows about the same degree of damage to be repaired as with the first surgery," Mark said.

"That's comforting. Have you two talked with Uncle Martin?"

"He gave us all the details. Did you know he arranged to

have a law enforcement officer stationed outside the door to this room?" Pam asked.

"I've been too groggy to notice anything outside my room."

"I'll tell you something else you don't know," Mark said.

"I'm all ears."

"Sheriff Covington located the Whitfield meth lab and closed it down. He arrested several people, including three Central Americans who've already confessed to putting the bombs under your cars at Ralph's direction."

"I wonder how Sheriff Covington convinced the three guys to confess?" Teddy asked.

"As you must know, Bruce Covington doesn't always adhere to strictly legal or politically correct methods," Pam said.

"The confessions appear to have been made in short order after the arrests," Mark said.

"How did the Central Americans get onto our property?" Teddy asked.

"They came in from the woods in the back."

"You didn't mention Ralph Whitfield," Teddy said.

"He's in the wind. That's why the security outside this room 24/7."

"Uncle Martin joined the search for Ralph?"

"Sheriff Covington talked Martin out of the idea. Instead, Martin spends a lot of time supervising the repairs to the Big House and the garage. He's also taking charge of purchasing new trucks needed for the business."

"Mom, please tell Uncle Martin not to bother with replacing my vehicles. I might want something different."

Martin entered the room. "You can tell me yourself." He leaned over the bed to give Teddy a light kiss.

"I don't want to spend the rest of my life looking over my shoulder for Ralph. What are we going to do about him?" Teddy asked Martin."

"Bruce, Hack, and I have a plan."

"Don't tell me you want my daughter to be bait again," Pam said.

"What?" Mark asked.

"Exciting times I'll tell you about later," Teddy said.

"Exciting for you, beyond excruciating for me," Pam said.

"Could we talk about the definition of 'bait' after Teddy's surgery?" Mark asked.

***

"Mark, I've been in this hospital too long. I need to get back to work," Teddy said a day after her surgery.

"I'm dismissing you this afternoon. Any chance whatsoever that you would agree to work from the Big House for the next several days?"

"The probability of that happening is vanishingly small."

"That's what I expected. What do you have in mind for your next vehicle or vehicles?" Mark asked.

"Let's get to the essentials. Until I make up my mind about a new car, I figure someone can drive me back and forth to the bank in one of the new F-150s Uncle Martin bought, or you can take me to the bank in the mornings when you leave for the hospital and then take me home after you finish work."

Mark sighed. "Exactly what propels you to get back to work at the bank? It would be much easier to protect you at the Big House until law enforcement apprehends Ralph Whitfield."

"If I hide out at home, Ralph will think he's won this round. Besides, I feel better about the bank when I'm working there."

"I hope you're not micromanaging," Mark said.

"I'm not. I simply think things go better when I'm there."

"What did you mean the other day in the hospital when Pam and Martin were talking about using you as bait?"

"I'll tell you the full undiluted story of Mom and Jason falling in love, and how Mom and I were freed from the pervert. Oh, and we also took down a major crime lord."

"Who is we?"

"Primarily Hack, Uncle Martin, Jason, Sheriff Covington, and me."

"I've already heard bits and pieces of the story, not the full details," Mark said.

"How much time do you have?"

"All we need unless I'm called away for an emergency."

"Sit back and listen," Teddy said.

CHAPTER 40

The next day, Sheriff Covington appeared at the Big House in time for the afternoon cocktail hour. Once he was seated, Pam gave him a double Glenmorangie, which he gratefully accepted. "Martin, good to have you home again, and I'm glad you agreed not to go after Ralph on your own," Sheriff Covington said, raising his glass in a toast.

"Good to be here," Martin replied.

"I hope we can stay. I'm tired of the West Coast lifestyle," Shanna said.

"No more modeling or working in the entertainment industry?" Teddy asked.

"I'll concentrate on writing my children's books. I may even write an adult book." Shanna grinned.

"What would be the subject of this book?" Martin asked.

"A novelized history of the Andrews family, suitably disguised."

"A guaranteed best seller," Mark said.

Martin raised his eyes upward. "Oh Lord, in your mercy."

Sheriff Covington looked at Martin. "Now?"

"As good as any, better than most," Martin said. "JJ and Martin Jackson, we need to have an adult-type conversation. Please occupy yourselves somewhere else in the house and don't attempt to listen to our conversation."

"Are you guys going to talk about sex?" JJ asked.

"Not this time. Now scoot and stay out of trouble," Martin said.

"I'm trouble on the way to happening," Martin Jackson said.

"Stay out of mischief and we'll shoot tomorrow. I need to practice left-handed," Teddy said.

"We're outta here," JJ said.

"Teddy, do you know how to load and cock your pistol one-handed?" Sheriff Covington asked.

"Uncle Martin and Jason showed me when they were teaching me advanced shooting techniques. I need to practice."

"I'll help with the practice and supervising the boys," Martin said.

"I'm happy that you will be involved," Pam said. "Will I also be happy about what you men have in mind for Teddy?"

"We won't proceed unless everyone agrees. In fact, we may not need to do anything," the sheriff said.

"You think Ralph can be caught soon?" Teddy asked.

"We've issued a nationwide BOLO on him for attempted murder and skipping his bond, along with several other charges," Sheriff Covington said.

"BOLO?" Pam asked.

"Be on the lookout," Sheriff Covington clarified.

"Do you think Ralph has left the area?" Shanna asked.

"My highly trained lawman's gut tells me he hasn't. I think Ralph's obsession with Teddy and his craziness will drive him to come after her again."

"Ralph probably won't quit until we kill him," Martin said.

"Will you try to arrest him, if he's found?" Mark asked the sheriff.

Sheriff Covington kept his face impassive. "That would be the legally preferred course of action. But even if we can arrest Ralph, he's likely to escape going to prison by mounting a diminished capacity defense."

"He would be sent to an institution for treatment of his mental illness, wouldn't he?" Pam asked.

"Ralph has a near genius IQ. What if he convinces the shrinks that he's no longer mentally ill and they release him back to his family? I have no confidence that he won't once again come after Teddy," Sheriff Covington said.

"Will you make a good faith effort to arrest him?" Mark asked.

"Once we find Ralph, he can choose to be arrested or to pursue another option."

"What's your plan to make Ralph resurface?" Mark asked.

CHAPTER 41

Joan Mitchell, the editor of the *Alexander County Messenger*, met with Teddy and Allison Jameson in her law office.

"Good to see you, Joan," Allison said.

"Happy to be here," Joan replied. "Mrs. Fredericks, I understand you have a story to tell about the unfortunate events that transpired at the Vickery Bank and Trust, and at the Big House over the past several days."

"I hope you'll agree to print the story above the fold on the front page in the next edition of *The Messenger*," Teddy said.

"We've already reported the previous events. Am I correct that you have another purpose in mind other than rehashing what has already happened?" Joan asked.

"Why don't you let Mrs. Fredericks tell you what's on her mind? You can then decide about publishing the interview," Allison said.

"Sounds good to me. First, Mrs. Fredericks, when do you expect Miz Lizbeth home from China?"

"Miz Lizbeth, Jason, and Mr. Jackson should be home in three to six weeks," Teddy answered.

"Any word on her therapy?"

"Miz Lizbeth has responded better than expected."

"Wonderful news, for your family and for this county," Joan said.

"We're grateful," Teddy said.

"How long have you known Ralph Whitfield?" Joan asked.

"Since we were students at Alexander County High School."

"Did you know him very well?"

"Not at all. He asked me to go out with him on a number of occasions."

"Did you accept his invitations?"

"No, despite his persistence," Teddy said.

"Why?"

"I was, shall we say, adopted into the Andrews family. Over time, I learned about the long-standing enmity between my family and the Whitfields. While those past events did not directly involve me, I was skeptical about beginning a friendship with Ralph. Furthermore, he acted as if he were doing me a favor by asking me out."

"Any other reasons?" Joan asked.

"I thought he was more than a little off, as recent events have proven."

Allison held up her right hand. "Joan, from a legal point of view, please change 'have proven' to 'suggested.'"

"I agree. But, Mrs. Fredericks, what do you mean by more than a little off?" Joan asked.

"Ralph never looked directly at me on the few occasions when we talked. He constantly fidgeted, couldn't sit still. When I refused his advances, he said I was a typically conceited Andrews, and that one day I'd be sorry I rejected him."

"Did you think he might try to harm you?" Joan asked.

"Not at the time. For the present, let's review some facts. We have a recording of the encounter between Ralph and me in my office. Ralph was arrested and charged for his actions at the bank. He was released from jail on bail. He presumably has skipped bail and disappeared. Sheriff Covington and his deputies located and destroyed a meth lab on Whitfield property in the woods along the Broad River. The three Central Americans captured in that raid confessed to setting the explosives under my cars at Ralph's order. The resulting explosions destroyed our garage and damaged the other vehicles in it as well as the front of the Big House."

"Not to mention the harm to you personally from the explosions," Allison added.

"We've reported that Sheriff Covington was at the Big House at the time of the explosions. He has been noncommittal about Ralph's potential involvement," Joan said.

"As he should," Allison said.

"I believe Ralph was operating the drone that was surveilling our property at the time of the explosions. I further believe Ralph set off the explosions remotely through the drone," Teddy said.

"Yet, you have no proof for your contentions," Joan observed.

"An arrest warrant has been issued on Ralph for several charges growing out of the events at the Big House and the meth lab, as you well know." Teddy smiled and looked at Allison. "Presumably, a trial on the charges will either convict or exonerate Ralph, assuming he can be brought to trial."

"I sense you're building up to the real purpose of this interview," Joan said.

"Ms. Mitchel, I want this community and Ralph to know that I consider him a coward. Yes, he came into my office to accost me; however, he ... allegedly sent three Central Americans to do his dirty work in trying to kill me. Again, allegedly, he observed what was happening at the Big House and set off the explosions. If Ralph believes he did not act cowardly, let him come out of hiding and face me. I'll be ready."

Joan pursed her lips and took a deep breath. "You want *The Messenger* to flush Ralph out of hiding."

"That would be a welcomed outcome of publishing this interview," Allison said.

"Let's come back to that issue in a few minutes. Mrs. Fredericks, why did Ralph come to your office at the bank in the first place?" Joan asked.

"We have proof, which we have provided to law enforcement, that Ralph mounted a concerted and persistent attack on our computer systems, including at the Vickery Bank and Trust. We determined the attack came from a computer belonging to Ralph. A counterattack was undertaken, which according to Ralph destroyed the Whitfield information systems."

"We will not comment further on the alleged counterattack," Allison said.

"Allison, you're the lawyer for *The Messenger* as well as for the Andrews family. Do you see any adverse legal consequences if we publish substantial portions of this interview?" Joan asked.

"Pragmatically, no. Who would attempt to sue the paper for libel? In order for Ralph to sue the paper, he would have to come out of hiding, which would result in his arrest. And, to invoke an old legal principle, 'The truth is the best defense against libel.'"

"Mrs. Fredericks, you do realize that publication of this interview could put you in tremendous jeopardy?" Joan asked.

"We have that contingency covered," Teddy said. "In fact, we want Ralph to become even more irrational."

CHAPTER 42

For the third day in a row after *The Alexander County Messenger* published Teddy's interview, Sheriff Covington drove the county's tactical vehicle to the Big House. Teddy, wearing a bullet-proof vest and helmet, walked without apparent concern from the door of the Big House to the vehicle. Once Teddy was seated beside Sheriff Covington, he drove away from the Big House.

"Good to see you again this morning," Sheriff Covington greeted Teddy.

"Same to you, Sheriff. Any Ralph sightings?"

"Nothing confirmed," Sheriff Covington said as he turned onto Sweet Gum road headed toward Vickery.

"Sheriff Covington," a voice sounded on the two-way radio.

"Go ahead, Sergeant Willis. Has Snoopy seen something?"

"An eighteen-wheeler followed closely by a black Suburban with tinted windows traveling at excessive speed toward you."

"How far away?"

"You'll probably meet at the bridge."

"That won't happen. Tell the other deputies to block the road after the semi and Suburban pass."

"Roger that, Sheriff. What will you do?"

"I'll block the road on this side of the road as planned. Covington out . . . Teddy, semis are restricted from using Sweet Gum Road. Ralph probably thinks a big truck can wreck this tactical vehicle."

"What's next?" Teddy held the Glock 17 in her fanny pack.

"Buckle up tightly and hang on." Sheriff Covington abruptly made a tire-squealing U-turn . "Teddy, many people in this area would call what I just did a bootlegger's turn."

"My eyeballs are still rotating."

Sheriff Covington brought the vehicle to a quick stop. "Keep your seat. I'll be back in a jiffy." He exited the vehicle, went to the back, and removed a set of tire spikes that he unrolled across both lanes of the road. Once back in the vehicle, he drove another twenty-five yards and made a second U-turn so that he and Teddy faced the direction of the oncoming semi and Suburban. "Teddy, things may get a little hairy in a few minutes." Sheriff Covington spoke into his cell phone. "Martin, you aware of what's going on?"

"I'm within a hundred yards behind you."

"Good. Come on up here. Teddy, please exit this vehicle and walk as fast as you can toward Martin. I don't want Ralph and his minions getting to you."

"What will you do?"

"You'll see. Now, go. Martin will give you more instructions."

Teddy walked to where Martin was standing in front of a new F-150.

"If you're feeling adventurous, Teddy, stand beside me."

"Uncle Martin, you really are trying to incite and infuriate Ralph, aren't you?"

"That's the plan." Martin held a Heckler & Koch MP5.

Martin and Teddy saw the eighteen-wheeler rush across the bridge and hit the line of spikes. The driver managed to keep the truck on the road when the front tires blew out. Sheriff Covington opened fire with an AR-15, smashing the windshield. The truck stopped. The Suburban drove on the shoulder to pass the truck without hitting the spikes. Sheriff Covington loaded a fresh magazine in the AR-15 and opened fire, aiming at the front tires of the Suburban, which caromed off the road.

Sheriff Covington's voice boomed over the tactical vehicle's loudspeaker. "Driver, exit the Suburban with your hands in the air or my next rounds will blast you to hell."

Nothing happened for about a minute until the driver's side front door opened. Ralph, holding his own AR-15, stood behind the opened door, which gave him some degree of protection from Sheriff Covington.

"I've come to kill the bitch!" Ralph shouted.

"No way, Ralph. Drop your weapon immediately or you're dead."

Martin, Teddy, and the sheriff saw a deputy walking quickly toward Ralph from the direction of the bridge. Teddy raised her left hand above her head with her middle finger extended.

"Why don't you meet me halfway, Ralph, and we'll settle things once and for all," she shouted.

"No, bitch. I'll shoot you."

The deputy fired his Taser X3 at Ralph's back. The approximately 50,000-volt electric charge from the two released darts knocked Ralph to his knees. His AR-15 fell to the ground.

"Tase him again," Sheriff Covington ordered.

The deputy complied. Ralph fell face down on the ground, violently shaking.

"He's out for a while, Sheriff."

"Please check the cab of the truck for survivors."

Two more deputies arrived on the scene. After a short interval, the first deputy shouted, "Two men, alive for now but wounded."

"I'll call for EMS." Sheriff Covington walked toward the newly arrived deputies. "Put handcuffs on Ralph, wrists and ankles.

We'll get him into the tactical vehicle, and I'll drive him to the county jail and throw away the key. You deputies can stay here until the EMS bus arrives."

***

On the way back to Big House, Teddy said, "I'd better stay home for the rest of the day. Gabby will call if she needs me."

"Good idea. If you feel the need to work off any tension, we can take the boys shooting. How's your shoulder?"

"Mark says he's pleased with my progress. I wish the recovery could go faster."

"Mark's a good man; glad he's in the family."

"So am I." Teddy was silent for a few moments. "Uncle Martin, do you think Ralph will survive the trip to jail?"

"Most likely. Too many people saw Ralph placed into the tactical vehicle handcuffed at his wrists and ankles and only semi-conscious. Be hard to make a case he tried to escape. Do you want him dead?"

"I prefer that he rot in prison like his grandfather. Do you think Ralph can mount a diminished capacity defense?"

"Think about how the events unfolded today. What he set in motion required detailed planning, which belies diminished capacity. Ralph's not insane; he's overcome with jealousy and resentment."

"I hope things work out that way," Teddy said.

"I'm interested in the agency claiming first dibs on prosecuting Ralph."

"You mean the feds or Alexander County?" Teddy asked.

"That's right. Ralph committed several federal crimes with his actions toward you and the bank. The feds probably will assert rights to the first prosecution."

"If I remember correctly, there's no parole in the federal system. Ralph could be imprisoned for a long time," Teddy said

"Longer than you might think."

"How so?" Teddy asked.

"Knowing Bruce Covington as I do, he'll undoubtedly agitate with the county to prosecute Ralph in Alexander County on a set of charges different from those the feds will invoke. Once convicted on both sets of charges, Ralph could face sequential long prison sentences."

"Interesting idea," Teddy said.

"We may not need to worry about Ralph ever getting out of prison, regardless of the length of his sentences." Martin turned off Sweet Gum road onto the Andrews property.

"You think he won't survive prison?"

"His personality will likely lead him to antagonize some very mean inmates. I don't see Ralph going gently into the long dark night of incarceration."

"Maybe the feds will put Ralph into a super max prison for his safety," Teddy said.

While driving to the Big House Martin said, "Teddy, why don't you call Mark to fill him in about everything that happened today. Maybe he can come home to be with us."

"Sounds good. Mark can be on call for emergencies."

"I'll contact Jason in China to let him know the Ralph situation has been contained. Miz Lizbeth will pitch a hissy fit if we wait until she returns to let her know what happened."

CHAPTER 43

Martin parked the family's Honda Odyssey so that the passenger's side sliding door opened at the foot of the wheelchair ramp leading to the porch of the Big House.

"Miz Lizbeth, are you steady enough after your long flight to walk up the ramp?" Pam asked.

"I am," Miz Lizbeth said.

"I'll be right behind you. Mr. Jackson and Jason will walk on either side of you," Pam said.

"Let's get on with this demonstration. I want my afternoon martini, maybe more than one." Miz Lizbeth walked slowly and steadily down the ramp leading out of the Odyssey and up the ramp to the porch. When she reached the porch, the rest of the family standing by the front door broke into applause.

"Thank you," Miz Lizbeth acknowledged the greeting. "Let's not stop here; I'm going to the den." Jackson and Jason held her arms as she sat in her usual chair in the den. "Enough showing off for today. As you all witnessed, my Chinese therapy worked a miracle to some extent."

Martin Jackson embraced Jason. "I'm really glad you're home."

"Happy to be here. I've had enough Chinese food to last the rest of my life," Jason said.

Miz Lizbeth motioned for JJ and Martin Jackson to come near her. "I believe you two have each grown six inches while I've been away."

"The result of great food and good clean living," JJ responded.

"Along with a lot of exercise," Martin Jackson said. "We're training for when Sister Woman's shoulder heals."

"Why?" Miz Lizbeth asked.

"We don't want her to be at a disadvantage when we outrun her," JJ said.

"That'll be the day," Teddy said on the way to kiss Miz Lizbeth. "Welcome home, Elizabeth."

Miz Lizbeth held Teddy's hands and looked deeply into her eyes. "You're pregnant, aren't you, Theodora?"

"Mom did the test to confirm."

Jason hugged Teddy. "Well done. What does Mark say about becoming a father?"

"He's cautiously ecstatic," Teddy said.

"Sister Woman's pregnancy should give us nine or ten months for more training before she can race again," Martin Jackson said to JJ.

"Right. We don't want to take advantage of Auntie Teddy," JJ said.

"Jackson, where's my martini?" Miz Lizbeth asked. "We have a lot to celebrate."

"JJ and Martin Jackson, please distribute the drinks," Jackson said. He gave Miz Lizbeth's martini to JJ, who immediately put it in her hands.

"Mr. Jackson, club soda on ice with a slice of lime for me," Teddy said.

"JJ and I have wondered why Sister Woman has been abstemious the last couple of weeks. Now we know," Martin Jackson said.

"Abstemious. That's the right word. Where did you learn it?"

Pam asked her son.

"JJ and I have been working our way through the Big House library rather than spending so much time playing computer games," Martin Jackson answered.

"Hence the many Shakespeare quotes you two have been blessing us with," Teddy said.

"That's right," JJ said.

Miz Lizbeth raised her glass to Shanna. "I see we're in time to welcome another grandchild into the family."

"You returned in plenty of time," Shanna said. "Hopefully, this grandchild will be born under calmer circumstances than when JJ made his debut."

"Martin, did you secure the job at Alexander County High School?" Miz Lizbeth asked.

"I'll be the new head football and basketball coach," Martin said.

After another round of applause, Miz Lizbeth asked, "Martin, you're confident we no longer face threats from the Whitfields?"

"For now, unless the younger Whitfields continue the feud."

"Good. Theodora, I understand you performed magnificently during the recent troubles. I look forward to a blow-by-blow account of your heroics," Miz Lizbeth said.

"Elizabeth, I'm not sure heroics is the right word. Maybe tomorrow at cocktail hour Uncle Martin and I can give you all of the details."

"Sounds good. JJ, Martin Jackson, please help Jackson refill everyone's glass. I have a momentous and happy announcement," Miz Lizbeth said.

The two boys distributed the second round of drinks. Jackson then stood by Miz Lizbeth's chair. She raised her glass.

"Jackson and I will announce this Sunday in church that we've been married for many years." Jackson leaned down to kiss Miz Lizbeth as applause and cheering again filled the room.

"About time," Martin said. He shook hands with Jackson. "We've suspected for many years that you and Miz Lizbeth have been married. Glad to have the formal announcement."

"We've been waiting for this joyful occasion." Jason kissed his mother and shook hands with Jackson.

"To quote the Bard, 'All's well that ends well,'" JJ said.

Martin Jackson, not to be outdone, gave his own quote from Shakespeare: "What's past is prologue."

ACKNOWLEDGMENTS

First and foremost, I acknowledge the great support my beloved Andrea often gave me, albeit with some reservations that what I wrote might embarrass her, especially among her childhood friends.

I also acknowledge the support my two daughters, Anne-Marie Frosolono Schultz and Christina Frosolono Sell, both accomplished authors, have given me.

I often say I accomplished two great things in my life: (1) convincing Andrea Ernestine Cheek not only to marry me but to remain in the marriage and (2) siring two absolutely amazing daughters.